DOUBLED

BY RALPH HUGHES

DORRANCE
PUBLISHING CO
EST. 1920
PITTSBURGH, PENNSYLVANIA 15238

The contents of this work, including, but not limited to, the accuracy of events, people, and places depicted; opinions expressed; permission to use previously published materials included; and any advice given or actions advocated are solely the responsibility of the author, who assumes all liability for said work and indemnifies the publisher against any claims stemming from publication of the work.

Dorrance Publishing Co
585 Alpha Drive
Suite 103
Pittsburgh, PA 15238
Visit our website at www.dorrancebookstore.com

ISBN: 978-1-6853-7141-8
eISBN: 978-1-6853-7984-1

CHAPTERS

CHAPTER I

April 2017, Riyadh Saudi Arabia

John Thorn finished packing a medium sized suitcase and a small carry-on bag in preparation for his unscheduled trip to Washington. This would be his first trip back to Hqs after arriving in Riyadh as the CIA's Chief of Station (COS) some nine months previously and he was anxious about the trip. He was reviewing in his mind the events of the last nine months when one of his assistants arrived to drive him to the airport. Given all that had happened since his arrival, John had chosen an ex-Delta Force trooper, Sam Butterfield, to drive him.

Upon entering Sam asked, "Are you ready to go, John?"

"I am. Let me kiss Alice goodbye and we can go."

After a quick exchange with Alice, John climbed into the passenger side of the armored GMC Denali. As soon as he got in Sam explained, "We will not be taking King Salman Road but rather the long way around to the Ring Road. I have a few of our guys strategically stationed along our route, just in case we have some company."

"I'm glad to see you have bought into my admonitions about security," said John. "And I hope you will maintain that posture while I'm away."

"Don't worry, John, you and the recent events have convinced all of us of the necessity to be extremely cautious."

As they left the Diplomatic Quarter of the Safarat neighborhood they continued along Makkah Al Mukarramah Road rather than taking the more direct route via King Salman Road. They had not proceeded much more than a few miles along that road when Sam exclaimed, "We have a tail, Boss. I think this means trouble. There may be two vehicles on us."

Sam removed the encrypted Motorola radio from its cradle and pushing the talk button said, "Alter, Alert – we have a tail. What is your position?"

A voice immediately responded, "We are only a half mile behind you and I think we see the problem. Our other vehicle is about 5 miles in front of you. I'll put them on alert."

Sam was grim faced with an intent look about him. "I see a black SUV well behind our tail and that should be our guys. I'm going to speed up and see if the entire party follows suit."

Sam gunned the Denali, pushing the speed up to 80 MPH. "I see that only one vehicle, other than ours, is keeping up with us. So it appears we have only one trouble maker behind us. We should be able to deal with him, therefore, I'm going to slow down."

As the Denali slowed to about 40 MPH, the White Toyota Land Cruiser continued the higher rate of speed. Not sure if this really was a tail or just another erratic Saudi driver, Sam allowed the Toyota to pass him. However, once the Toyota came along side of the Denali, shooters appeared from both the front and rear passenger windows. As they opened fire with handguns, John and Sam both reflexibly ducted down as they heard the *rat a tat tat* against the windows. However the small caliber rounds were not capable of penetrating the armored windows of the Denali. Recognizing that these weapons were ineffective the Toyota began to swerve into the Denali, forcing it to the shoulder of the road. Sam shook off his initial fearful reaction and immediately plotted a course of action in his head. He slowed his vehicle, allowing the Toyota to assume a blocking position. But just as the Toyota was slowing, Sam slammed on the brakes and came to an abrupt halt. This gave him about 10 yards between the vehicles. As soon as the doors on both sides of the pursuing vehicle open, Sam gunned the Denali's big engine. Just as he intentionally clipped the left rear bumper of the Toyota, he noted that the gunman now were armed with Kalashnikov's, which could possibly penetrate his vehicle. However, when he rammed the rear bumper the gunman who were exiting their vehicle went flying in all directions like bowling pins. One gunman on the driver's side of the vehicle was trying to catch his balance when the Denali's front bumper lifted him high in the air. Both Sam and John heard him bounce off the roof of their vehicle. Another gunman was trapped between the opened door of his vehicle and the oncoming Denali. Sam closed his eyes and winced as his vehicle hit the would-be attacker, crushing him against the Toyota's open door. When he opened his eyes he was free of the Toyota and found that there was only superficial damage to his SUV.

While Sam made a quick exit from the scene, the-would be attackers were in a state of total disarray. It was at this point that the other American vehicle was arriving on the scene. The driver of that vehicle, Norman Halderman, radioed to Sam, "Get out of here. We'll handle this mess."

As Sam sped off, Halderman raced his vehicle in front of the Toyota and then stomped on the accelerator in reverse. The rear, reinforced bumper of Halderman's vehicle slammed into the front of the Toyota, smashing open the radiator and sending the occupants into further disarray. As Halderman sped away he radioed to Sam, "That Toyota will not be going anywhere tonight. I'll stay on you all the way to the airport but I don't think you are going to have any more problems."

John safely arrived at the airport with no time to spare. Fortunately a Saudi official was waiting at the airport to expedite him through immigration and airline controls. Within the hour he was trying to sleep in the jumbo jet as it made its way to London but he was too charged to find sleep. The rest of his journey was trouble free and after a brief transfer in London he was on his way to Washington.

Upon arrival in Dulles Airport, John quickly picked up his rental car and started out toward the CIA. His stomach growled and churned as he drove along the GW Memorial Parkway to the back entrance of CIA's headquarters in Langley Virginia. The feeling of apprehension caused a physical reaction – his hands were shaking on the steering wheel. This drive was one that John normally cherished. He particularly relished it at times like this when he had just left some drab Arab country. In the past, the drive would have fostered a peaceful feeling in contrast to the chaotic streets of Riyadh that he had just left. Everything appeared so orderly. The smells of freshly cut grass and the picture perfect colors from the spring's azaleas and Dog-wood trees contrasted so sharply with the dirt and sand that blew so harshly in the Arab spring. But today, John's thoughts were preoccupied. *I killed five people.* He shuddered. *The decisions I made killed four others and left several others wounded. There can be no accounting for these kinds of results.*

With a sense of foreboding John entered Hqs that morning. On his right was the large wall with so many Stars on it, representing those CIA employees who had fallen while in service to their country. Many of those Stars were dedicated to close friends of his who were involved in operations in which he too participated. Now additional Stars would have to be chiseled into that wall. He knew that he would not be able to look at those new Stars without seeing a finger pointing at him saying, "*You* did this."

He retrieved his badge from the security office and proceeded to Paul Brant's office. Paul was the Director of the National Clandestine Service (D/NCS), also known as the "nation's spy master". Paul's office was located on the seventh (top) floor of the building and upon entering John glanced through the floor to ceiling widows at the panoramic view of the wooded Virginia country side. This view generated a rather peaceful and serene ambiance that contrasted sharply with the typical business that was conducted here. The office itself was relatively large with a credenza against the far wall and an executive desk in front of it. That section of the office also included two straight-backed chairs that faced the desk. In the middle of the room was a small conference table that could seat 8 persons. On the near side of the office was a sofa flanked by two arm chairs. Rounding out the office on the wall opposite the windows was a huge, colored world map dotted with many notations.

Paul was seated behind his desk and as John walked in he noticed the Chief of the Near East Division, CNE, sitting opposite Paul. Both were John's long-time friends but he also knew they took their jobs very seriously and were anxious to get to the bottom of the troubles in Riyadh Station. He was fearful that Paul was going to tell him that he and the Director decided to fire him.

John sat in the other chair facing Paul's desk and after a very brief 'catching up' on family and friends, Paul decided to get to the point.

"What the hell is going on in Riyadh, John? This past six months have been an absolute disaster like *nothing else* I have seen in my career. We have read all your messages but we want to hear all the nuances and whatever else you may have left out of official messages. You started off with a bang and I thought you were going to immediately transform your station into a model for others to emulate, but then it all went to hell in a hand basket."

"A few months ago," John began, "I thought I was going to enjoy coming back here to the Hqs and explaining how I went about turning things around in Riyadh. But today I was reluctant to enter this building. I know that you expected, rightfully so, better results from me. But I can tell you that I am more down on myself than either of you two could be. That being said, I don't know that I would change any of the operational decisions I made. There is something very wrong going on but at the moment, I'm not sure what that is."

Paul said, "I'm not going to try and sugar coat this for you John, you are indeed the commander in the field and you must take responsibility when things go badly, just as you readily take ownership of successes in your Station."

CNE Jim Harding chimed in, "That's right John. I expected better from you. I have never seen flaps like this in all my time at the Agency. If you do your job correctly and have your officers using good tradecraft, you shouldn't have dead bodies and compromises on your hands."

Jim was a friend and his rebuke startled John. He wondered, *Why the hell was he piling on? I know I am responsible but to suggest I'm a total fuck-up is out of line. Until I have found some answers, I'll have to sit and listen to his sniping, but I don't like it one bit. His record sucks compared to mine so I wonder if this is just jealousy talking.*"

Paul abruptly broke in, "That's enough Jim. John's record tells me he knows how to run operations and he knows he is responsible when things go badly. Also, John, I know you had an extremely difficult decision to make and I will address that later. And while we are going to hold you responsible, John, I want you to know that we are here to help you discover why things went sideways and how to fix it."

"I didn't mean to be overly critical, it's just that I am so disturbed by what has gone wrong" Jim contritely murmured.

John was quite relieved at Paul's attitude and then he look at Jim, "How the hell do you think I feel? I am taking responsibility but I am more concerned now about finding the reason or reasons for the flaps and how we can rectify the situation."

Then turning to Paul, "I'm very pleased that you understand. I must say that I feared a Washington *cover your ass* response, not from you personally, but from Washington in general."

Paul removed his glasses and began cleaning them, "Jim, can you give us a moment. I need to talk to John alone for a bit." After Jim left, Paul said, "Don't dwell on the negative, John. I know you well enough to be certain that the troubles in your Station are not of your making.

You made a hard decision, which produced a horrific result, but it was the right thing to do and we are proud of you. For the present, however, keep this whole thing under wraps. Don't brief the Ambassador or anybody else until I tell you otherwise. The President wants to see how this plays out in the press before deciding who should know what really happened. The President did tell the Director that not only does he believe you made the right decision but he considers you a hero."

Paul told John that he has some new information that will shed some light on the problems, "Before revealing that," he added, " why don't you start from the beginning John and give me a blow by blow account of what took place over the last nine months or so."

"Okay, here goes."

CHAPTER II

August 2016, Riyadh, Saudi Arabia

The first thing John did when he arrived in Riyadh was to review the operational goals and objectives of Riyadh Station. These goals and objectives are provided to every CIA Station at the beginning of each year. Then he compared those goals and objectives to what the Station had accomplished during the year. The comparison was not good.

The primary objective, even before the Russians, was to counter terrorist operations by penetrating the most aggressive terror groups, al-Qaida and ISIS. Additionally, the Station was tasked with running anti-terrorist operations against the Houthi rebels in neighboring Yemen. Due to the tenuous security situation there, the Station in Yemen, currently in Aden, rather than its traditional home in Sana'a, was in no position to organize para-military type operations. So the onus of this task fell to Riyadh. The situation in Yemen had become increasingly unsettling and the U.S. was beginning to play a major role in the fight against the Houthi movement and its Iranian supporters. In addition the growing threat from al-Qaida, known there as Al-Qaida in the Arabian Peninsula (AQAP), needed to be addressed by the Station.

Other objectives of the Station were to report on the dynamics of the Saudi Royal Family, the Saudi economy with particular emphasis on Petroleum and the Saudi financial institutions.

So it was on that hot August morning that John finished his review of the Station's targets and objectives. He had a limited exposure to Riyadh's capability from Washington but now that he was in Riyadh and had a firsthand look at the situation, it distressed him. To accomplish any of the objectives mentioned, the Station needed to penetrate the organizations involved and that meant recruiting spies – in the past year there were zero recruitments.

John's career in the CIA was stellar. As a junior case officer he recruited valuable spies -designated as "agents" in the CIA - in every Station to which he had been assigned. He had come into the Agency with a burning desire to help his country and he found the CIA's mission to be conducive to achieving his desire. He had worked his way up to be a Chief of Station rather quickly, and once he did, he proved to be a very able manager.

The part of the job John most enjoyed was mentoring younger officers and watching them blossom into first rate case officers. He assumed that his biggest challenge yet was going to be here in Riyadh. It was incumbent upon him to breathe some new life into this Station. He assumed he would have to be a hard ass with most of the officers but others might respond to a more 'motherly' approach. He told himself he would reserve judgement on this issue until after he had a better assessment of each officer.

John had had some exposure to his deputy, Tim Haggerty, in the past and he had not been impressed. In fact, he had tried to get Tim reassigned so that he could pick his own deputy. But Tim had been in Riyadh for a year and was expected to be there for another year before his tour was complete. John had already decided that there would be no extension to Tim's tour.

So on this first morning he decided to start with Tim. He walked over to the next office and asked Tim to come into his office for a chat. Tim, with a year under his belt in Riyadh, was familiar with all the operations and the pros and cons of the various officers. Tim was about the same age as John but look older. His hair was almost all white, while John had a more distinguished sprinkling of grey. Tim was also shorter than John with a growing paunch that tended to make him look older. Tim was more of the studious type and his face had that pallor look of those who seldom ventured outdoors. He was a graduate of Yale with an advanced degree in political science, and his wife Denise was similarly inclined, as she too was a Yale graduate with a master's degree in political science. Tim had a profound understanding of the political situation in the Arab World and its players. However, he was not well suited for operations since he was more comfortable reading a book about the area rather than sitting in coffee shops arguing current affairs, something that John loved to do.

Starting out John said, "Tim, from my read of the Station's objectives and our accomplishments, I don't think we are doing very well. This Station hasn't recruited a new agent in over year. Also, our reporting on terrorism in general is pathetic. What are our ops officers doing with their time?"

Tim was calm in his response, "John, I know we have not set the world on fire here, but you have to agree that recruiting agents to penetrate ISIS and al-Qaida is extremely difficult. These terrorists are hard nuts to crack and they are extremely loyal to their leaders. Likewise, recruiting Saudis is next to impossible. They have all the money in the world and they are not exactly courageous types who would risk the wrath of the regime, which has no tolerance for any kind of disobedience."

"I understand that", John said, "but agents are difficult to recruit everywhere. Being a traitor to one's country or cause is not something that comes natural to many men or women, but our agency has been finding ways to recruit agents all over the world since its inception and we are going to do it here."

Tim nodded in agreement, but later that night told his wife, "John doesn't know what he is up against here. I think he is just another one of those hard chargers who will soon learn that things are different in Saudi Arabia. I've decided to let John huff and puff for a while until he comes to understand that Washington's expectations for Riyadh Station are unrealistic."

John sensed that while Tim was agreeing he had that "I know better look" about him. So John said, "here is how I want to proceed: I will be in the office every morning at 7 AM to read the intelligence reports that have come in during the night and the operational messages as well. That will take me to about the time I have to attend the morning meet with the Ambassador and heads of other key agencies at 9am. Typically that will not last longer than 45 minutes, except on Tuesdays when we have the larger Country Team meeting."

Just thinking about the Country Team meetings caused John to groan. He assumed that because Riyadh was a large mission, the Country Team would be huge, consisting of agency chiefs like the Drug Enforcement Agency,

Agriculture Department, Commerce Department, at least two Military reps but probably more, the head of AID[1], and the various heads of the Embassy sections. So unlike the smaller meetings that were held on a daily basis, almost half the attendees of the Country Team didn't have high security clearances, and that meant John would just have to sit there and listen but not offer any comments or advice.

"In any event", John went on, "most days I will be out of those meetings by 10 am and I will then want to start short, one-on-one meetings with each ops officer, starting with you Tim. I will want to review what each officer has accomplished in the past 24 hours and what he expects to do in the next 24 hours. However, before I start that process, I want to have a general meeting with all ops officers to convey to them my expectations and my general philosophy about being an intelligence officer."

"Boss," Tim interrupted, "do you really want to micro-manage everything our officers do?"

John had been accused of being a micro manger before and he had to admit to himself that there was some truth to it. However, his assessment of the accomplishments and activities of Riyadh Station told him that almost everyone on his team needed good kick in the ass. He didn't get to be one of the Agency's top ops officers at a relatively young age by not being aggressive, detail oriented and sometimes a real bastard of a boss.

"Look Tim, many of our officers may come to dislike me because I will be all over them and demanding. I don't care if I am not liked – you can be the nice guy. However, I take my responsibility as the COS here very seriously. If I have my way we are going to be recruiting agents and running both espionage and para-military operations on a much broader scale than we have thus far. Those operations will be risky, particularly for the agents involved who will be putting their lives on the line. So when I approve an operation, I want to have all the details because if anyone loses their life, it will be on me. From my standpoint, without good agents we will not have good information. Without good information decisions I make may be flawed, but more importantly, the bigger decisions made by our policymakers could be dead wrong. Lastly, I know the Director is expecting me to turn

[1] Agency for International Development

this Station around and start producing results, and that is what we are going to do."

Tim walked out of the COS' office thinking that he was going to have a rough few months with the new chief. As he passed John's secretary, JoAnn Sabinski, he said, "What an asshole. This guy is going to make all of our lives difficult with his rah, rah, rah stuff. He thinks he is the only one who knows anything about operations. Wait until he finds out how many counter-terrorist agents the Station is going to add, or how many Saudi agents. I can tell him right now – none."

JoAnn verbally said nothing but the look on her face spoke volumes. She was seething; she did not like Tim Haggerty!

John spent the remainder of his day familiarizing himself with the Stations administrative personnel, the physical layout and security practices. He was particularly concerned about access to and the construction of the "bubble", a rather large conference room within a vaulted room. The bubble itself was made of clear, 2 inch thick and hard plastic on all sides so that any object attached to it could be readily identified. The bubble sat on "stilts" so that even the floor could be examined for any foreign objects. Additionally it had electronic sensors to detect any signals in the area, as well as an electronic field that would block any signals attempting to enter or emanate out of the bubble. This was the most secure area of the Station – indeed in the entire Embassy - and a place where ops officers could come to write their operational reports and read sensitive material. For John, this would be the place where he would hold all his operational discussions and meetings. The computers were linked to an encrypted telecommunication system that ensured all messages, both incoming and outgoing, were secure and could only be read on Agency computers.

The Station was located on the third floor of the Embassy. In order to access the elevator in the Embassy, one had to enter a four digit code, and in order to have the elevator stop at the third floor, another code had to be entered. Finally, in order to gain entry through the main door to the Station, one had to provide a four fingered print on a glass pad.

Satisfied that the Station was physically secure, John spent some time with his secretary explaining how he wished to organize his days. Having a "secretary" was a bit antiquated these days as most offices favored the "administrative assistance." But John liked to have the old fashion secretary who would take dictation and transcribe all but his most thoughtful reports. JoAnn Sabinski was in her late 40's, had never married nor had children. She had been in the Agency for most of her adult life. She was tall, 5' 8", but not a very attractive women, although she was well groomed and kept herself in prime physical condition. She was extremely efficient, not particularly friendly or jovial, but very serious about her job. In a word, she lived for her job and was dedicated to the COS - just what John wanted and why he chose her for the position.

Typically John like to stay relatively late at the office, unless he had an early evening social engagement. Late hours at the office were almost a must for responsible COS' in the area because Hqs was 8 hours behind. So if John stayed in the office until at least 7 pm, when it was 11am in Washington, he would get the initial responses to high priority cables he and his staff had dispatched that day. On this day he was prepared to leave at 7:30 and was surprised to see that JoAnn was still at her desk. Other than the communicators and the Marine guards, they were probably the only ones left in the Embassy. On his way out John ask JoAnn why she was still at the office. She replied that it was her habit to read through all of the operational and intelligence reports of the day so that she would be better equipped to handle any request of the COS. John was mildly pleased with this state of affairs, but over time began to worry about JoAnn's obsessively long hours. Sometimes he would note that she had logged out of the security system at close to midnight.

The next day he had his first meeting with all the ops officers. "Let me begin," he told them, "by letting you know that my assessment of this Station's accomplishments is not very positive. I don't think any of you have been going about your job in a fashion that produces results. OK, so now you are saying to yourselves, 'here comes this guy right out of Hqs and he acts like he knows more than us about operations in the Kingdom.' Well guys, maybe I do and maybe I don't but you have to admit that operations are moving at a snail's pace here. Is there anyone among you who is satisfied with the progress you have made in the past year? Anyone? Anyone NOT satisfied with their progress in the past year?" At this point most of the officers either nodded yes or raised their hands.

"It seems we have a consensus – almost nobody is satisfied with their progress. I noticed that you Peter seemed to be one who is satisfied with the progress you are making. Would you please stay on for a few minutes after this meeting to give me some details of your ops activities?

Peter Christopolis said, "Sure John, I'd be happy to give you a complete run down of my developmentals"

John continued by saying, "As for the rest of you, why not do things my way for a while and let's see if we can turn things around. I have spent many years in the Arab World and have a number of good recruitments under my belt. There is no big mystery how it's done, so give me a chance to help you. First of all, good ops officers have to be out almost every night meeting potential agents. You have to be imaginative about this. Find out where there will be lectures on political subjects and attend those lectures. Go to coffee houses that attract the young, inquisitive minds and make sure you hit every diplomatic function you can. Get yourselves invited to as many events as possible.

The only way to start assessing people as potential agents is to meet them first. The more people you meet and assess, the more successful you are going to be. Someone once said if you meet 100 people there is probably one agent among them. But if you don't get out and meet 100 people, you won't recruit a single agent. Is this news to any of you? Do any of you have any questions about what I just said?" There were no responses.

Before starting again John noticed that his deputy Tim Haggerty had begun to drum his fingers on the conference table and it was getting louder and louder. "Tim, am I boring you or is there something you wish to say?"

"Oh sorry boss, I was just day dreaming".

"Given your lack of operational activity, I suggest you start paying attention," John retorted. *If Tim is trying to play some cute power game in front of all the officers, I'm going to have my foot so far up his ass, I'll lose my shoe.*

John then turned his attention back to the entire group, "Also, I want to impress upon you that we are the eyes and ears of our policy makers. It is incumbent upon us to give them the best information available so they can formulate the best policies for our nation. In doing that you must strictly adhere to the truth. We have a sacred trust that must be held to the highest standards. In the past I have seen ops officers inflate intel reports so that they look good. That simply will not be tolerated. It is our mission to tell the truth to our consumers. Now we may engage in repeated falsehoods in our efforts to recruit foreigners and to perform some operational tasks, but our operational and intelligence reports to our customers and those at Hqs who support us, must uphold the highest standards of honesty. Am I clear on that point?" A resounding chorus of "yes sirs" followed that, except for Tim, who just nodded.

"I didn't hear your response Tim, did I not make myself clear to you."

"Sorry," said Tim, "I fully agree with you."

"The final thing I want to emphasize to you is the tremendous importance of tradecraft. I will be paying particular attention to how you prepare for agent meetings and the tradecraft you employ in those meetings. You all have had extensive training at the Farm and elsewhere on agent handling but all too often I have seen officers disregard their training and become exceedingly sloppy. Remember, the agents we recruit rely on us to keep them safe and alive. We have an obligation of the highest order to maintain a level of tradecraft that ensures our agents will come to no harm. If you think you may have some difficulty keeping your agent safe, come to me and together we will devise a plan that will."

"Lastly, I want to tell all of you that I love my job. Every morning when I get out of bed I feel that I can't wait to get to work. I want all of you to have that same feeling. The spy business is very serious and very important but it can be, and should be, a lot of fun. Once you recruit your own agents and those agents begin to provide you with valuable intelligence information, you will feel that you are really contributing to your country's well-being. Are there any questions? No? Was I that clear? OK, I'll get off my high horse and allow my words to sink. Go do your jobs!"

The officers began to file out of the bubble, discussing the comments of their boss with some exuberance. Peter Christopolis stayed behind and approached John, "Can we have our little chat later? I have a scheduled meeting that I should attend."

"Sure, Peter. Just come and see me when you are free."

After leaving the meeting Tim Haggerty and a couple of the officers congregated in the open space outside of Tim's and John's offices. Tim said to them, "well, your lives are going to be miserable for a while. You might as well get used to spinning your wheels for a period of time until the boss realizes what we are up against here."

One of the officers, Kim Malloy, chimed in, "I don't know, Tim, I think perhaps we should be buying into John's philosophy; you have to admit we haven't been very successful this past year."

Another officer, George Willis, said, "I agree! I'm actually excited about going all out for new recruits and making this a hard-charging Station, a Station we can all be proud of."

After those comments, a red-faced Tim Haggerty said nothing as he wondered back to his office.

So in those first few weeks as COS Riyadh John settled into his routine at the office – early morning arrival to read all the intel and ops messages; attend the Ambassador's morning meetings and then start his round of interviews with his ops officers. He originally planned to spend about 15 minutes with each officer and then concentrate on his own operational tasks but he found in those first few weeks that 15 minutes was just not enough time. His meetings with DCOS Haggerty were frustrating. Tim saw himself as a Station administrator, and as the DCOS, indeed he was. Tim was au courant on almost every political situation in the Middle East; he knew all the details of every operation being run by the Station, and he made sure the administrative staff was functioning like a well-oiled machine. But as far as John was concerned Tim was supposed to be an ops officer above all else, not an administrator. He was having a hard time motivating Tim to start his own operations. In actual fact Riyadh Station was rather large as Stations go in this part of the world but *this is not really a large organization requiring extensive management. I can handle most of the management myself – I need Tim to be more operational.* Also, the last thing he needed was for his deputy to try and undermine him. He thought he better address that issue up front and clearly.

With fury in his eyes John said, "Tim, I don't know what you think you were doing in our meeting the other day, but let me be clear with you. If I think you are trying to undermine the directions I am giving our officers, I will have you out of here in a blink of the eye. That doesn't mean I don't welcome dissent and opposing views, I do. But snide undercutting I will not tolerate. Now, do we have a problem?"

Tim claimed that John simply misinterpreted him. "I'm all on board with your program and ready to help in any way I can," Tim calmly responded.

The next officer to be interviewed was George Willis. George was an interesting case, as the nephew of former DCI (Director of CIA) Peter Willis, he was expected to be a rising star in the Agency. Both the Director and the D/NCS had told John in no uncertain terms that they expected him to groom George into one of the best ops officers in the Agency. After a few minutes with George, John concluded that his superiors' expectations were not unfounded. George was a handsome, tall man at 6' 2", and in great physical condition. He looked like the California surfer poster boy with his light sandy hair, good looks and deep tan. Additionally, it very quickly became apparent that George was quite bright and adept at languages. Having studied Arabic for only a year, he was quite proficient in the language. George had been a Marine Corp captain before joining the Agency and he tended to maintain his Marine conditioning regime. He was married to Amy Fielding, whose great grandfather was a tycoon in the steel business. The couple did not have children but they had only been married for a few years. John had been told that there were some problems in the marriage but he didn't know anything more than that. Amy was a pleasant woman, but not very attractive, nor was she particularly bright; she was however, loaded! John would on occasion question George's character – *why would a good-looking, bright, dynamic man marry someone who, bluntly put, was so dull.* There was an obvious answer but John did not wish to voice it.

In the first few interviews it became clear that George was doing all the right things. John asked George what he was doing with his time and George replied, "I am out almost every night, attending a reception, dinner, lecture, political discussion or some other type of function that will bring me in contact with potential targets for recruitment. I have three individuals I am seriously developing: a Saudi undersecretary in the Ministry of Foreign Affairs; an Egyptian diplomat and a Palestinian woman who is an executive in a charitable fund."

When John probed his young officer rather intensely about his developmentals, George said, "I met the Saudi Foreign Affairs official almost immediately after my arrival about a year ago. We have become fast friends since the Saudi, Abdullah bin Saud, was educated at Georgetown University in Washington, D.C. He is bright, athletic and, most importantly, he is an official on the American Desk in the Ministry of Foreign Affairs. That means he has access to potentially important intelligence information.

"George, during this year long development period, have you noted any vulnerabilities in Abdullah's character or some situation in his life that would make him vulnerable to recruitment?"

"I have looked carefully but thus far I don't see any issue that would cause him to consider a recruitment pitch. However, I intend to keep on looking."

John shook his head and said, "Look, you have gone through all the right steps in the recruitment cycle; you *spotted* Abdullah as a potential recruit; you made an *assessment* that he had *access* to potentially important intel; then you *developed* him for the past year. That development has not revealed any vulnerabilities for recruitment. In fact, it has told you that Abdullah is a loyal Saudi who would not betray his country. He may on occasion give you a tidbit of information, but he is not a candidate for recruitment. One of the hardest things to do in this business is to let go of a developmental when we realize he is not recruitable and move on to another target. That is not to say that you should cease your friendship with Abdullah, but you have to manage your valuable time so that you can move on to other potential targets."

George admitted that he was coming to the same conclusion but was reluctant to let go. Now that he had his marching order he would.

As for the Egyptian Diplomat, Mohammad al-Masri, John saw much more potential. Mohammad, like most Egyptian diplomats, was quite sophisticated and bright. He spoke four or five languages fluently, had a PhD in history from Cairo University, had been a diplomat for about 15 years and worked hard at his profession. Mohammad was well-known in Riyadh's diplomatic circles, since he attended as many functions as he was able, and being a fellow of good cheer, he tended to be invited frequently. Mohammad's brother was a military officer in Cairo and in previous years had been the aide-de-camp to now Egyptian President Abdal-Fatah al-Sisi when the latter was Commander-in-Chief of the Egyptian Armed Forces. So, not only did Mohammad have access to potentially important Ministry of Foreign Affairs intel, but he also had potential access to military and presidential information. He could be a very valuable agent!

As for any potential vulnerabilities, George reported that Mohammad terribly missed having a good scotch whiskey – not that he was an alcoholic, but he liked his booze a bit more than most. Additionally, as is the case with most Egyptian government officials, he was severely underpaid. Living in one of the wealthiest countries in the world whose citizens loved to flaunt their wealth, he could not help but feel the pinch. So, when George first offered Mohammad a bottle of Johnny Walker Blue, Mohammed had set aside his pride and quickly accepted. George was quick to learn that the Station's supply of secretly imported liquor was one of his best operational tools in Saudi Arabia – a country where the import and consumption of alcohol is banned. More importantly, Mohammad complained bitterly about the slave wages Egyptian diplomats were given.

All of this was very familiar to John from his earlier years of service in Cairo. He recalled that Egyptian ministers were paid the equivalent of $600 per month, and yet, they all drove Mercedes cars and lived in opulent homes. Where the funds to support such lifestyles came from was a frequent question, and the answer was always some form of corruption. So John encouraged George to continue his development of Mohammad by periodically offering him some form of financial support that would not be so blatant as to offend his dignity. George was encouraged to ask for Mohammed's thoughts on various political events and then to present his "gifts" to Mohammad as repayment for the "insight" provided by him. Hopefully, the remuneration for these insights would turn into a more formal and regular payment for something more than insights, and once it did, Mohammad's recruitment would just be a matter of time. John knew that once the Egyptian started to receive regular payments, it would be extremely difficult for him to live without them.

George's other developmental, Amal Ansari, was the most interesting. She was the effective administrator of a charitable fund, of which she was well suited due to her degree in finance and accounting from the American

University of Beirut. From George's description, John learned that Amal was only 28 years old and apparently quite attractive. Her parents were Palestinian refugees who were resettled in South Beirut's Shatila Refugee Camp. Thus, Amal grew up in squalor but because of her academic brilliance, she earned a scholarship to AUB, the Middle East's most prestigious institute of higher learning, not counting schools in Israel.

It was not uncommon to find a Palestinian managing the funds or finances of various organizations or individuals in Saudi Arabia – they were well-known and well-suited for such positions - but it was unusual for a Palestinian woman, in fact any kind of woman, to be running a financial office. It turns out the Amal was unusual in many ways – a spirited woman who was fluent in English, French and Arabic. As a very well read women she had opinions on a wide variety of subjects and felt no apprehension about voicing her views. But as John tried to get a better grasp of what kind, *if any*, intelligence she might have access to, he was hitting a dead end. George could not explain exactly what kind of charitable fund she managed, nor what the objectives of the fund were.

Many charitable funds in Saudi Arabia were known to have supported radical movements throughout the area, as well as some terrorist organizations. Amal had hinted that her organization may support some radical groups, so John instruct George to learn exactly who these groups were and what kind of support they received.

Meetings with the remaining ops officers followed the one with George Willis. John was not happy with any of these meetings. For instance, he finally met with Peter Christopolis, the officer who earlier claimed to have several good developmentals. Peter was in his late 30s and on his third overseas tour. He was a rail thin individual who tended to almost always wear braces and occasionally an ascot or bow tie rather than a conventional necktie. Because he had such a skinny neck, Peter appeared to have an oversized Adam's apple. When he spoke, Peter's Adam's apple seemed to bob up and down his neck. John found this most distracting.

When John asked Peter how he was spending his evenings and who was he developing, Peter went into great detail about an Italian diplomat, whose wife had Royal linage, and how this couple was the darling of the diplomatic circuit. Peter said, "This Italian considers me to be his best friend. I am also *very close* to a Belgium diplomat who provides me with many tidbits of information about what is happening in the Saudi government.

John asked Peter if those two were the developmentals Peter had referred to in their previous meeting and Peter confirmed that they were. Trying to mask the frustration he felt, John began, "Peter, you have all the good makings of a strong FSO, Foreign Service Officer in the State Department, but I'm not sure you are cut out for the spy business. We are *not* interested in tidbits of information about the Saudi government; we want to steal their secrets! You know that don't you?"

Peter countered by saying he thought both of his European contacts were plugged into Saudis who were providing them with information that was not readily available to the public. John, again trying to disguise his frustration, responded, "Then perhaps you should be looking at those Saudis *directly*, rather than the European intermediaries.

"If these Europeans have any usefulness to the intelligence business, it is as an access agent, not as a penetration of a government. We typically think of an access agent as someone who can initiate the first steps for us in the recruitment cycle of a hard target, like a Russian. Well, Saudis can be considered a hard target too and if your European friends can start the recruitment process for you by giving you a good assessment of their Saudi interlocutors, then maybe you should try to recruit them for that purpose."

"No, neither of my friends would ever consider being an agent of the CIA for any purpose."

John stared at him in exasperation. "Drop them! They are not developmentals if they cannot serve a purpose in the recruitment cycle. You are wasting your time, Peter. You are not here to collect 'tidbits' on the diplomatic circuit; you are here to steal secrets and in order to do that you need to recruit spies. Where have you served previously, Peter?"

"I previously served in Brussels and Bonn.

John then asked "Why are you now in an NE Division Station?

"It wasn't my choice," Peter replied, "my last COS recommended that I have a tour in NE, so here I am."

"Do you know why he made the recommendation and who was that COS?"

Peter said his former COS' words were something like, "maybe you'll learn a thing or two in NE."

When Peter identified his former COS in Bonn, John recognized him immediately as an old NE hand with whom John had served in earlier days. Then John understood why Peter was here – he was in Riyadh to learn how to be an ops officer. John made a mental note to keep hammering away at him until Peter learned the difference between a developmental and a friendly contact.

With the exception of Kim Malloy, the meetings with the remaining officers went along the same lines as the meeting with Peter Christopolis. Each officer had one or two agents he was handling but none were seriously developing someone who had the potential to become a productive asset, or had access to a productive asset. John's message to each of them was the same: "I want you to attend some function every night that will allow you to meet a potential agent." He reviewed for them the agent acquisition cycle, something that should have been drummed into them at the Agency's training facility, 'The Farm'. The first step in the agent acquisition cycle is to "spot" a potential agent and you can't do that sitting at home he would tell them. He ended his review with each of them with the solemn warning that their tours in Riyadh would be extremely short if he did not see some positive movement and they certainly would not like the grades on their fitness reports. Indeed, "Unless there was some dramatic improvement," he warned, "this could be your last overseas assignment."

CHAPTER III

About half of John's time was consumed with liaison.[2] The Station had regular contact with three organizations – the Istikhbarat al-'Am or General Intelligence (GI), the Mubahith al-'Am or General Investigations Department, and directly with the Minister of Interior. For the most part John dealt with GI and the Minister of Interior, while DCOS Haggerty met with the Mubahith. The intelligence exchange with the various Saudi services had developed into a very professional exchange over the years. Initially it had been pretty much a one-way street with the Station providing intelligence from all over the world to the Saudis, while the Saudi side provide only a bit of local color. However, over the years the Saudis had become more sophisticated and their current collection efforts were robust, particularly in the Middle East.

With the elevation of Prince Mohammad bin Nawwaf to the position of Crown Prince, meaning he was next in line to be King, his position of Minister of Interior and general tsar of intelligence made him even more important. John first met Prince Mohammad in the latter's office in Jeddah when John first arrived in August. The heads of the Saudi Government move to Ta'if, which is in the Mecca Province, during the summer months because Taif is about 6000 feet above sea level and therefore much cooler than Riyadh. However, senior government officials tend to meet non-Muslims in

---

[2] In CIA parlance,' liaison' refers to local intelligence services with whom the Station cooperates.

nearby Jeddah, not in Ta'if. So when John received a call from one of Prince Mohammad's aides in early October telling him the Prince was back in Riyadh and wanted to see him the following morning, he was a bit surprised. First off, he didn't know the Prince had returned to Riyadh. Secondly, meetings with Prince Mohammad tended to be at the request of the American side and they were almost always scheduled in the afternoon or evening. *This must be important,* John thought.

As he was led into the Prince's office he was taken aback by its size and grandeur. It seemed as if the Prince's desk was about a football field away from the office's entrance and the long walk to the seating area was adorned with beautiful Persian carpets. Finally reaching the desk area the Prince rose to greet him and John said, "sabah al-kheir sumu amir." To which the Prince replied, "And good morning to you John. I see your Arabic pronunciation is excellent but I believe my English is better than your Arabic, so let's proceed in your language." John knew that Prince Mohammad had studied at an American college and therefore was fluent in English but John was fluent in Arabic.

Before John could respond, Prince Mohammad said, "I asked you to come in today John because we have received an important bit of information about a meeting to be held in Yemen between some of the leaders of al-Qaida in the Arabian Peninsula, which I believe you refer to as AQAP. Our understanding is the meeting will take place in the village of Yuwan, which is northwest of the port city of al-Mukalla. There is a strong possibility that the notorious bomb maker Hassan al-Asiri will be at this meeting. Al-Asiri's presence leads us to believe that the purpose of the meeting will be to plan a terrorist attack outside of Yemen - most probably against a Saudi or American target. We must develop more information on this potential meeting but the little we know now tells us it will be held in the home of an AQAP member."

John asked the Prince about the timing of the meeting but Prince Mohammad could only say that it was "Weeks away".

John said, "I am not intimately familiar with that area; what else is there?"

"Nothing, John, the place is pretty desolate. I am hoping your people back at Langley and in the Pentagon will put all your resources on this. Track the senior members of AQAP and see if you can learn if any of them are planning to travel. You know they are very disciplined in the use of their communications so we will need to cover this target with everything you and we have. But our info tells us that this meeting is important and and disrupting it could lead to an intel coup, resulting in the take down of the participants and recovery of their documents, cell phones and computer hard drives. With all that info we could track these guys down and eliminate a major threat to both our countries."

"The location of the meeting, probably eliminates an air strike of any kind. This is a small village in which most of the residences are close together and multi-storied, making it difficult to hit a target without serious collateral damage. Besides, an air strike would rule out the possibility of capturing one or two important terrorists and the collection of highly important counter terrorist information. What do you think?"

John was unhesitant in his response, "I totally agree with you. I am going to recommend that we immediately start planning for a special ops team to infiltrate the area, attack the meeting site, capture as many participants as possible and kill the remainder. Of course Washington will ask for a lot more intelligence before giving approval for a special ops attack. Just to be clear, you are suggesting that this will be a U.S. operation but we will share the intel with you, is that right?"

"Not entirely", said the Prince, "we want to have limited participation in the planning. Naturally all the operators will be your guys, but we want one Saudi officer to tag along."

"Hmm, that might be difficult, you know how precise a mission like this has to be. The troops on the ground have to instinctively rely on each other and know the others' moves even *before* they make them. That means they have trained together for extended periods. Having an outsider along could put the mission in jeopardy."

The Prince was insistent that a Saudi officer accompany the team as an observer who would be completely under the command of the American team leader. So John told him that he would try to get Washington onboard with having a Saudi participant.

Back at the Station John noted that it was too early to call Hqs. and he thought it might be more useful to send a message detailing the meeting and his recommendations so that when he did call later, Hqs would have had time to coordinate with the Pentagon. He wanted to think this through and draft his message carefully. So he did not dictate the message to JoAnn but rather drafted it on his computer. In doing so he recommended that his special ops team in Riyadh not be the action team. He had assigned to him a 5 member special ops group but he thought an operation of this importance would probably require a team at least twice the size as his. However, if there was to be a Saudi observer, he wanted the Station's military specialist Norm Halderman to also be included. Norm was a former JSOC[3] officer with extensive special ops training. He would certainly not be a hindrance to any team. Unfortunately John could not say the same for the Saudi officer that the Prince insistent on including.

Of course, a tough decision had to be made regarding whether an insertion team should be deployed. These types of operations were extremely dangerous and required extensive planning. If the AQAP meeting took place soon, there would not be sufficient time to plan for a raid. And even if there was enough time, Washington may deem it is too risky and, therefore, opt to take out the participants with missiles regardless of the risk of collateral damage.

John began by stating the obvious – much more information was required to plan for this kind of operation. Intense satellite coverage of the area should begin immediately. NSA[4] must be directed to give special attention to any comms in the area. Trusted agents in Yemen should be put on alert to report on any unusual activity. He wrote that the Saudis will allow U.S. forces to stage from their base in either Najran or Khamis Mushait, with Najran being the closer of the two and Khamis Mushait the larger with more available services.

If a decision is made to attempt a raid with a concomitant capture of al-Asiri, John suggested that a Twin-Otter aircraft be brought in to conduct a reconnaissance mission. He further suggested that the actual reconnaissance team be composed of paramilitary officers from the Station. The Twin-Otter

[3] Joint Special Operations Command. A military unit composed of troopers highly trained in the use of deadly force from various military commands. Its primary mission is to conduct highly classified, and dangerous para military operations, often in conjunction with the CIA.
[4] NSA: The National Security Agency. This Agency is responsible for collecting signals intelligence and that includes all types of communications and other data transmitted electronically.

had been around for a long time and is well suited for this type of operation. It can fly low, land in remote desert areas and take off with limited space. John knew the Agency's team was very adept at conducting this kind of operation and their recon info could mean the difference between success and failure of the follow-on operation. Satellites and drones can produce a lot of information but they are no substitute for 'on the ground' reconnaissance.

John addressed his message "Eyes Only" to D/NCS Paul Brant, CNE Jim Harding and C/CTC[5], and a few hours after sending it, he made a secure video phone call to Langley. All of the addressees on his message were conferenced into the call and there was an obvious excitement within the group. Dan Clark, the head of CTC, was particularly enthusiastic about the possibility of capturing al-Asiri, plus the collection of cell phone, computer and other forms of information that potentially could lead to the identification of terrorist both inside and out of Yemen. Clark suggested that this op had the potential to lead to the decimation of the entire terrorist organization.

D/NCS Paul Brant was more reserved, having seen too many proposed operations come apart before they got off the ground. Paul said, "This has great potential but we must have more intelligence before we and JSOC can make a decision as to which path we are going to follow. John, you have to get back to the Saudis and tell them we need details. We can't come up with a plan based on the sketchy info they have provided. Meanwhile, we have already tasked NSA to step up their collection of comms in Yemen and we have directed more intense satellite coverage of the area. We might also put some drones over Yuwan but we don't want to alert our targets that we are watching them. So drone coverage will be limited."

"I know we need more info, Paul," John replied, "and I have said as much to Mohammed. I just wanted to get all of you in Washington on board so we can start thinking about the options available to us and determine which would be the best one for our set of circumstances."

"Ok, I understand. John. I think your suggestion of going in there with a recon team is a good one; I have already alerted the guys in our Air Branch to start planning such a mission. Meanwhile I have also briefed the Director about this. He wants to wait until we firm up our plan before briefing the

---

[5] Chief of the Counter-Terrorism Center

President. However, the Director asked me to tell you that you should do whatever is necessary to bring about this operation. This is the kind of news the President likes to hear, and of course if it is successful, he will share it with the Nation."

John groaned, "publicizing this operation is the last thing I want to see happen but I guess it's inevitable."

The next morning John called Prince Mohammad's office to set up an appointment and he was told to come that evening at 8 PM. He did not want to wait until evening but the Saudi side was insistent. When he met Prince Mohammad that evening, the latter apologized for the delay. He said, "John I know you were anxious to meet this morning but our ops officers were having meetings today with agents whom I thought could provide us more detail on the AQAP meeting, and they did. I have several important updates: First, Al-Asiri definitely will be at this meeting and secondly, the meeting is set for November 14th. We have not been able to determine who else will attend but it is clear from the arrangements being made, they must all be important. There will be a 10 man protection team from AQAP at the meeting and this rarely happens. Typically they have two or three security types at most guarding their people. The size of the protection detail alone is indicative of the importance of the members attending the meeting. Our assumption is they are planning a major terrorist op and want to keep knowledge of it restricted to just a few individuals. Have you picked up any intel from your side about the meeting?"

John said that he had not heard back from Washington but was not surprised that he had not. Yesterday all collection sources had been tasked and they should start reporting back soon. He told Prince Mohammad that their initial thought was to send in a recon team to scout out the area in advance. They would use a Twin-Otter. So, most likely, they could stage the op from Najran because that aircraft does not require any support facilities other than fuel. John also said that Washington was objecting to the prospect of including a Saudi in the action team.

Prince Mohammad was firm in his response, "John we are risking several of our sources on this operation and we think it will be for your benefit. It is not too much to ask that we include one of ours. The officer we have selected has gone through the U.S. Army's Special Forces and Ranger schools. When you meet him, I am sure you will agree that he is up to the task."

John could tell from the Prince's tone and facial expressions that this was not going to be negotiable so he decided to refrain from making it an issue.

Over the next 10 days information about the Yuwan meeting began to dribble in from both the Saudi and the U.S. side. Hqs. assigned a cryptonym for the operation - CAPTURE. It was CIA practice to give all major operations, agents or any sustained contact, a cryptonym that was used in all correspondence. This practice had started in the first days of the CIA when so much of the correspondence was via "dispatch" that would be delivered via a courier from overseas to Hqs. The thinking then was if a diplomatic pouch containing CIA dispatches was ever intercepted, the receiving party would have a difficult time making any sense out of them. This would be even more difficult because while agents and other contacts had cryptonyms, CIA officers and staff had pseudonyms that were used in all correspondence. Even Agency programs were assigned cryptonyms, making Agency correspondence almost unintelligible to an outsider.

Two more attendees of the proposed meeting in Yuwan were identified by both Saudi and U.S. intelligence sources and both were leaders of AQAP. Satellite coverage of the area indicated that there were no hospitals in Yuwan but there was one small school. This information would be useful only if the decision was made to attack the meeting remotely with missiles. Background traces of the known attendees indicated that one of them, Ahmad al-Tuwayjari, was actually born in Yuwan and his family still lived there. The family home would have to be identified, as it was the probable meeting site.

John decided it was time to brief Ambassador Fred Wagner on the potential operation. When he did, Wagner was enthusiastic and offered to do anything he could to support the operation. He volunteered to raise the issue with the King but John asked him to allow Prince Mohammed to handle the Saudi side. "There is no way Mohammed would proceed with this 'joint' operation without first getting the King's full support," said John.

Wagner agreed but told John he wanted to be kept fully informed about this operation.

Next John worked on getting the "Recon Team" ready for action. The Twin-Otter was on its way with two pilots. He planned to involve 3 members of the Station's para-military team who were specialists in reconnaissance. The team would be flown into Yemen during the middle of the night and would determine the best landing zone (LZ) or drop zone (DZ) for the raiding party. The decision to enter the actual village or not would not be made in advance. This decision would be left to the recon team and would be based on what they learned during the recon and what kind, if any, obstacle they encountered. At first, they will use night-vision equipment from a distance to determine the best entry and egress points. They would also seek to obtain other anecdotal information that satellites could not. If all appeared safe, they would actually enter the village and photograph the presumed target house – the Al Tuwayjari family home - which had been identified on their maps, and its surroundings.

One of the first things the recon team determined was that there would only be a sliver of a moon on the night of the recon – great for reconnaissance. This contrasted sharply with the knowledge that on the night of the AQAP proposed meeting there would be a "super full moon". This fact was most discouraging because the super full moon, the first since 1948, would significantly light up the area, discounting the advantage the American team would have with sophisticated night vision equipment.

Norman Halderman chose two former JSOC troops to accompany him on the recon. The two former troopers, Sam Butterfield and Bill Lucas, had conducted many surreptitious recons and were well suited for the job. The team took off from Riyadh early evening on October 29th and landed in Najran 3 hours later. The Twin Otter had to be refueled and the troopers wanted to make last minute checks of their equipment. They were armed only with AR-15 assault rifles with suppressors and thermal scopes. They also wore video capturing helmets and carried low light and thermal cameras. Having thoroughly studied the satellite imagery of the area, they felt they could practically move about blind folded.

Shortly after midnight the Twin Otter took off for what they anticipated to be an hour and 40 minute flight. It was pitch black out that night but the pilots were confident they could safely land about 2 kilometers from Yuwan where there was a small flat area in what was otherwise a very rough terrain. The pilots too had conducted many surreptitious flights into "denied areas". To the casual observer it would appear that the entire group was on a routine flight back in the U.S. or some vacation spot. The troopers were humming tunes and the pilots were casually examining their instruments.

Finally the co-pilot announced "10 minutes to touchdown." The landing was quite rough; had everyone not been strapped in they would have been thrown around the inside of the aircraft. But it very quickly came to a halt. The team immediately deplaned, fanned out and determined that they were quite alone in the area. Indeed, they could not see a living thing or structure because of the mountainous terrain. They quickly moved in the direction of Yuwan without saying a word to one another.

As they approached the village, they could see that it was backed up to a wall that was part of a mesa overlooking the village. They communicated through hand signals and decided to climb to the top of the mesa in order to obtain a wide view of the entire village. As they approached the top of the mesa, several dogs from the village began to bark. At first, they were fearful that the villagers would assume there were intruders in the area, but soon, jackals began to howl back at the barking dogs. The team relaxed because of the "cover" the jackals were providing.

After obtaining a broad view of the entire village from the mesa and capturing it with their cameras, they decided to move in closer. Climbing down from the mesa they approached the village from the West. The first couple of buildings they observed appeared to be abandoned shacks – the windows were all broken and doors were hanging from their hinges. Nothing with heat emanated from these building so the team was quite certain they were unoccupied. As they moved in closer Sam Butterfield entered one of these shacks and was hit by the stench of animal waste. Clearly no one lived in these buildings.

So they moved on to the next group of buildings that were not as decrepit as the first but they appeared unoccupied. Their equipment did register some heat from one of the buildings but this was most likely from animals. The team signaled Bill Lucas to enter that building, which was directly in front of him. Bill crawled to the entrance and from ground level looked closely into the room. Lying there on the mud floor was a small Yemeni, a boy of about 15, sound asleep with a baby goat lying next to him. Bill looked closer and he could see that one cheek of the boy was bulging out as if a large balloon had been placed in his mouth. Clearly the boy went to sleep while still chewing a large wad of *Khat*, the narcotic leaves that almost all Yemeni men, and many women, start chewing in the late afternoon. This boy must have gotten a late start since the khat was still in his mouth. That meant he was receiving a continuous drip from the narcotic. He certainly was high and would not wake any time soon.

Intelligence had identified the house of AQAP leader Tuwayjari's relatives, and the team wanted to photograph the house before leaving. It was easy to identify the house, as it was in the northern most part of the village, which was backed up to the wall of the mesa. So the team stealthily moved through the streets until they approached a large, mean-looking dog. The dog had its lip curled back and appeared to be ready to attack Norm Halderman, who was in the lead at that moment. As the dog emitted a low growl, bent its hind legs, and prepared to spring, Halderman was ready with a piece of steak laced with an anesthetic. He threw the meat toward the dog who quickly swallowed it. Norm knew that the anesthesia would have put a medium-sized dog to sleep for about 30 minutes. But this dog was huge. Norm waited a few seconds for the medication to take effect. Instead of losing conscious, the dog simply dropped to its stomach and casually watched while the three moved on.

In short order they identified the target house; took photos of it and made some sketches of it and the surrounding area. Once that was accomplished, it was time to abandon the village proper and return to the aircraft. Their mission told them that this was a sleepy village with no nighttime guards, except for the dog. The surrounding terrain would give cover to troopers coming in for an operational raid. The outlying buildings could actually provide temporary shelter to invading troops, if that was necessary.

They had been on the ground for more than two hours, and therefore, they needed to retreat quickly in order to take off from the area before the first signs of daylight. As they began to move quietly through one of the streets, Norm almost jumped out of his boots when he felt something warm and slimy rub against his leg. He looked down and there was the supposedly ferocious dog wagging its tale in hopes of receiving another goodie. Sam obliged and they moved out of the village. All in all, they considered the mission a success.

CHAPTER IV

Back in Riyadh the next day John met with the recon team first and was pleased to hear their report. Their success put him in a jovial mood and he could not help but digress when he heard about the boy high on khat. He told the team that many years ago he made his first trip to Yemen and it appeared to him when he arrived in Sana'a that Yemen was bursting into the 13th century. Indoor plumbing was widely available, but with the lack of sewers, waste simply emptied into the streets. Almost all homes were constructed from mud. Indeed John stayed with the then COS, who lived in a mud house. At six feet tall, John had a sore head most of the time he was in Yemen. Most doorways were not much higher than 5'8" and John was forever banging his head.

John recounted how he was an experienced souk negotiator at the time and was attempting to purchase a Yemeni *jambiya*, which is a dagger with a severe bend. Typically in Yemen, they are placed in a very decorative sheath, and men attach them to their midriff with a wide belt. John and the jambiya seller were locked in serious negotiations over the dagger when John decided to use the traditionally successful negotiating tactic of leaving the shop and returning hours later.

John chuckled, "At the time, I was unaware of the use of *khat*, but I sure learned about it that day. Because when I returned a couple of hours later, it was afternoon, and the shopkeeper had begun chewing *khat* for the day. His cheek was bulging, and his eyes were glassy. I attempted to get a low price for the *jambiya*, but the proprietor waived me off. So, I told him that I would accept the last price he had announced that morning, and the proprietor waved me off again. It soon became apparent that he had completely lost his interest in anything but *khat*."

John had one more story he had to tell of that trip and khat. "I had wanted to visit a museum that the Egyptians had helped the Yemenis build at the end of the 'Royal' war in the 1960s. The museum was in the city of Ta'iz, about 170 miles from Sana'a and about 3,000 feet lower in elevation. Trying to experience real Yemeni life and to get serious practice in Arabic, I booked 2 seats in a share cab going to Ta'iz, rather than flying there. Once I was squeezed into the back seat of the Opel station wagon I wished I had booked three seats. Anyway, when Yemenis travel and when on vacation, they don't wait until the afternoon to start enjoying khat – the start first thing in the morning.

'Unfortunately the driver of the share cab believed that he too had to join in the joyful mood of his charges, so he too stuffed his cheeks with the narcotic leaves. As they began down the steep mountain road, with twists and turns the likes of which I had never seen, the driver continuously looked back over his should to make a point to one of the passengers. I was the *only one* grasping a handle with white-knuckles. The sheer drop of *hundreds of feet* did not seem to faze the others. It was an experience I would never forget, more so because during the frequent stops of the trip, I, the rich American, could buy nothing. The Yemenis *insisted* I was their guest and it was forbidden for me to pay for a tea or *bebsi*[6]."

Having exhausted his Yemen stories, he thanked the entire team for a job well-done and told them their efforts may be the difference between success and failure of this operation.

John next started his morning meetings with his ops officers and this morning the first was Kim Malloy, who was becoming his most promising young ops officer. Kim was rather short with a completion of someone who has never seen the sun but eyes that reflected high intelligence. Kim was on his first tour and after his initial meeting with his COS he took to

---

[6] Arab pronunciation of Pepsi since there is no P in the Arabic alphabet.

heart John's message. He was out almost every night attending some kind of function that would bring him in contact with potential targets of opportunity. Kim had the tools to be an excellent ops officer: he spoke native Arabic and was at home in this male dominated society. Kim, the son of Christian missionaries, had grown up in Egypt where he became an authority on antiquities in the Middle East. Additionally, he loved to fish and hunt and was an accomplished athlete. The Saudis and other Arabs took to him immediately.

During their meeting in the "bubble", Kim reported that he had three individuals he considered 'developmentals'. The most interesting, Kim reported, was Hussein al-Biladi an engineer working for Aramco[7]. Now a Saudi company, Aramco is still populated by many Americans and almost no Saudis, except at the executive level. Kim explained that Hussein was an Iraqi petroleum engineer and had been working for Aramco for nine years. John asked Kim to explain what was so interesting about Hussein that would make him a potential target for recruitment.

Kim began to explain that in Hussein's opinion Iraq was slowly coming under the influence of Iran and its Ayatollahs. Hussein was a Sunni Muslim and the Shia' were now dominating Iraq to the great disadvantage of Sunnis. So he was more comfortable in Saudi Arabia, even though he did not adhere to the Saudi version of the Sunni sect, called Wahhabism. Indeed, Hussein believed that the Wahhabis had misinterpreted the Quran and that the Saudi Royal family was using the religion as a tool to control their society and keep themselves in power. Hussein believed that Islam should be more moderate than either Saudi Arabia or Iran preached.

Also, since Hussein had been working at Aramco, he had extensive working and social relationships with Americans. Kim said that Hussein had grown to admire the work ethic and sense of fair play the Americans demonstrated to not only other Americans but to everyone.

"Look, Kim," John interjected, "that's all well and good, but we want someone who is of intelligence value, not just a good guy."

---

[7] American/Arabian Oil Company, now known as Saudi Aramco. It is one of the largest companies in the world and the most profitable company in the world. Founded by Standard Oil Company and Texaco in 1938.

"I've saved the best part to last," Kim said, grinning. "Hussein's cousin is a senior member of ISIS. The two grew up together in Baghdad and used to be extremely close. In recent years they have not had an opportunity to see much of each other, but they do correspond by email and occasional phone conversations. The cousin, Rifat al-Biladi, lives in Syria but frequently travels to Iraq, Yemen and occasionally to Saudi Arabia. I'm relatively sure I can recruit Hussein to report on his cousin's activities but I have the impression that Rifat is extremely cautious about anything he says in correspondence or on the phone, and since he was a very infrequent visitor to Saudi, reporting from him would be sporadic at best."

"This is great stuff, Kim. I think you may be on to a major recruitment."

Slightly bewildered, Kim asked, "How so?"

"Well, I think we have to go after the bigger prize and that is Rifat himself."

Kim shook his head, "Boss, Rifat is a radical, he would die before selling out ISIS to America."

"I understand that," John replied, "but he may well be susceptible to a false flag recruitment. Do you think Rifat might agree to report to a Saudi prince's organization that secretly supports radical and Jihadi movements?"

"I never thought of that but it has real possibilities."

John explained that the traditional false flag recruitment involved a case officer impersonating someone with a different nationality, or 'flag'. By way of example, some East Germans, before the collapse of communism, had been recruited by American case officers who claimed to be Russians. While the East Germans would never spy for America, they had little compunction about spying for the Soviet Union. "In this case," said John, "we are not trying to impersonate a nationality but rather a cause."

Kim said he understood, but his first step was to recruit Hussein, get him on the payroll, and then run various false flag scenarios by him.

"Kim, I like the way you think," said John. "First let's get the operational approvals from Hqs to proceed with the recruitment. I think you should draft an 'immediate' message to Hqs in which you outline our plan and ask for an expedited POA." Kim almost leaped out of his chair so he could get to his computer and draft the cable to Washington. He hoped to have the *Provisional Operational Approval* (POA) within a couple of days.

Next John met with George Willis to discuss his development of Amal Ansari the female executive running a Saudi charity fund. George had visited Amal at her office and while there it became abundantly clear that there was a "shit load" of money passing through this organization. Amal talked about business contacts she had in Afghanistan, Syria, Libya, Iraq and Lebanon. Amal hinted that she disapproved of many of the disbursements the charity was making. At that point in the discussion both of them noticed that her staff was paying close attention to George and that was making them both nervous, particularly as Amal was being critical of the charity's activities.

Eventually she said to George, "faddal shi?" to which he replied, "I'd love some tea." But Amal surprised him by saying, "why don't we visit the coffee shop around the corner where we can relax a bit more. It was clear that she was uncomfortable talking in her office. Once they settled into the coffee shop, Amal was more frank about her disillusionment over the disbursements being made by the so called charity. She said she was essentially closing her eyes to what she suspected was large payments to various radicals in other countries, some of whom may even be terrorists.

Amal went on to complain about her life in Saudi Arabia, most particularly the way the system and Saudi men treated women. "I have lived her long enough to know that I am smarter and more competent than 95% of the Saudi men, yet they treat me as some inferior being. Many men in my home country Lebanon feel the same way about women, but I can tell them to go 'stuff it' and there is nothing they can do about it. If I said that to a Saudi, I might find myself receiving the sting of a whip."

"I would like to be a fly on the wall when you tell a Saudi to go stuff it – I'm sure he would be so flabbergasted that he would be speechless."

"Well, I'm not going to do it just to satisfy your curiosity, George Willis."

George noted there was a big smile on Amal's face as she teased him. In fact, her smile was rather contagious; it wanted to make him joke and laugh with her. He was surprised by the way she captivated and allured him. Her casual banter came across as the most engaging discussion he could have. There was something about this woman that projected sincerity, honesty, brilliance, all coupled with a sense that she really cared about people, particularly him!

When George reported all this to John, the latter said "we have to move her along to recruitment George. I think she could provide us with some very valuable information on how some of these radical groups get their funds, how much they get and who among the Saudis knows and approves of these disbursements." As he did with Kim, John instructed George to get out an immediate message asking for a POA to recruit Amal as a penetration of the Saudi fund.

As it turned out, the POA for Amal was almost instantaneously issued and sent to the Station. John told George to make an appointment with Amal and start the recruitment process. So George called Amal at her office and suggested they meet for tea at the coffee shop where they last met. Amal left no doubt that she was anxious to meet George, so they agreed to meet at 2 o'clock that afternoon, about the time she closed the office for the day.

At the coffee house they began talking about their hobbies and interests. Amal told George that she had a large collection of Roberts Prints that she brought from Lebanon. George was familiar with the work of David Roberts. He was the Scot who travelled through the area, mostly the Holy Land and Egypt, in the first part of the 19th century and made some spectacular sketches of the places he visited. Roberts turned the sketches into wonderful lithographs that became quite popular. Indeed, Queen Victoria commissioned an entire set of his lithographs and they are still part of the Royal Collection. Amal said she was particularly fond of two colored prints she had of Baalbek.

"They must be beautiful," John said

Amal confirmed that indeed they were and then asked if George would like to see them. He enthusiastically agreed, thinking the coffee house was not a very amenable venue for making a recruitment pitch. If Amal reacted badly to the pitch, he would much rather they not be in public.

"I live close by, just behind the Al-Yamamah University," Amal said and she proceeded to give him her address and the directions.

"Great, why don't I follow you to your place."

"I'd rather you didn't," she quickly responded. "You know the Mutawa, the Saudi religious police, are constantly on alert for single women having male visitors. If we women are discovered bringing a man to our homes, we most likely will receive a one-way plane ticket out of here. So why don't you give me about 10 minutes and then come to my place. I'll leave the door open a crack so you can walk right in."

This was even better, George thought. Not only was he being provided with a private place to make the recruitment pitch, but there was a level of clandestinity being introduced into the relationship. This could only bode well for the future.

Amal left first and George waited the suggested 10 minutes and then left the coffee house for Amal's home. Approaching her home George could see that the door indeed was open a crack and he walked in. Amal was in her small kitchen making coffee for them when he entered. He was immediately struck by her appearance. It was the first time he had seen her without an abayah or hijab. She never wore the niqab, or veil, as most Saudi women did, but outdoors she, as required of all women, did cover her head and body. George was amazed at what the abayah and hijab had hidden from him. This woman was beautiful and had the body of a super model. Her long raven colored hair had a brilliant shine to it as it hung mid-way down her back. She had beautiful dark, almond shaped eyes, coffee colored skin, round full breasts and an ass that George had difficulty taken his eyes off of. No woman had ever quite had this effect on him. He felt like a teenage boy with nervous energy and totally unsure of what to do.

Amal turned and catching his lustful look at her, she replied with a shy smile. Amal put a coffee service down of the table in front of George and asked how he likes his coffee. Still slightly flustered and embarrassed, he said, "black is fine."

Having served him coffee, Amal brought out her two colored prints. Both prints were magnificent portrayals of Baalbek's Temple of Bacchus but from different angles. Amal explained, "In Roman times Baalbek was known as Heliopolis and The Temple of Bacchus was commissioned by the Roman Emperor Antoninum Pius. Now it is one of the best preserved Roman Temples of its size in the world."

George was very impressed. "The prints are truly magnificent," he remarked.

After discussing the prints for a short while, George moved the conversation to Amal's work and in particular the charity. He asked if she knew all the recipients of funds.

"I don't really know any of them. I mean, I see their names and account numbers on paper. I have also heard rumors about some of them and what I have heard I don't like."

"Give me an example."

"Well there is a fellow in Lebanon that my father hates. He told me this fellow, his name is Ahmad, is 'dirt' and a 'son of a dog'.[8] My father told me the guy claims to be religious but has killed others without remorse. He is hateful and a bully on top of it."

George tried to hone in on this subject by asking Amal to further identify this Ahmad and to tell him more about him. However, Amal firmly resisted, "George I invited you here because I like you and we seem to have an easy time talking to one another. But this subject is depressing to me and this evening I want to be happy."

George could see the handwriting on the wall. He was moving too fast. He had to slow things down and develop their relationship a bit further on a social plane. He decided to take off his recruitment hat for the night and try to become her close friend. So for the rest of the evening they talked more about art, Arab culture and the travails of women living in Saudi Arabia. They laughed a lot and generally enjoyed each other's company.

After an hour or so George said he had 'push off'. But before he left he returned to the subject of her fund, "I don't want to upset you but I want you to know that the disposition of all that money in your fund is of interest to me. I would like to talk to you again about it."

"I sensed that interests you, George, and that is not a problem. It's just that *tonight* I wanted to get away from it. I'm not usually in this kind of mood so perhaps the next time we get together I'll be more amenable to discussing it."

"Not a problem. I'm glad we did have the conversation about Baalbek and the Romans. I find it fascinating and envy you for being so close to this historical area your entire life. I really find you so easy to talk to," George added with a smile, " and I hope we have many more such conversations."

Amal got up and moved toward the door - a sign that George was to leave. When they got to the door, she said, "Don't try to figure me out based

[8] ibn kelb – a frequently used Arab cuss word equivalent to 'son of a bitch' in English

on this evening, George. I'm in a strange mood for some reason but I still enjoyed our time together." With that she reached up and gave him a peck on the cheek and opened the door for him to leave.

As George walked back to his car he tried to recreate the evening and he just couldn't bring much sense to it. In part, he thought, he was so unnerved by the sheer beauty of this woman that he was not at his best. Additionally her compassion and warmth produced a comfort level within him that was very pleasing. She affected him in a totally unfamiliar way.

The next day at their morning meeting John immediately asked George how things went with Amal. George was not his usual effervescent and confident self. He detailed the previous evening's conversations and mood to his boss. "The vibes I received told me this wasn't the time to pitch her. I felt that there was some kind of barrier, so I backed off and concentrated on building our relationship on a more solid foundation."

John told George not to worry saying, "I'm glad you proceeded as you did. Good case officers learn to trust their instincts and a lot of instinct goes into a recruitment pitch. You have to feel the timing is right when you make the pitch. It's better to solidify the relationship first. When you make a recruitment pitch you are unmasking yourself and giving information to your target that she can use against you. So when you make the pitch, you must feel extremely confident that the answer is going to be positive."

John could tell that George was disappointed but he knew he would get over it. Whether or not Amal was agent material was still an open question and he knew George would make the right decision with regard to a recruitment attempt.

The following morning George received a phone call from Amal. She apologized for being out of sorts on the night of his visit and suggested he might want to drop by that evening. She said she was in a much better mood and that she would like to discuss the matters that interest him. George readily agreed and it was decided that he would come by around 8 that evening. He was quite elated after the phone call, particularly because of her reference to 'matters that interest him'. He was sure this meant she was prepared to provide him some details about her fund.

About 7:45 that evening John parked his car in one of al-Yamamah University's parking lots and then walked the rest of the way to Amal's. He arrived precisely at 8 pm. After one short knock on the door, she answered. She had a beaming smile on her face and it was clear her mood was euphoric. She was dressed in a short skirt and a top that showed just a hint of cleavage. Tame by Western standards but in this part of the world it was scandalous.

She told George to have a seat while she prepared coffee for them, "or perhaps you would like juice or something," she asked.

George had all he could do to mumble that coffee was just fine. He simply could not take his eyes off of her.

Amal turned to him and said, "George, you look as if you are undressing me with your eyes, have you never seen an Arab woman up close and dressed like this before?" George tried to say something but his mouth felt so dry nothing would come out. As Amal moved close to him he could smell her and feel the warmth of her body emanating toward him. Her closeness generated a shock wave through his entire body with every nerve ending coming alive. She leaned into him and as they began to kiss she slipped her tongue into his mouth.

George lost almost all sense of control. His entire body simply wanted to take this women. However, a small voice in the back of his head is told him that "this is not professional, what will you tell the COS, what will you tell Amy?" George ignored the voice and plowed ahead.

Amal matched his abandon, as she clutched his neck and pulled him to her. Soon they were tearing at each other's clothing and quickly he was inside her. George felt as if he could not get deep enough into her and she had a similar sensation as she attempted to pull him closer into her. Loud moans from George signaled he had exploded into her but she was not ready to release him. She implored him not to stop and he did not disappoint. He continued to thrust into her until she emitted a low groan a satisfaction. George rolled off of her but continued to admire her body, particularly now that perspiration was dribbling down between her lovely breasts.

Finally, George said, "I really didn't expect this when I agreed to come to your place tonight."

Amal smiled, "I hope you are not disappointed. I really didn't plan for what happened, but I welcome it."

George was still a bit surprised by the turn of events, particularly with an Arab women, and he said as much to Amal. Amal explained that she is a woman first and then an Arab, and went on to explain that Arab woman have sexual needs just like all others. She conceded that most Arab women try to deny their natural desires and they are greatly assisted in that endeavor by Arab men. Amal further explained that for an Arab women she is liberated but because she lives in an extremely conservative society, she hides her independence. She confessed, "I am *immensely* attracted to you - you are a beautiful man – and because you are not a Muslim, I can demonstrate my liberation with you. I hope you don't find me too forward. The night before last when you were here, I began to have these feelings for you and I suspect that is why I acted rather strangely. I didn't expect to act out as I did this evening but I did tell myself to be true to my feelings."

By now a bit of guilt had begun to creep into George's consciousness. After all, he had always been faithful to Amy and generally considered himself to be a "stand-up" sort of guy, even though he knew he was in a troubled marriage. Now he had been seduced by this woman, or did *he* seduce *her*? He wasn't quite sure. In any event, he recognized that he had crossed a line, one that affected not only his marriage but his professionalism. The guilt eventually led him to tell Amal that he was having difficulty coming to grips with their involvement.

"Amal, you know that I am married, and most likely, there isn't any long-term future for us." Having said that, he had to admit to himself that not only was Amal more beautiful than Amy, but he loved her spontaneity and sexual aggressiveness. Besides, her self-assuredness and comfort with herself made her very easy to be with.

"George," Amal began, cutting off his thoughts, "I have no expectations from you. I am very attracted to you, and from what just happened, I think we are very physically compatible. I simply like being with you and talking to you. I see no reason why we cannot continue to enjoy each other privately and keep it from the outside world. I'll never ask more from you."

This was music to George's ears. Amal was suggesting for all intents and purposes to enter into a clandestine relationship. He decided it was time to reveal his true affiliation to Amal and make a recruitment pitch for her to report on details of her charitable fund's activities. So he said, "Amal, I have to be perfectly honest with you if we are to have such a relationship. I am not a diplomat, but really a CIA officer. What really drew my interest to you in the first place was the questionable disbursements from your fund."

"So *this* is what you were after – I am a simple tool for the CIA to use."

"No, no, Amal. I did not intend to have a physical relationship with you. It just happened and I will not be able to explain that to my bosses. That part of our relationship will only be between the two of us. That is if you agree to continue to see me, which I sincerely *hope* you do. Having been with you once, I cannot conceive of not having you again.

That's what I hoped to hear", responded Amal. "Let's cement this relationship by you ravaging me again."

Later as the two lay in bed thoroughly exhausted, George began to explain what kind of information he wanted from Amal. Simply put, he needed to know the source of funds – was there a long list of donors, or was it a few individuals. Who decides on how the funds are distributed and on what basis? Does she have the recipients' names or only account numbers? If there are names, what does Amal know about these people? Where do they live? Do they head an organization of some kind? If so, what are the details of the organization?

"George, I have a lot of the information you want," Amal began, "and I believe it will be useful to you because I am *convinced* we are supporting radical groups. However, I have to be careful. If I am discovered giving you this information, I will not only be fired, but I could be in great danger."

George began to explain that they would be very careful with the information she provides and the two of them will be very careful not to be linked together. He suggested that they continue to meet at her home, with him parking his car a good distance away and walking to her residence. Their 'cover for action' if anyone ever discovered they were secretly meeting would be the obvious – they are having an affair.

Amal said, "That's fine for you, George, but having an affair will get me fired."

George told her he could not make any promises at the moment, but he would seek approval to resettle her in a Western country or the U.S. He said, "Such a resettlement would include finding you job at least as good as, if not better than what you have now. Of course that would only be the case if you lost your job because you have been helping me." He explained that this is something they do for their trusted sources who become compromised, and in her case having an affair discovered would mean she had been compromised.

Amal said his proposal was very acceptable to her, as she would much prefer to be in the West rather than Saudi Arabia or a similar country. Although for the immediate future she was very content to stay where she is in order to continue their relationship. George then told her that she should be compensated for her work on behalf of the CIA and proposed that he put her on a retainer of $1,000 per month. George's training told him this was an important step in finalizing a recruitment. Once an agent began accepting a steady income, human nature made it almost impossible to stop the arrangement.

Amal whipped her head around, "What do you think of me – a paid whore?"

George had to quickly calm her. He told her that she would be more than earning the retainer by the risk she was taking. Also, because she might have to move quickly and start life all over, she needed to build up a nest egg for contingencies.

Amal reaction to that was that $1,000 a month would not build much of a nest egg and it certainly was not worth the risk she would be taken.

George conceded that it wasn't commensurate with the risks but more would be available if her production was good. And if she did have to be resettled somewhere else, the Agency would make sure she was comfortably situated financially. He had not anticipated this conversation and he silently cursed himself nor not obtaining prior approvals for resettlement. The monthly salary would not be a problem but he was not sure the Agency would be inclined to provide a comfortable resettlement. He supposed that it all depended upon how valuable her information was going to be. Of course if it was not very good intel, he would have to terminate their relationship and there would be no commitment. And if her information was really good, Hqs would have no problem in approving a resettlement plan.

George and Amal worked out meeting arrangements. They would meet two weeks from that date at 9 pm and if for some reason the meeting had to be cancelled they would meet the following week at the same time. Amal's small home had two levels with her bedroom on the second level. They agreed that she would leave her bedroom drapes open as an all clear sign, but if for whatever reason he should not enter her house, the drapes would be closed. If George needed to cancel a meeting, Amal would receive a text message in appearance from Saudi Telcom in which STC is offering free minutes. If George believes she is in danger, the STC message will say that she is in danger of losing her service unless her bill is paid immediately. George told her if she ever receives such a message she should attempt to go to the American Embassy forthwith, where she will be expected. He told her not to be alarmed by his plans as they are just for contingency purposes and will most likely never have to be used.

Having taken care of meeting plans and signals, they began to discuss intelligence information. They agreed that Amal will copy the names, account numbers and whatever other data is on her computer about the fund's recipients. She promised to have that info at the next meeting. She will also copy details of the charity's management team and its contributors.

On his way home George felt pretty good about himself. He had just made his first recruitment, and it could be a very valuable one. He was, however, undecided about what, if anything, he would tell John Thorn about the sexual component. On the other hand, there was no doubt that he would say *nothing* to Amy about it.

CHAPTER V

Early the next morning John instructed his deputy, Tim Haggerty, to make a quick trip to Najran. John wanted to make sure that the facilities there were such that they could stage a 15 man special ops team and their helicopters without drawing undue attention. Lt. Col. Brad Armstrong, the JSOC team leader had arrived the previous evening and he would accompany Tim to Najran. Tim had to make a quick trip home to gather some belongings and then he planned to meet Armstrong at the Riyadh Airforce Base.

So that morning John started his meetings with ops officers without first meeting with Haggerty. First in line was George Willis who was pacing impatiently outside the bubble waiting to brief his boss on the previous evening's developments. John had seen this kind of behavior before and assumed he was about to hear some good news. Sure enough, George got right to the point and blurted out that he made his first recruitment. He did, however, neglect the sexual component to the evening.

George expressed his regret for not foreseeing the possibility of a resettlement and getting Hqs' views on it. John was excited about the potential and told George not to worry about resettlement. "Firstly," said John, "if we run this operation correctly, there should be no need for resettlement. Secondly, if she provides us with good intel, Hqs will have no problem with approving a resettlement plan. Thirdly, if she doesn't have good intel, we will turn her loose and there will be no reason for a commitment. The only potential problem I see is if her intel pinpoints a terrorist op that we have to thwart and the finger points to her for leaking the information. That is always a problem with counter-terrorist ops; sometimes we have to take action that will blow our asset. George, write this up and ask Hqs to approve a resettlement commitment for Amal, if it becomes necessary."

Next, John met Kim Malloy. Malloy reported that he had met the Aramco engineer, Hussein al-Baladi, the previous evening. Kim reminded John that he had not received operational approval from Hqs to proceed with a recruitment pitch. Kim explained that he thought he could have pulled off the recruitment the previous evening. He told John, "I danced around the issue by telling Hussein that he would have to carry the real burden if his cousin Rifat were involved in a terrorist act in which someone got killed. I told him that if he really made the effort, he could learn what Rifat was planning and make it possible for us to stop Rifat and prevent any casualty. But doing nothing about it would make him almost as responsible as Rifat. After I said that, he asked me what he could possibly do to stop him. At that point, I would have lead into a recruitment pitch, if I had the approval."

John had read all the operational messages that had come in overnight and it was clear to him that Kim had not. John said, "I have good news for you Kim, Hqs approved your proposal – it just came in this morning." Get together with Hussein and make the pitch. Have you given any thought to how you are going to frame the false flag recruitment?"

"Yes I have. I have based it on a Saudi prince named Meshal al-Talal. There are rumors abound in Riyadh that suggest Talal is a radical and is backing foreign radical groups financially. I plan to tell Hussein to make the pitch to his cousin along the following lines: Prince Talal was spending a considerable amount of money on radical groups and felt that he was not getting the most out of his contributions. The Prince wanted independent, inside information on radical or terrorist groups so that he could better channel his funds to deserving organizations. Talal had heard good things about Rifat and wanted him to be his eyes and ears in ISIS. Furthermore, the Prince was prepared to offer financial compensation to someone who was in a position to provide him confidential information about their organization, as long as they could keep their mouth shut about what they were doing."

John said he liked the plan and commented on how venal he had found some of the most extreme radicals to be. "We often see these guys who claim to be extremely religious as anything but when given the chance to sleep with a good looking woman – actually they don't have to be good looking - or to enrich themselves, they are all in. So, I think this will work, Kim."

CHAPTER VI

The original plan for CAPTURE, the cryptonym for the proposed paramilitary operation in Yemen, was to insert 16 combat equipped shooters using two MH 60M Black Hawk stealth helicopters. Given the fact that almost all housing units in Yuwan were multi-story and very close to one another, it was decided that the Black Hawks would deposit the shooters about 1 kilometer from Yuwan. The team would then approach the village high above on the mesa and repel down the mesa where the targeted house was located. Given that there would be a full super moon that night it was thought that bringing the Black Hawks any closer to the village would certainly alert someone.

However, shortly after Haggerty and Lt. Col Armstrong left for Najran, John received an urgent message informing him that intercept comms were indicating that almost twice as many AQAP members as originally believed would be in Yuwan for the meeting. The indications were that most of the additional members were part of a protective force. This meant that top officials of AQAP would be attending but it also meant that the American contingent would be outnumbered. Thus, both Hqs and JSOC had agreed to double the size of the CAPTURE team and the number of aircraft.

John wished that Haggerty and Armstrong had not left so early because their aircraft did not have secure comms, making it impossible for him to bring them up to speed on the latest developments. However, Haggerty was carrying a secure satellite phone that could be used once they landed in Najran. In the meantime, John decided to seek an urgent meeting with Prince Mohammed in order to inform him of the change in plans. Fortunately, Mohammed was already in his office when John called and he told John to come right over and to bring Norm Halderman, John's military specialist, with him. Prince Mohammed said he wanted to introduce them to Hasan al-Sudari, the Saudi captain who would be part of the insertion team. John was pleased with the prospect of meeting al-Sudari. He had received very favorable reports about al-Sudari from the Special Forces school in Fort Bragg, North Carolina. Indeed, the reports were so favorable that it was hard to believe this guy was a Saudi. He was at the top of his class and was described as "tough as nails" – certainly not your average Saudi.

Within half an hour John and Halderman were in Prince Mohammad's office and sitting with the Prince was a young man dressed in traditional Saudi style – a white thobe covering the body from neck to feet, a white gutra covering the head and an 'agal, the black cord that holds the gutra in place. As the young man stood to meet the visitors, John was sure this was Captain al-Sudari. He stood about 6'2", and even under the all covering thobe John could see this man was all muscle. Unlike most Saudi men, he was clean shaven and presented with a vice like hand-shake. John had seen many Saudis in the company of Prince Mohammed and almost all of them appeared rigid, meek and obsequious. *Not this guy.* He was very relaxed and in good humor. He had one of those contagious smiles that put people at ease. It was immediately apparent to John that this was a confident man who was comfortable in his own skin.

As Prince Mohammed introduced Hasan to John and Norm Halderman, Hasan said, "I think I have met several CIA officers previously, but this is the first time anyone has owned up to it."

John laughed and said, "now that you know, I might have to kill you."

There was a glimmer in his eye when Hasan replied, "I wouldn't try that if I were you."

Naturally this was all in good humor, but John thought to himself, *No, I don't think I would try anything like that with this fellow.*

Without any further small talk, John got down to business by detailing the latest reports about the increase in numbers expected at the Yuwan. The

Saudi side indicated they had not received any similar information and wondered how accurate the American intelligence was. John told them that this was not human sourced intel but basically from intercepts. Prince Mohammed said, "Well in that case, I agree with your plan to double the size of the insertion team."

Hasan asked what kind of arms and other equipment the team would be carrying. Norm Halderman had the answer to this question, as he replied, "Essentially in terms of weapons, they will have both AR-15s with suppressors and/or the M4A1 Colt Carbines, as the standard rifle depending upon the shooters preference. The Carbines will be fitted with the SOPMOD Kit, which includes a grenade launcher, a holographic sight, a CCO sight, a PEQ2 aiming laser, and the insight flashlight. All troopers will also carry a side arm, the 9mm Beretta. They had not previously planned to bring other weapons but now that the team was expanded, they will also bring two M249 SAW machine guns. Additionally they will have four M24A1 SWS sniper rifles with silencers. Other equipment will include repelling equipment, flash-bangs, explosive devices for breaching doors, night vision goggles, as well as thermal cameras and secure comms built into their helmets.

Prince Mohammed had a bewildered look on his face and finally admitted he didn't know half of what Halderman was talking about. Hasan casually brushed aside Mohammed's concern as he said he was familiar with all this equipment. He then said, "I just want to be sure that I will be issued the same equipment the U.S. shooters are going to carry. He seemed satisfied when Norm assured him he would be equipped with the same weapons and night vision equipment that the American troopers will carry, and that he could choose between the AR-15 and the M4A1 Carbine.

Prince Muhammed conceded that he was a bit concerned that the Saudi source had not reported about the increased numbers. He did say that they only had periodic contact with their source and it was not easy to communicate with him. However, he was bothered by the fact that such crucial information was not independently known to them.

The next day the 28 JSOC operators, a term they used for themselves rather than 'shooter', arrived at King Khaled Airport in Riyadh. Norm Halderman and Hasan al-Sudari were at the airport to meet them. Hasan had complete command over the security elements at the airport so that the team was whisked directly from the aircraft to a secure room adjacent to the Royal VIP lounge. Their luggage tags were taken from them but not their passports.

Entry to and exit from Saudi Arabia required visas and multiple stamps in one's passport. These passports had neither an entry nor will they have an exit visa and no stamps would be put in them. Moreover, the flight manifest of the Saudia flight on which they arrived did not contain their names. For all intents and purposes, they were never in Saudi Arabia. Once their checked baggage was retrieved, they were put on two VIP Mercedes minibuses and taken to Riyadh Air Force Base where they were housed in plush living quarters.

Norm had been involved in a number of operations with JSOC in the past and he noted that these operators were similar to those he had previously known. For one thing, they did not appear to be the spit and polish type of military man. Some had facial hair, others did not. Some had shoulder length hair, while others were trim cut. Some were tall; others were short. There was no identifying type, except for their calm demeanor and steely eyes, which were often difficult to see because they tended to have their baseball caps pulled down to their eye level. The casual observer would be hard pressed to identify them, if asked. What was really interesting was how easily Hasan blended in with them. It was as if there was some sort of an internal beacon they all had that told them, 'this guy is one of ours.' A couple of the operators were proficient in Arabic, but they were pleased that a native speaker would be with them.

Once they were all settled, Norm called them all together and gave them the latest details that were available. He told them that they would have a final briefing tomorrow before heading down to Najran, where they were to spend two days making final preparations before commencing the op. They would meet up with the flight crews, the so called Night Stalkers, in Najran. The actual helicopters were to be ferried to Najran aboard C-130s. Once the operators, weapons and aircraft were all together in Najran, they were to have a series of simulation runs. Norm explained to the troops that Hasan and he would be part of the insertion team, as would two other members of the CIA Station. Norm explained that those two others, Sam

Butterfield and Bill Lucas, were ex-JSOC operators and had been part of the recon team that recently scouted out Yuwan. Their "on-the-ground" knowledge could be invaluable during the operation. The troopers took all this in without comment or question. Their simple nods of the head indicating that they liked what they heard.

Meanwhile, John called Najran and spoke to Haggerty on the SAT phone, briefing him about the change in team composition and the latest intel on the number of bad guys that were expected in Yuwan. Haggarty noted that there was not much for him to do in Najran, so he suggested that he return to Riyadh. But John told him that he wanted to have a senior member of the station in Najran until this operation was complete. "Tim, you stay there and be my rep. You know Murphy's Law – if it can go wrong, it *will*. With you watching things there and me here, maybe we can defeat Murphy for a change. Let me know as soon as the Black Hawks arrive and you have had a chance to assess the crews. From what I've seen here, this insertion team is first-rate, and our Saudi addition fits right in. I'm feeling fairly confident that this op is going to be a success."

John did not need to be concerned about the air crews. The 'Night Stalkers' were from the 160th Special Operations Aviation Regiment of the U.S. Army. These pilots were the best helicopter pilots in the world. Their regiment was started after the 1980 catastrophe in the Iranian desert during an attempt to free U.S. hostages in Iran. After that failed attempt the Night Stalkers were formed and have participated in almost every high risk, secret operation calling for the use of helicopters. These pilots had and could do things with their aircrafts that were simply amazing.

The next morning the Saudis provided a VIP outfitted Boeing 737 to take the team from Riyadh to Najran. The plane was big enough to transport all the operators, their equipment and weapons, which had arrived the previous evening aboard a U.S. Air Force C-141. Norm Halderman was visibly excited, if not a bit nervous, to be starting on the first leg of this mission. In contrast, all the troopers, to include Hasan al-Sudari, appeared nonchalant and almost on the verge of being bored. Once the plane landed in Najran they were taken immediately to a fenced off area that contained a military style barracks and a small building with a classroom that would hold about 50 people. The windows of the classroom were blackened and a Saudi security team had performed a "sweep" of the entire building and barracks to ensure that there were no transmitters or other type of listening devices active.

Lt. Col. Armstrong was in command from this point onward. He gathered the men in the classroom and displayed a large map of the Yuwan village and surrounding area. He indicated that there would essentially be four teams and he appointed a team leader for each team, and an overall unit commander. He indicated that he wanted the Saudi, Hasan, to be in the first team in case they encountered a local and need his language and cultural knowledge. Armstrong said there was always the possibility there will be a shepherd or some other individual wondering around the outskirts of the village. If the team encountered such an individual, they were to a. search him to be sure he had no arms; b. immobilize him with plastic zip cords, and a gag; c. convince him that he was safe, as long as he followed direction and did not attempt to escape, and d. then place him in secure holding area.

Next Armstrong indicated on the map the insertion point and said that the Black Hawks would arrive exactly 3 minutes apart. The operators were to alight from their aircraft via fast rope because the topography in the area is very uneven and, therefore, not a very conducive one for helicopters to land. The fast rope technique is similar to rappelling but there is no equipment involved other than a thick, braided rope that has an uneven surface. The uneven surface helps the operator to maintain a secure grip on the rope, which is absolutely necessary since the only things holding him to the rope are his gloved hands. The rope dangles free from the helicopter and there can be as many as three men at a time, separated by at least six feet, on the rope. That means a helicopter with 8 men can probably deposit the men in less than 30 seconds.

Armstrong went on to explain that the Black Hawks will retreat to a flat area about 1 kilometer from the Drop Zone and wait there until the troopers have completed their mission. Armstrong explained that the village was not visible from the DZ because it sat in a bowl below the mesa. The plan, he said, is for the 1st team to quickly move toward the top of the mesa, which is also the back end of the village. He cautioned that they did not have the luxury of darkness because of the supermoon that would be shinning, so speed was essential.

Once arriving at the precipice of the mesa they were to begin securing rappelling ropes for the entire unit. The second mission of the 1st team was to assess the situation around the target building, count the number of guards on the outside of the building and pinpoint their location. If they were all in the front of the building, away from the wall of the mesa, the teams would be able to rappel down the mesa before encountering any opposition. Because the entrance to the building was in front, the team should assume that most, if not all, the guards would be in front. "Any questions thus far," asked Armstrong. There were none.

Armstrong went on to explain that the plan was for no action to take place until the entire unit arrived at the mesa and the rappelling equipment and ropes were in place. If the guards were not all in front of the building an assessment would have to be made as to whether the guards on the periphery and back of the building should be taken out from atop the mesa or could a small number of operators rappel down the outer sides of the mesa and then neutralize these guards with either knives or their silenced 9mm's. The aim of the 1st team, explained Armstrong, was to take out all of the external guards with stealth so that the main force, which will be composed of the 2nd and 3ed teams, could enter the building with surprise, and thereby be able to capture, rather than kill, bomb-maker al-Asiri and AQAP leader Tuwayjari.

At this point Armstrong placed large pictures of the two terrorists on an easel for all to see. "We want to bring these two assholes home with us," said Armstrong. He went on to say that he wanted the team to take the hard drives from all the computers in the house and to collect all the cell phones. He appointed 3 troopers whom he knew had the required technical know-how to perform the task. The rest of the team was to conduct a thorough search of the building and capture all papers, notes, calendars or anything else that might hold intelligence value. Lastly, the fourth team would maintain a protective perimeter around the target building during the entire operation.

"Does everyone understand their job now," asked Armstrong. There were indeed a few questions that essentially had to do with the position of the various troopers within a team. Armstrong provided detailed answers to the troopers' satisfaction.

Armstrong then noted that there are trees and other vegetation on the east side of the village. The team was to exfiltrate on that side because the Black Hawks could get close to the ground just on the other side of the vegetation and may even be able to land. With the armed opposition eliminated, the team should be able to secure an area for the choppers to come in close and retrieve the teams, their captives and the drove of data it was expected they would capture.

Armstrong went on to say that there is an area nearby Najran with topography very similar to Yuwan's and during the next 36 hours they would practice their op in this area. At this point Armstrong addressed Hasan and said, "Captain, I know you outrank our operators, but when we are out on a mission, the team leader I appoint is boss, regardless of his military rank. You must accept that you will take orders when given to you and not hesitate because it is coming from an enlisted man.

Hasan said, "Colonel, I know the drill. I respect these men for their abilities, knowledge and experience – I would *never* second guess them." The Saudi could not have said anything better. It was clear he was now a respected member of the unit.

During the next day and a half the unit went through mock infiltrations over and over. Lt. Col. Armstrong changed the scenario from time to time in order to provide various options that the team may encounter during the actual operation. It was important that each member of the team knew what the others were doing and could perform his own individual responsibility with a high degree of confidence. Fortunately the AQAP meeting was set for evening and not during daylight hours. Not that they would have much in the way of cover, given the super full moon that was expected. However, even the small amount of darkness gave them some cover and advantage.

In the first helicopter was going to be Butterfield and Lucas, who had participated in the recon, and Saudi Captain Hasan al-Sudari. The plan was for these three to be the first off the aircraft and together with the remaining five operators, they were to secure the DZ. Two of these 5 troopers were snipers and a third carried one of the machine guns. The second and third helicopters each had 8 fully combat ready operators armed with either the

AR-15 or Colt Carbine. In the last helicopter was Norm Halderman, who had secure communications to Lt. Col. Armstrong back in Najran, and the two other snipers, plus a trooper with the remaining machine gun.

When it was time to commence the operation, the team was fully confident in their ability to successfully complete the mission. Lt. Col Armstrong gathered the men together shortly before launch time. He made a quick review of the operation's objectives and asked if anyone had any doubts about their tasks or objectives. There were no questions so Armstrong asked, "So everyone is comfortable with the mission and their own specific tasks? Is there anyone who would like to back out of the mission? This is the last opportunity to do so." There were a few chuckles but no one wanted out. With that Armstrong wished them luck and told them he had full confidence in them.

They boarded their helicopters for their approximate three hour flight shortly before sun set. The Black Hawks would have to be refueled about half way though their flight to Yuwan and again about half way through their return. The refueling would be accomplished in mid-air with a MC-130 aircraft. Fortunately, the air defense system in Yemen was unsophisticated at best and non-existent in most places. Therefore, refueling could be accomplished with minimal risk of detection. And so it was that about half-way to Yuwan, two MC-130s met up with the Black Hawks to refuel them. The troopers appeared to be dozing off while the refueling took place. Indeed, when not checking their gear, they tended to sleep.

Finally, the pilot of the first helicopter announced, "10 minutes." The team remained calm as they began making last minute checks of their equipment, but the adrenaline was *really* flowing now. According to plan, the 1 st team was off the helicopter and in position in less than 90 seconds. The second Black Hawk's team started down their ropes 90 seconds later. Just as the last troopers were descending from the 2 nd aircraft **all hell broke loose.**

From a hill just above the DZ rifle and machine gun fire was directed at the team while RPG 7s[9] were aimed at the helicopters. The first helicopter

---

[9] Rocket Propelled Grenade 7, an unguided, shoulder launched grenade launcher. The RPG 7 was originally a Soviet anti-tank weapon but has been used extensively by terrorist and other groups because of its simplicity and availability, particularly in the Middle East.

was already out of range but the second was clearly within the firing range of the RPG-7s and indeed it took a glancing hit.

Instantly Butterfield sensed the magnitude of the problem as he saw his buddy Lucas take a round to the head, just below the helmet line. Lucas' helmet contained much of the blood and brain matter from splattering out the back side but Butterfield could see both dripping down from underneath Lucas' helmet. There was little doubt his buddy was dead.

Butterfield immediately communicated with Halderman, who was on the last helo, and reported that they were under fire. "We are being hit hard by an ambush" he yelled into his mic. "They were waiting for us. Lucas and an operator are KIA; al-Sudari is hit. *Do not* enter the DZ area. Repeat, *do not* enter the DZ." Halderman asked, "Can you estimate the size of the enemy?" Butterfield responded, "Appears to be 30 to 40 jihadis. They are trying to take out the helos with RPGs. They are in a semi-circle between us and the village and shooting down at us from a hill." As he was reporting this, Butterfield glanced over at al-Sudari who was in obvious pain from the hits he took. Nonetheless, the Saudi calmly assumed a prone shooting position and was taking precision shots at the enemy.

Halderman told the pilots to abort landing and "hold one", which is military speak for "wait a minute". He then apprised Armstrong back at Najran of the developments. Armstrong told him to abort the mission but to allow the unit commander to devise a quick tactical plan to defeat the ambush and extract all the teams from the area. It was clear to Armstrong that there was no AQAP meeting and therefore no leaders to capture. The best scenario now was to get the troops out as quickly and safely as possible.

The pilots and the unit commander made a quick assessment of the situation. First it appeared that the ambush party had expected only two helos and 16 men, otherwise they would not have opened fire when they did. Secondly, there was about 1 kilometer between the bad guys, whom the pilots could distinctly visualize with their thermal equipment, and the village. They quickly concluded that the two remaining teams could be dropped behind and above the attackers, which is what they did.

While the attackers were not clearly visible to the first two teams, the latter two teams had them in full view and began firing down on them. Also, the Night Stalkers made several passes by the ambush party and gave them a taste of their M134 mini guns, which could fire up to 6,000 rounds a minute. What was a calm, moon filled night just minutes before was now pure calamity. The jihadis were firing on full automatic most of the time and were simply aiming in the direction of the Americans. Meanwhile the U.S. operators and the one Saudi were not wasting any shots; every shot they took was well aimed to kill the opponent. The same was not true for the mini guns on the helos – they were spitting out rounds with such velocity that it scared the hell out of the Jihadis, regardless if they hit their intended targets or not. The two SAW machine guns were also firing with precision but at a much faster rate than the standard rifles. Small arms fire was coming at the terrorist group from all directions and the fire power was devastating. The jihadis had assumed they were going to knock out the entire raiding party but they soon discovered they were being massacred by the Americans. Very quickly the discipline among the AQAP group evaporated and they began to flee in all directions – maybe two or three were able to avoid the deadly aim of the highly trained U.S. troopers.

The designated unit commander was in communication with each of the team leaders, and he asked if it appeared that any member of the enemy group still posed a threat. All reported that the enemy was either dead or had left the area. One team leader indicated that his team had witnessed two jihadis who appeared to be wounded but not killed flee the area to the West and away from the village. Since the plan was to evacuate on the northeast side of the village, the commander assumed they were in no danger from those two. "Let's get the hell out of here," the unit commander announced once the scene was secure.

The two teams that were above the ambush party moved downhill to join their fellow troopers who had sustained the brunt of the ambush. In doing so, they had to pass through the area where the jihadis had been positioned. They examined the battlefield and found that all of the jihadis that were lying on the ground were indeed dead. They carefully took count of the dead enemy, which came to a total of 38. Once all the teams had joined, the unit commander asked the team leaders for a headcount. All team leaders other than that of the first team reported that their teams were all accounted for and safe. That leader of the first team reported that all were accounted for but two were KIA. Satisfied that nobody would be left behind, the unit commander ordered the teams to quickly scout a nearby LZ.

As the Black Hawks descended into the area, it was clear that they could and would need to land. Four wounded operators were receiving first-aid, and two KIAs needed to be loaded onto the helos. The troopers formed a secure perimeter around the LZ while the casualties were loaded. Then, all of them boarded an aircraft very quickly and headed back to Najran.

The pilot of the helo that had taken a hit reported that he thought he could not make more than 100 kilometers. He said he was losing oil and running hot. When Armstrong received this report he immediately arranged for a C-130 to "pick-up" the Black Hawk in an area of relatively flat terrain area between Najran and Yuwan. Again, the lack of a sophisticated air defense system was working in their favor.

The embarrassing results of operation CAPTURE were recorded in an "after-action" report prepared by Lt. Col. Armstrong, and it was quickly communicated to Washington where it was briefed to the President, the Secretary of Defense and the chairmen of the House and Senate Intelligence and Armed Forces Committees.

Meanwhile, John prepared his own damage assessment that he planned to send to CIA Hqs. He would use it as a basis to brief Prince Mohammad and, perhaps, the King. John concluded in the after-action report that at some point, the opposition had learned of the American plan and set up the ambush. If there was ever going to be an AQAP meeting, which he thought was debatable, it was certainly canceled after AQAP had learned that the Saudis and the Americans were aware of it. All indications were that the Saudi agent was in fact a double, and it was he who had set up the Saudis and the Americans to fail.

John based this assumption on the fact that Prince Mohammad had told him that they had not been able to contact their agent after his initial report. If the agent was a double, it would be natural for him to "disappear" when he knew there was going to be a lot of finger-pointing. In this case, the fingers would ultimately be pointing at the agent. John wondered if the Saudi handler of this agent had revealed to him the fact that a raid of the meeting was being planned along with any details about the raid. John suspected that he had. And since the agent had not been in contact with his handler after first reporting about the meeting, the handler could not have told him about the increased size of the American team. That is why AQAP had been unaware the Americans had doubled the size of the invasion party. The agent may have had the initial information about the raid but had fled before the plan was altered to double the number of men.

To answer some of these doubts, John had to meet Prince Mohammed. Before he could request a meeting with the Prince, he received a phone call informing him that the Prince wanted to see him immediately. As soon as he arrived, John received an apology from the Prince. "I have concluded that it was our agent who sold us out," he said. "We had contacted him once after his initial report, but since then, it appears that he has dropped off the face of the earth. He must have been doubled against us by AQAP. At least, that is my conclusion. If you have some other reasonable explanation for this disaster, I would like to hear it."

"I do not have any other theory," John replied, "and I was coming to that same conclusion myself. My question to you, however, is this: Did your agent handler reveal to this agent *anything* about our plan to raid the meeting?"

"I don't know the answer to that," replied the Prince. "My officer should not have shared any such information with the agent, but I can understand why he may have. You see, we were trying to be as helpful as possible to this raid, and in doing so, we gave our agent some detailed requirements to report on regarding this meeting. We had to share some information with him to refine his reporting back to us. In doing so, we had to give him some indication that an intervention of some sort was being planned. Additionally, we wanted to be sure that our agent was not around during the meeting – we didn't want to get him killed. So, my officer may have warned the agent to steer clear of the meeting."

John told the Prince that it was clear to him that AQAP was aware of the raid but their information was based on our original plan. They were unaware of the fact that the size of the unit was doubled.

"Yes, that makes sense," The Prince responded. "We had no contact with this agent after it was decided that the unit's size would be increased. So, this is our fault, John. The King would like to meet you to personally offer the Kingdom's apology for what happened. Additionally, we want to make certain arrangements for the families of both men who died in Yuwan. We wish to make a cash donation of $1 million to each family. I want you to personally convey our condolences to them and make this cash offer as a token of our grief."

John told the Prince that it would be appropriate to include the Ambassador in any meeting with the King. "The Ambassador was not particularly happy the last couple of times I met the King. He quite correctly assumes that meetings with the head of state are within his realm of responsibility. As for the cash payment, I don't know what to say about that. On the one hand, we work in a dangerous business, and we understand that when we take up this mantel. If we don't take risks, we will not be successful. I know that both of the men who died fully understood the risks involved, and like the rest of us, they were prepared to risk their lives to better protect their country.

"On the other hand, you know that one of those killed, Bill Lucas, was part of my team here in Riyadh. I know his family well, and I can tell you they are *devastated* by Bill's death. Bill was a middle-level government official, so he didn't make a lot of money. From that point of view, I suppose the cash donation would be well-received by his wife. Likewise, the JSOC trooper was an enlisted man in the U.S. Army, and I have been informed that he has a wife and three small children. The U.S. Military and Veteran Affairs Department will provide them with assistance, but there is no doubt that they will struggle financially with the relatively small annuity they will receive."

The Prince shook his head as he said, "John, I was not asking for your permission to make the donations. We *are* going to do it unless you tell me it's not enough in which case, we will increase the amount. As for the Ambassador, I am not concerned about his feelings. But if you want him to attend the meeting, you better get him on the phone now because you and I are leaving for the King's palace in five minutes."

John excused himself and went out of the office to call the Ambassador. The Ambassador's secretary answered the phone and told John that the Ambassador was busy in a meeting, but she agreed to get him on the line when

John told her it was urgent. Once the Ambassador was on the line, John told him about the upcoming meeting with the King. "John, I want you to postpone that meeting so I can attend," the Ambassador replied. "I have a phone call booked with the Secretary in 20 minutes, and I can't stand up the Secretary of State, not even for the King."

"Look, Fred, I am in no position to dictate to the Prince and King when and where we will meet. You are going to have to make a decision here."

"It's *your* fuck-up that has caused all this, John," snapped the Ambassador. "Now, I have to explain it to the Secretary."

"I am not going to argue with you about the merits of our operation and whose fault it is. If you believed the operation was a fuck-up, you should have said something to that effect before we launched it. Right now, I'm going to see the King, and I am advising you to do the same."

"Tell Prince Mohammed I requested a delay in the meeting."

"I'll pass on your request, but I'm not making any promises."

John walked back into the Prince's office and told him that the Ambassador had asked to delay the meeting. Prince Mohammed smiled and said, "Message received. Now, let's get going. You're riding with me."

John had not ridden with the Prince previously, and he hoped it would not be like a ride in a Saudi VIP motorcade. The Saudis seemed to believe that motorcades must travel at top speed, and he recalled many visitors grabbing hold of their seats with white knuckles and saying, "I'm going to die in a car accident before any terrorist can get me." As it was, the Prince had only two GMC SUVs as security around his Mercedes 600, and they drove at a high but reasonable speed.

John had been to the King's palace a number of times previously, but no matter how many times one visited, one had to be awestruck entering the palace. It dripped of gold everywhere – the door fixtures, drapery rods, columns, chairs, tables. The rooms were immense, particularly the entry hall. Crystal chandeliers were in every room and some of them looked to be 10 feet wide. The floors were lined with the finest Persian carpets with their vibrant colors - they were true works of art.

Meetings with the King usually took place in either his office or his majlis. The majlis was a vast room with more than 100 chairs lining the walls. Just above the throne where the King sat, there was a huge portrait of King Abdalaziz ibn Saud, the founder of the Saudi monarchy and father of all the past and current Kings. Thus, the last name of all of the offspring kings was "bin Abdalaziz," meaning "son of Abdalaziz." Ibn[10] Saud, as the first King was typically referred to in the West, used his majlis at least weekly to hear complaints from and for visits with his subjects. Bedouin would use the majlis as a court to settle disputes over such things as watering holes or camels. That practice was continued by Ibn Saud's successors until March 1975 when a disgruntled Prince who had recently returned to Saudi Arabia after spending 11 years in the U.S. assassinated King Faisal in his majlis. Since then, the majlis sessions were still held occasionally, but attendance was strictly controlled and the security was tight.

This meeting, however, was in the King's office, not the majlis. Although not quite as large as the majlis, the office certainly was no cubby hole. It was the size of a football field. The trappings and furniture were meant to impress, and they did. As John and Prince Mohammed entered the office, an aide to the King motioned for them to sit at chairs on each side of the King's beautifully carved desk. The Prince brushed aside the aide's directions and went around to the King and kissed his hand and both cheeks. Then, they traded greetings in Arabic.

The King then turned to John and said "Ahlan wa sahlan[11] Mister (pronounced Meester) John. To which John replied "Tisharufna inno yashufkum mara ukra, Jalalitkum; inshallah bil kheir."[12] The King continued in Arabic by asking John to pass on his greetings and blessings to the President. He said that he wanted John to personally convey to the President his sincere apology for the disaster that occurred. The King went on to say that he had approved sharing of the information they had collected with the CIA and the staging of the raid from Saudi soil. Based on everything Prince Mohammed had told him, the Saudi side had believed in their source and had been quite confident about the information he had provided. Had the King

---

[10] This is another way of saying "bin," meaning son.
[11] A common but poetic way of saying welcome.
[12] It is an honor to meet you again your Majesty, God willing all is well with you.

had any doubts, he would not have approved the operation. He added that the Saudi side felt an obligation to make amends to the families of those killed, and as Prince Mohammed had already explained, they were prepared to make a generous contribution for the future of these families.

John thanked the King and then said, "Your Majesty, we live in dangerous times. Your Kingdom and our democracy are threatened by terrorists who claim to be doing their bidding in god's name. We must defeat them for the sake of our countries, and to do that we must take risks from time to time. We took a risk this time and the results were not to our liking but that is the nature of intelligence and anti-terrorist work." John was prepared to make additional comments, to include a tribute to Captain al-Sudari, but the King got to his feet and offered limp handshake, signaling the end of the meeting.

Outside Prince Mohammed told John that he liked what he said to the King and he was sure the King took it to heart.

John replied that he had wished that he could have said a few words about Hasan and the stand-up performance he put on.

"Don't worry about that; his Majesty is well aware of Hasan's perform-ance and has thanked him personally," said the Prince.

John told the Prince that he expected that due to the deaths of the Amer-icans, the media would get wind of the operation and its negative results. "For the time being," said John, "we are going to give the standard reply that we do not comment on intelligence or sensitive operational matters. If it comes to pass that there is some leakage, most likely from either a Con-gressman or a Congressional staffer, the Embassy will refer questions to Washington. We hope that you will do the same."

"We will have an easier time deflecting the press than you will, so don't worry about us."

As John left the Prince to return to the Embassy, he could not help but reflect on the meeting with the King. He had met this Saudi King and two of his predecessors, and all were similarly meek and retiring. He could not help but compare this meeting to those he had had years ago in Amman, Jordan with the late King Hussein. Hussein was anything but meek and retiring. The first adjective that came to mind while thinking of King Hussein was gracious. He recalled how Hussein would make his visitors comfortable by suggesting that it was he who was the beneficiary of the meeting and thanking his visitors for being so kind as to call on him.

John recalled a specific incident when he was waiting outside King Hussein's office to meet with him. There was a group of four or five Bedu also waiting to see the King. They were hot under the collar for some perceived injustice they had encountered as a result of a decision the King had made. One Bedouin was talking in a loud voice, proclaiming something about the camels he had lost because of the King – he was going to give the King a piece of his mind. The Bedu were received before John and they marched into his office with fury in their eyes and persistence in their steps. They were in with the King for about 20 minutes. When they came out of his office they were walking on air. This was vintage King Hussein - clearly a natural born politician, he had charmed them and soothed over their complaints in very short order.

The second impression one had of King Hussein was his commanding presence. Although diminutive in size, King Hussein had a contrasting deep baritone voice of a giant. The first time anyone met Kind Hussein, he or she was struck by the loud, commanding voice that emanated from such a small frame. John had not met Hussein's son Abdullah, the current King, but he was given to understand the Abdullah had the same qualities and disposition as his father.

Back at the Embassy, John was told the Ambassador was waiting to see him. The Ambassador was fuming because John had gone ahead with the meeting with the King without him. , "Look, Fred," John began, "you would have done the same thing. You *know* I couldn't have asked Prince Mohammed to tell the King to hold his pants on because Ambassador Wagner wasn't ready for the meeting.

"Besides, your absence from these kinds of meetings suggests that you were not involved in the planning and execution of the operation. Some day, you may want to deny knowledge of an operation gone badly, and you may not be believable if you insist on being present in all meetings. If one of my officers makes a pitch to a Saudi government official and that official rejects the pitch, he most likely will then report it. The next thing you will know is that the Minister of Foreign Affairs will be calling you in to explain why your officers are trying to get Saudis to spy against their own government. You will, of course, deny any knowledge of it, but will you be believed? Not if you have demonstrated in the past that you are fully conversant with my operations."

Fred said, "Of course you are right, I just wanted to show a united front and take some of the heat off of you for an operation that had ended badly. I also don't want the King to feel that he can go around me and talk to anyone in the Embassy that he pleases.

"You *know* that is not going to happen, Fred. The King is not going to talk to some lowly official in the Embassy. I'm surprised that he deigns to speak to *me*. In any case, the reason for the meeting was that the King wished to apologize. Can you believe that?"

Fred was surprised when John told him that it was the Saudis who were apologetic and that they had taken full responsibility for the flap. John then explain to the Ambassador the situation with the now missing Saudi agent and the consensus that the agent was either a double to begin with or he had been doubled sometime before the commencement of the raid. John told Fred that the King had asked him to personally convey his apology to the President for the death of the two Americans.

"How do you plan to handle that?" asked Fred.

"I will report this back to Washington and let *them* decide who tells the President and when, but I suspected the Director will do so in the morning when the President receives his PDB[13] briefing. Fred said he would communicate this back to the "Secretary" just so that latter was not caught off guard should the President raise it with him.

"Good idea," said John, "but if you are going to put that in a message, be sure to limit the distribution to a select few at State." With that, all seemed to be smoothed over with the Ambassador and he was his very gracious self again.

John returned to his office to report on the meeting with the Prince and King. In his cable he asked whether there was any other reporting to the effect that AQAP had doubled an agent. He also asked that the damage assessment he knew Hqs would conduct, specifically try to determine if they had been misled from the beginning, or was there really going to be a high-level AQAP

---

[13] Presidential Daily Brief, which is prepared every morning by the CIA and briefed to the President, often with the Director of the CIA present.

meeting that was cancelled in favor of the ambush? The answer to that question would give John some indication of whether the Saudi agent was doubled sometime after his initial report, or if he had been doubled all along – meaning the report that there was to be a meeting in Yemen was a ruse to draw the Americans in and kill them.

John still had some doubt in his mind about whether it was the Saudi agent who sold them out, or was there some other mole involved. John's thinking was that if he were in AQAP's shoes, and he had a double agent reporting on this operation, he would not have pulled the double out of the scene until the very last minute. Presumably, if the Saudi agent was indeed the cause of the failure, he might have been able to report to AQAP about the increased deployment of troopers and helicopters had he not been pulled out of the operation so early. *That would probably have resulted in a massive disaster for the Americans,* thought John.

CHAPTER VII

As he had been entirely wrapped up in the planning and the aftermath of the CAPTURE operation, John had not had time to meet his ops officers and go over their operational developments. So, he told JoAnn to ask Tim Haggerty to join him that afternoon for the meetings with the ops officers and then to schedule meetings with the ops officers in the bubble starting at 2 PM. JoAnn reported that Tim and Lt. Col. Armstrong were at Riyadh Airforce Base doing a final debrief of the JSOC team before they left that evening. She said that Tim was expected to return soon and she would have him join the ops meetings as soon as he arrived. She also informed John that she had scheduled a meeting with George Willis at 2 PM and Kim Malloy at 2:30 and was trying to round up the others for later.

At the meeting with Willis, the latter said his meeting with the boss was fortuitous, as he was scheduled to meet MONEY that evening.

John asked, "Who the hell is MONEY?"

George told him that was the cryptonym Hqs had assigned to Amal Ansari. John should have guessed as much, as it was common practice for case officers to refer to their agents by their crypts and not their real names.

George said this would be the first meeting with 'MONEY' since her recruitment. He said he was hoping that she would have a significant amount of data for him. John wanted to know the details of the tradecraft George had planned for the meeting. George reminded John about the danger signal they had devised with the open or closed drapes in her bedroom and of the STC text message signals. He also went over the fact that he would be meeting in her home and their cover, if ever they were caught, would be that they are having an affair. George said that Hqs had approved a resettlement provision for Amal but without details.

John said, "OK, good George, so what about security of the meeting. How will you get there and have you arranged for an SDR[14]?"

George replied that he planned to park his car near or in the University of Al-Yamamah and walk a couple of blocks to her home. He said he had never used a SDR for a meeting, except in training at the Farm. He went on to say that he didn't know of anyone at the Station that had used and SDR.

"Well you are going to start using them now. I want you to plan a SDR route that will take an hour and a half at least for you to get to the meeting. Get together with a couple of other people from the Station – they don't have to be ops officers – and have them position themselves at various places along your SDR route. All of you should be in radio contact so that if any of them spot surveillance on you, they can signal you to abort. I also want you to park your car at one of the malls in town and then take one or two taxis before you get to the University area. From there you can walk to her home." John wished George good luck on his first meeting and said he hoped George came back with some hot intel.

Just as George was leaving the bubble, Tim arrived and asked if he could bring John up to date on the JSOC departure. John said, "Let's wait on that Tim, Malloy is about to meet with us to go over his latest operational developments."

"Sure," Tim said, "I don't have much to report anyway."

John had noticed Kim outside the bubble pacing back and forth. He had that same enthusiastic step that John had noted in Willis when the latter made his first recruitment.

Kim entered the bubble and blurted out, "al-Biladi is on board."

Tim, who had been tied up with the JSOC operation recently, had a quizzical look on his face. He asked, "What are we talking about here?"

---

[14] Surveillance Detection Route

Kim quickly reviewed his development of Hussein al-Biladi – now FLAG – an Iraqi engineer working for ARAMCO. He told Tim that Hussein has a close cousin, Rifat al-Biladi – now encrypted "COUSIN" – who is a leader in ISIS. He said that he pitched Hussein with the scenario that he in turn recruit his cousin Rifat to work for Prince Meshal al-Talal, a Saudi Prince who is known to favor radical groups. Hussein –or as he reminded Tim, FLAG - thought this was a great idea and even he had heard rumors about Prince Talal supporting radical groups. He thought his cousin would buy into the idea of helping the Prince better direct his support, particularly when he learns that Talal is ready to put him on a retainer.

John asked, "When do you think Hussein will make contact with Rifat in order to make the pitch?

Kim told him that Hussein was going to send, or may have already sent, Rifat a message telling him he had some important news for him. He hoped that Rifat would come to Saudi Arabia and the pitch could be made here in Saudi but that depended on the response from Rifat. Kim said that Hussein had voiced some concern that perhaps Talal was already supporting ISIS and it could be possible that Rifat and he already knew each other. That could spell disaster in the future.

John said that he too had considered that possibility, and as a result, had asked Hqs to make a thorough check on Talal to see if he had any direct contact with ISIS members. The response was that Talal is very circumspect about his support, if any, to radical groups. Hqs' best guess is that Talal may have radical inclinations but he has not acted on them. It appears that he is one of those guys without any balls to back up his convictions.

Kim said he wanted to brief them on another interesting developmental he had. He said the guy's name is Hisham an-Nassar an engineer working for the Saudi Ministry of Energy, Industry and Mineral Resources, which until earlier this year was known as the Ministry of Petroleum and Mineral Resources. Hisham actually works in the Minister's office and is privy to the latest Saudi plans and intentions with regard to oil and other energy issues.

Kim explained that Hisham was educated at the University of Oklahoma, where he received his Ph.D. in petroleum engineering. Kim further explained that Hisham spent about eight or nine years at Oklahoma, having done both his undergraduate and graduate work there. When he first arrived in Norman he was quickly "adopted" by a well-meaning Oklahoma family, the Robinsons. They took him in and treated him as if he were a son. They were those simple, gracious and generous people so prevalent in the Midwest. They were good Christians but they never preached or otherwise tried to foist Christianity on to Hisham.

Kim added, "Hisham went back to Saudi Arabia after completing his undergraduate work and married a Saudi girl, Ayesha. He return to Norman with Ayesha to complete his graduate work and during those four years Ayesha bore two children, a boy and a girl. The Robinsons took to the Saudi children as if they were their own grandchildren. Indeed, Hisham says the children still refer to the Robinsons as their American grandparents. With a great deal of pride, Hisham told me that the Robinsons visit every Christmas and come with a load of presents for the children, whom he proudly proclaims are natural born Americans.

"Hisham generally agrees with Saudi energy policies, but he is very disturbed by what he calls the royal family's intolerant policy toward its citizens. He believes that the majority of those in the royal family are hypocrites and deny their citizens some very basic human rights. He also disagrees with the Saudi interpretation of Islam. He believes that Wahhabism is intolerant though Mohammed taught tolerance, particularly of Judaism and Christianity. While Hisham came back from America slightly at odds with the Kingdom's policies, Ayesha is almost *radically* opposed to the Kingdom's treatment of its citizens, particularly women. In Oklahoma, Ayesha used to drive her minivan with the children in the back *every day*. Now, to be told that somehow getting behind the wheel of a vehicle was sacrilegious made no sense to her except as an expression of how the regime encourages male control over all women.

"Given that as background, plus the fact that Hisham was starting to provide me with information on sensitive oil planning and policies, leads me to believe that Hisham is ready for recruitment."

Both John and Tim readily agreed with him, with John instructing Kim, "To get all the traces on Hisham from Hqs, plus the approval to move forward with a recruitment."

"But Boss, the traces came in this morning on Hisham" said Kim, "I'm surprised you haven't seen already seen them."

John said, "I normally would have gotten those traces early this morning, but I have been up to my ass in alligators these past couple of days, given the CAPTURE operation in Yemen that has just gone to hell in a hand basket."

Tim also admitted that he was severely behind in all his reading, as he had been out of the Station for more than a week.

"There is nothing to be concerned with, "said Kim, "the traces on Hisham were all positive. Indeed, there was some domestic reporting indicating that while at OU Hisham was already voicing his discontent with the Saudi regime."

What was supposed to be a half hour meeting had already turned into a one and a half hours meeting. "We have to wrap this up," said John. "I have a lot of bureaucratic work to get done, and I'll have to beg off the other officers today. However, I want you to move forward with the recruitment of Hisham. I think the best approach would be to say that you appreciate the information he has been providing, but you fear that if you and he continue to see each other openly, Hisham will eventually be in trouble with the regime. Then, you can suggest to him that you meet clandestinely *without* using that word. Once you get him into a clandestine relationship with him being aware that you are expecting him to provide sensitive information and he goes along with it, you can then formalize the recruitment. This is the so-called 'let the agent recruit himself' approach, which I am not very fond of, but in this case, I think it is the best way."

John stayed at the office until 8:30 that evening, writing and reading reports. As he put his papers away and locked his safe, he noted that JoAnn was still at her desk. He asked if she ever got out of the office at a reasonable hour. Her response was the hour of her departure was reasonable *to her*.

When he got home, his wife Alice was waiting with his favorite meal, a Yankee pot roast. Because of his busy schedule he and Alice had not had much of an opportunity to talk much during the past couple of weeks. It had been his practice to confide his inner most thoughts with her, even those based on highly classified information. Alice had been an Agency employee when they first met and she had worked in a Station after they were first married. So she had all the security clearances that go with an Agency employee, and that means Top Secret and higher. Alice was a good judge of people and was often able to provide John with a perspective of an employee that he had not considered.

John's home was given a periodic sweep by the Agency's technical security team to check for bugs. But even so, when they were about to have a confidential discussion, he and Alice sat near their audio speakers and turned up the volume. So, after John returned home, they sat close to one another, each with a glass of wine that was left over from dinner. At times, John wondered if he exaggerated the need for the audio cover just so he and Alice could cozy up to one another. Not that he needed an excuse, but he certainly enjoyed their "togetherness."

John told Alice that he was going through an emotional crisis. He could not help but feel that had he paid slightly more attention to the details, asked more penetrating questions, or had been skeptical of the Saudi information, he could have prevented the death of a couple of good men. Rather than attempt to reassure John that it was not his fault, Alice just let him vent. She knew from experience that clichéd remarks from her would not be useful. At the moment, John needed to talk, and by talking it out, he would eventually feel better.

John revealed to her that he was not quite satisfied with the accepted conclusion that it was a doubled Saudi Agent who had alerted AQAP to the U.S. plan. He said, "In my opinion, AQAP would have kept their double agent in play until the last minute."

"You have been in the intelligence business for many years so of course you are going to see the better options of running an operation. However, maybe these jihadis were not sophisticated or experienced enough to think of that."

John shook his head. "These guys may be uneducated, but they are not dumb. They are very shrewd. Besides, they value one's life much less than we do. If their agent had been caught and executed by the Saudis, AQAP wouldn't lose much sleep over it. "It all seems too... *neat*. The answer is *too* easy. And since the blame's been placed elsewhere, we are all inclined to accept this explanation."

Alice told John that he was being too hard on himself and was overthinking the issue. "Maybe", he said, "but you can be sure that some little old lady back home in CIA's Counter Intelligence Staff is thinking the same thing I am and she will be checking every bit of intelligence and looking at all the players in this operation as a possible mole."

Alice said she thought he was right but that was a good thing, "If there is a mole on either our side or the Saudi side, we better discover who it is and soon."

John told Alice that the other, less important but more personal aspect of the disastrous operation was that it was going to reflect badly on him. "I know nobody is going to blame me, but in the back of people's mind a *big flap* occurred under my watch. You and I have sacrificed so much over the years – living in some god-forsaken places, being the target of assassination plans and having our kids subjected to it all.

John was referring to their time in Cairo and Tunis. In both cases, radicals had been attempting to kill the CIA chief in their country, which had happened to be John. It was an accepted assumption in both countries, but particularly in Egypt, that the CIA chief would be well known. Because so much of the COS' job in these countries involved working with a broad section of the local government starting right from the President, it didn't take long for it to become widely known who the CIA guy was. It was a fact of life that most COSs had learned to live with. And because they were well known, the COS often became the target of any group that opposed U.S. policy or actions in the area. Many locals believed that the CIA was behind every negative event in their country, and there were more negatives than positives in that part of the world. Certainly, the U.S. policy that favored Israel over the Palestinians was universally condemned in the Middle East. That policy alone had led some to want to retaliate by killing the CIA chief. Fortunately, the group that had targeted John in Cairo had not done their homework properly. They had gotten hold of a copy of the Embassy's phone book and looked up "security." Security, in embassies abroad, was the responsibility of the State Department's Bureau of Security, which was represented in embassies abroad by the RSO or the Regional Security Officer. Cairo had a rather large contingent of security officers, and they had been mistakenly targeted by the radicals who had equated Security with CIA. The security officers had been ambushed on their way to work one morning, but the radicals were as bad a shot as they were researchers. The security officers had been wounded, but none seriously. Later, a penetration of this group had revealed that they thought they had attacked the CIA chief and his assistants.

John and Alice talked for hours, and John wondered out loud if it was time for him to retire. Alice said, "We first got into this business because we wanted to contribute to our country's safety and security. Are you saying that you can no longer contribute? If so, I think you are wrong. I know your colleagues think highly of you, and as your wife, I see the dedication and devotion you give to the job *every day*. Do you honestly believe that you would not be sorely missed if you retired?"

John sighed, "Look Dear, we all fall into the trap of thinking we are irreplaceable but in actuality, none of us are. There are 10 guys back in Washington with substantial operational experience who would love to have my job and most of them would be quite good at it. I have to step aside at some point, and now that I am old enough to be eligible to retire, why not take the step."

"I'll give you one good reason", said Alice, "if you left now, you would be looked at as a loser. Indeed, the man I have been with all these years would not bail because he has sustained some professional setbacks.

John smiled, "Alice are you suggesting I'm a loser?"

They both laughed as Alice said, "Yes, and a dumb one at that."

John told Alice that the other issue that stimulated the thought of retirement was their two children. Both Gina and Jim were excellent students and both spoke fluent Arabic and French. Gina was in the 10th grade at the American International School – Riyadh, whereas Jim was in 8th grade, two years behind her. Because of their strong academic performances, language abilities and their international exposure, John assumed they would be accepted by some of the best colleges or universities in the U.S.

"You know what that means?" John asked Alice. "We are going to be hit with some university bills that we cannot afford on a government salary. I know I could make a lot more money outside the government, and for our kids' sake, I may have to do that."

This discussion brought John back to the beginning so many years ago. He thought back to his first encounter with the Agency more than 30 years ago. John was a Chicago boy, the son of a steelworker on the rough South Side. Not many boys from the neighborhood were successful, and many were serving time in prison. John was one of the lucky ones. He had earned enough money from summer jobs to pay his tuition to a Catholic high school that was also an athletic powerhouse. The priests at the school knew how to handle boys who thought they were *real tough*. Most boys quickly learned that education was a better way for them to succeed than hanging out on street corners. John himself was surprised to learn that he was actually a bright kid. The nuns in elementary school had convinced him that he was on the dumb side. He was also a gifted athlete, and that had gotten him a full scholarship to college at the end of his high school days.

He had dreamed of being a star college baseball player, but early in his college career, an injury had sidelined him. At the time, he was only just getting by in school because athletics had become his first priority. So, he decided to drop out of college for a few years to allow his shoulder and elbow to heal. He then joined the Army. During his boot camp days, he elected to take several Army exams, including the officer candidate school or OCS exam. Shortly thereafter, he was called by his company commander to meet some "civilians." They asked John many questions about himself but gave very little in the way of reasons behind their questions. At the end of the interview, the "civilians" had told John that he would be going on leave after training. "Go home and wait for us to call," they had said.

As his training had been coming to an end, John had mentioned to his company commander that he was told he would be going on leave after training. The Captain told him that everyone in the training unit was going to Korea and no one was going on leave. A week later, military orders arrived and everyone except John had indeed been ordered to go to Korea. John had been ordered to go on leave.

About three months had passed on leave, and John had begun to think that some way or another, he had slipped through the cracks and was going to be paid to stay home on leave for the rest of his military time. That was too good to be true. Eventually, he received the phone call and was told to book himself a flight to Washington as quickly as possible. It was only when he arrived in Washington that he learned that he was being vetted by the CIA, and the next step in that process was to sit for a polygraph examination. In no time at all, John had been on a flight, traveling as a civilian, to Tehran where he had served his military time with the CIA.

His time in Tehran had taught him that the CIA was filled with bright, dedicated men and women who put their country first. It was not unlike his own feeling of patriotism, but John thought he was better suited for life back in the U.S. So, at the end of his time in the military, he returned to college with a vengeance. He strived to achieve academic success instead of athletic success. He was recruited to play baseball again, but he found that the burning desire to play was no longer there. It just hadn't interested him as it had once had.

So, he had concentrated on academics and landed himself on the Dean's List semester after semester. However, as his college days came to an end and he thought more about a job, his thoughts repeatedly returned to those days of working for the CIA and the "family" of employees who were so focused on helping their country. He also missed the exotic places he had visited during those CIA years. With a burning desire to return to the Middle East, he had contacted the Agency and asked if they were still interested in him – they had been and thus had started John Thorn's career as a CIA officer.

John stood up and walked to the window, "I guess I should stop feeling sorry for myself and start working to get things back on track. There are actually a number of positive developments in the Station. Both Kim Malloy and George Willis are turning into first rate ops officers and both have already made a recruitment, with Kim having a second one already lined up. What is your take on their wives?"

"Amy, George's wife, is dumber than dirt, not very attractive and not very social," replied Alice. "By not very social I mean she could care less if she is involved with the rest of the Station's wives. Other than her money, I don't know what George sees in her, he being such a gorgeous man."

"I think you just answered your own question," John replied.

Alice continued to talk about Amy in a negative way, something she rarely did. She told John that because of Amy's upbringing, she was a spoiled, selfish person and a total narcissist. "And from what she has told the rest of the wives about herself, she apparently has little in the way of a moral foundation."

"What does that mean?"

"Well she apparently brags about her sexual adventures, a number of which have occurred since her marriage to George." If she is going to go screwing around, she should at least have the decency to keep it to herself. My feeling is that the marriage is not on solid ground and I doubt it will last much longer. I am told that George was more impressed by the power of her family, rather than the money, but he certainly cannot be impressed by Amy."

"You know what? George's new recruit is a woman, and from the way his eyes light up when he describes her, I'm beginning to think there may be a sexual component to that relationship. That could *really* complicate matters."

"I remember very vividly that you told me a good friend of yours had a sexual relationship with one of his first recruits," said Alice.

"Yes, he did," said John, "and he managed to keep sexual and professional matters separate. But the sexual aspect did confuse the professional relationship. I wouldn't recommend it. In fact, I will advise George against it. I can imagine a situation where an officer loses his perspective and is no longer driving the relationship but is *being* driven instead. That could lead to a security and counterintelligence situation with *serious* ramifications."

Alice asked John if he had actually asked George whether he was having sex with his agent, and John replied he had not. "If I ask him and he tells me he is having sex with her, I will be obligated to report that to Hqs. And, of course, that would be a black and white situation with Hqs, and they would direct me to have George terminate her. Personally, I think she is of limited value to us. Not that the information she can provide is not important, it is highly valuable. But after the initial data dump, any future information from her will simply be an update. Of course, we will want to keep her around for those updates, but that will not be anywhere near as important as her initial contribution. I'm thinking that after she provides the bulk of the data we want, I'll have George turn her over to another officer. That should prevent any potential conflict and obviate the need for me to make a damaging report to Washington."

"What about Kim's wife, Chloe?" asked John. Alice told John that Chloe Malloy had a good head on her shoulders and had a wealth of information on a wide variety of subjects. She had a master's degree in history from UPenn, but her knowledge extended well beyond historical subjects. In addition, she seemed to be a wonderful and loving mother to their three children. "I like her," Alice said. "She has a great sense of humor, and she's bright but doesn't take herself too seriously."

John asked his wife if she had had an opportunity to interact with Bill Lucas' wife before the latter had left Riyadh with the body of her husband. Alice said she had spent some time with Marcie Lucas the night before she had left, and Marcie had been inconsolable. John said he had been at the airport where they had arranged a small ceremony for Bill. He said that in his opinion, Marcie had seemed to be "holding it together" and had acted very brave.

"I'm sure the children were with her at the airport," said Alice. "When I saw her, the kids had been put to bed, and she was free to express her emotions. And boy did she do that! I really feel for her, you know."

"We have lost too many friends over the years," said John. "I hope we don't have to see another star engraved on that wall at the Agency's entrance. These deaths at the hands of terrorists are getting difficult to live with."

Finally, John asked his wife about Tim Haggerty's wife. Alice said she was having a difficult time getting to know Denise. "You know, she has both an undergraduate and a graduate degree in political science from Yale, so she has to be bright," Alice remarked. "But she is kind of quirky. She appears disheveled and unkempt most of the time. I've never seen her with any kind of makeup. Her hair always seems to need attention, and she dresses like a frump! When I get her engaged, it seems that she has a good sense of humor and contributes meaningfully to a conversation, but most of the time, I cannot get her engaged. She just appears disinterested."

"That's interesting," said John. "Tim is not unlike that except that he is quite fastidious about his attire and grooming. I have not been able to get a good fix on him though. He really isn't an ops officer's ops officer. I mean, he is not a people person. You know how every good ops officer likes people in general and loves a good argument? Tim appears to be quite content to just sit in his office and read. He is certainly very knowledgeable about this part of the world, but if he keeps it all to himself, he is not doing his job. He has been out of the office for most of the past couple of weeks, as I have had him accompany Lt. Col. Armstrong. I thought the exposure to active operational matters might bring him out of his shell, but it didn't." John uncrossed his leg and leaned back in his chair. "But I did enjoy not having him around."

CHAPTER VIII

That same evening, George Willis met his new agent. Before the meeting, he arranged for two of the fellows from the administrative staff to help with his SDR. One was a finance officer and the other a logistics officer. They were excited to participate in an operation even in their very limited roles. It was not very often that they were called upon to contribute, and when they were asked to, they responded with gusto. George provided them with a detailed map of his SDR, which had specific points at which they were to station themselves. George was going to be on foot as he passed their assigned locations, and it was their job to determine if anyone was following him.

It turned out that George was "clean" that evening. He proceeded to the university area by taxi and then to Amal's house by foot. The drapes of her bedroom window were open, indicating that it was safe to enter. He did not bother knocking, as he wanted to get in with the least amount of exposure outside her home. Amal was quite surprised when he simply walked into her home, and she mentioned as much to him. He told her that he wanted to spend the least amount of time standing outside her door and hoped she didn't object.

"I don't. It's just that I was surprised. From now on, I'll expect to see you walking through the door exactly on time as you did tonight."

"Amal, we have to be very precise in this business. When I say I'll meet you at 9 PM, I mean 9 PM, not 9:05 or some other time. Exact timing is something that is drilled into intelligence officers."

"I'm just glad you're *here*. Actually, I've been nervous all day. I copied all the data I could, and I feared the whole time that someone was going to ask me what I was doing. Then, on the way home, I almost convinced myself that I was going to be stopped and searched by the police."

"Listen, before we discuss anything else, let's set the next meeting arrangements. In fact, we will always do that first so that if we are interrupted and have to abort our meeting, we will have a new one already arranged."

They made arrangements to meet again at her house in exactly two weeks at the same time. They agreed that if the meeting was canceled for any reason, the alternate meeting would be the following week at 8 PM and every week thereafter until they did meet. Then, Amal approached George with a look that meant she was intent on ripping his clothes off.

"Before we start on personal issues," said George, "let's get business out of the way. Were you able to bring me something?"

"Indeed, I have," responded Amal. "I copied a list that contains all recipients of the disbursements from the fund for the past year. The list includes names, account numbers, bank names, and amounts. You will see that the list is not very extensive. I think there are only 12 recipients, but the amounts sent to them were substantial. I have also been able to determine that while Ahmad Battal is the nominal head of our organization, he is just a figurehead. The real figure behind the organization, that is, the person who contributes to the funds and decides who receives them is a Saudi Prince named Meshal al-Talal."

George could hardly contain his pleasure. He was mildly shocked to hear the name Meshal al-Talal, as Kim had mentioned that this was the name Kim was going to use for his false flag recruitment. Al-Talal was actually doing what Kim was going to portray him to be doing. This should back up Kim's whole recruitment scenario if anyone ever investigated the details.

"Let me copy all this down, Amal. I don't want to miss any of these details. Superb reporting, by the way! You are going to make me look good," he said with a grin.

"No need to write anything down," said Amal, "I have it all here on this flash drive, including some biographic information I learned about Prince Talal. As for making you look good, I don't see how you could look any *better*." She moved in and planted a big wet kiss on him. Then she slithered down to her knees, unbuckled his pants, and proved that an Arab woman can give fantastic blowjobs. Soon, they were tearing at each other's clothes with a passion that was filled with urgency.

When they finished, George remarked again about how surprised he was to find an Arab woman so full of passion and displaying unabashed sexual behavior. Amal told him that unlike most Western women, she regularly had to pretend to not have sexual feelings. She explained that she was so frustrated that when presented with an opportunity to fulfill her desires, especially with a man she was very attracted to, she was not going to pretend to be shy. "On the contrary," she said, "I'm going to seize the moment."

As they lay there physically spent, Amal revealed to George that he was the first American man she had ever been with. "You know, it is so unreal that it is you, an American, to whom I am so attracted. I say that because growing up in Shatila, the refugee camp in South Beirut, I was taught to hate Americans. I think that for most of my life, I did hate everything America stood for or at least what I *thought* it stood for. I still think that U.S. government policy, as opposed to its people and institutions, has been hypocritical and *dead wrong* when it comes to the Middle East. I can understand President Truman succumbing to the pressure and accepting the State of Israel in 1948, but the acceptance of Israel's military invasion of Arab countries in 1967 and the occupation of our lands should be an anathema to Americans."

"Do you know that Israel was so intent on making it appear that their 1967 invasion was a 'preemptive strike' that they attacked one of your intelligence ships that was collecting information about their invasion? The attack by both air and sea killed 34 Americans onboard the USS Liberty and wounded another 174."

"I have heard about that attack," said George, "but I don't have the numbers memorized as you so clearly do."

"Well, you should have," replied Amal. "What other direct attack on an American warship has occurred since World War II? If it had been Iran – an Arab country – or, god forbid, a communist country that killed American sailors, we might have seen World War III! Anyway, that incident just proves to me that American policy in the Middle East is based on a paradigm so different from that in any other part of the world.

"My parents survived the 1982 massacre of the Sabra and Shatila camps. That massacre was later termed a genocide by a UN commission. As many as 3,000 Palestinians were slaughtered by the Lebanese Forces while the Israeli Army guarded and blocked the entrance and exits to those camps, and none other than Ariel Sharon, later to be the Defense Minister and Prime Minister of Israel, had commanded the invasion."

"So, how was it that you had a change of heart about America?" asked George.

"It happened slowly," said Amal "and probably never would have had I not attended AUB. We had so many American professors at AUB who understood and were critical of US policy in the area. They criticized their own government, and I soon learned that many inside America did the same. And though they criticized the US *government*, they made it abundantly clear that they loved their country. Their expression of dissatisfaction with U.S. policy, I came to understand, was not limited to those professors in Beirut, but it was typical of all Americans who found fault with a policy or action of their government for one reason or another. That is what is so great about America. The people have the freedom to express their opposition without fear of retribution from any quarter.

"I also began to learn at AUB that Americans are essentially kind and fair people with a great sense of fair play. If you grew up where I did and witnessed what the Lebanese people did to each other, you would have to agree that the contrast is significant. So, now that I have opened my body and mind to you, George, you should be able to read me like a book. Do you want to share anything about yourself, or do you wish to keep a dark secret?"

"I didn't know I came off as being secretive." George cocked his head and smiled. "I always assumed I was pretty much an open book, free for anyone to read. And by the way, *I* opened my body to you too."

"Come on, George. You're a secret intelligence officer. How can you claim to be an open book?"

"Touché," George quipped, "but I still maintain that for the most part, I'm a pretty open person."

"Sure," Amal said, smirking. "You have made sweet love to me, and we have shared that kind of intimacy, but I know almost nothing about you except that you are *great* in bed." She sat up on the bed and turned toward him. "For instance, I don't know where you were born, what prompted you to work for the CIA, if you have any children, what your wife is like, or why you are fucking *me* if you really love her?"

"Didn't some famous philosopher claim that maintaining a bit of secrecy about oneself keeps the opposite sex interested?"

"Oh, you have captured my complete interest, George. You don't have to work on it anymore."

"Okay, Okay, Amal. What do you want to know?"

"There is nothing, in particular, that I want to know. I just…want you to share. Share some of your emotions, thoughts, history, and what not. In other words, George Willis, who are you?"

"Since I'm rather proud of my background and family, that should be easy," George said. "I come from a very patriotic family. My dad was a Marine officer and had commanded a unit in Beirut where they had been hit by a truck bomb in 1983. He left the Marines shortly after the Beirut incident, went back to law school, and is now a very successful lawyer in Philadelphia. My uncle, my dad's older brother, was the Director of the CIA a few years back. Like my father, older brother, and several cousins, I was a Marine Corp officer too. I did love being in the Marine Corps, but it didn't engage me mentally the way I wanted it to. So, when my time was up a few years back, I left and joined the Agency."

"What about your wife, George? Tell me something about the two of you."

"Okay. My wife Amy comes from an old Philadelphia family that was originally in the steel business. They were, and still are, some of the richest people in the U.S. I was attracted to all that – not the money but the *power* they hold and the influence they had. So much of that attraction has worn off now, mainly because Amy is rather superficial. She went to the best schools, but quite frankly, I don't know how she graduated. I suppose it was money that got her through. Although she is good to me, she is not a good person, and there is not much substance there. I probably should have left her by now, but if I'm being totally honest with myself, I would say I lack the courage."

"Wow, I…wasn't expecting that much honesty. Since we are being so honest, I want you to know where I'm coming from. I think you are adorable, and I am *very* infatuated with you. But I am not looking for a husband, so you should know that I do not expect you to leave your wife for me. I hope that didn't come across as presumptuous of me. I-I don't mean to be. I just… want to establish who we are together and let you know that there will never be *any* pressure from this quarter."

"Thank you so much for that, Amal. I believe we have and will continue to have a very unique relationship, both physically and emotionally. But both of us should know right from the beginning that it will end one day. That will be a sad day for me, but it *will* end."

There was a tear in Amal's eye when she said, "George, your honesty means a lot to me. Thank you."

After leaving Amal's home, George felt light-headed as he quickly walked back to the university area. Amal was having a profound effect on him even though he was trying to prevent that from happening. His relationship with her was becoming very complex. He didn't have a good feeling about their future, and he was beginning to anticipate a tragic ending.

The university was almost deserted, but a few students were hanging around. George hailed a taxi and had it take him to the mall where he had left his car. He decided that he did not want to store the flash drive at home overnight, so he drove to the Embassy. The Marine guard on duty saluted him and addressed him as Captain. "You know I'm no longer in the Corp, don't you, Corporal?"

"Once a Marine, always a Marine, Captain," the guard responded.

George smiled at him and then hurried upstairs to his office. He had initially intended to simply lock the flash drive in his safe and go home, but once he got to his desk, he decided to open the flash drive and take a quick look at the data on it.

George was astounded by what he saw. Amal's fund had paid out almost $500 Million in the past four years. George did not recognize any of the names of the recipients, but to his relief, he did not see the name Rifat al-Biladi, COUSIN's true name. If there had been a pre-existing relationship between Talal and Rifat, that would have undermined Malloy's upcoming false flag recruitment pitch. George was elated. *Analysts back in Washington are going to go bonkers over this detailed information,* he thought. Based on his casual perusal of the data, he was particularly interested in the fact that more than half of the funds passed through New York for distribution. If it was determined that the banks involved were privy to the fact that this money was being used for illicit purposes or if they declined to try to learn the purpose of the funds, they could be fined or even closed down. George was also convinced that regardless of how the funds were routed in transit, many of the banks failed to ask the mandatory questions to their clients about their source of funds. Most likely, that would violate the KYC[15] rule, which could leave the banks open to severe penalties.

The next morning, George was in early. He entered John's office and asked his boss to meet him in the bubble when he had a moment and then explained about the data Amal had provided the previous evening. John said, "I'll be right there. Wait for me." He told JoAnn to have Tim meet him in the bubble, but JoAnn reminded him that Tim was at Bill Lucas' home overseeing the packing up of the family's belongings. Bill's wife and children had already left Riyadh and would not be returning, so Tim and the station's logistics officer were there to make sure everything got packed properly.

John entered the bubble and asked, "Okay, George, what did you get?"

George had already inserted the flash drive into his computer and opened the first page of the document. "Have a look at this, John. Disbursements worth almost $500 Million have been made to various individuals and organizations in the Middle East, and, the *sole* source of these funds is Meshal al-Talal."

John immediately asked if COUSIN's name was on the recipient list, and was relieved when George told him it was not. Glancing over the list, John immediately recognized a few of the names as leaders of radical groups in Afghanistan, Algeria, and Libya, but most were unfamiliar to him. "I am impressed! This is really good stuff, George. Get together with the reports officer, and let's put this out as an intelligence report. But I want the distribution severely limited. This information is going to correct some misconceptions Washington has about Prince Talal. This woman of yours has

---

[15] KYC: Know Your Client requires financial institutions to satisfy themselves that their clients are using and transferring funds for legitimate purposes and are not involved in criminal or terrorism-related money laundering. These rules came into effect after the 9/11 attack on the New York Trade center buildings by Arab terrorists.

already earned her resettlement, at least in my view. By the way, how did your SDR go? Were there any tradecraft problems with the meeting?"

George explained that everything had gone smoothly and a meeting was scheduled with her two weeks from then.

As John was leaving the bubble, Kim Malloy came in and said that he needed to talk to John. John told him that he had to meet the Ambassador in a couple of minutes but would be back in less than an hour. At the meeting, the Ambassador asked if anyone had received any questions about the deaths of the two Americans. No one had. Thus far, it seemed that the press had not gotten wind of the failed operation. No one thought that it would last much longer. Once Congress was briefed about the operation, there would surely be quite a few leaks.

CHAPTER IX

John hurried back to the bubble after the mini country team meeting. Kim was waiting for him and immediately reported that FLAG had signaled him for a meeting yesterday and they had met the last night. At the meeting, FLAG had reported that he had heard from his cousin, COUSIN. The two had spoken on the phone, and COUSIN had wanted FLAG to meet him in Tripoli where he would be next week. FLAG had demurred because he wasn't sure that Kim wanted him to go to Libya and also since travel to Libya would involve several days away from his job. His superiors at ARAMCO would not be happy with him gone too long. Noting his hesitation, COUSIN had said he would be in Baghdad the following week and suggested that Hussein could meet him there. He had agreed to meet his cousin in Baghdad because he could claim he was going there to be with family, while he had no good reason to go to Libya. Additionally, Iraq bordered Saudi Arabia, which meant he could make a trip there and back quickly.

"I said to Hussein, 'You have shown good sense in making those arrangements. I think the arrangements you made are excellent. And don't worry about travel costs, I'll cover those," Kim told John. "So, I anticipate he will meet COUSIN within a couple of weeks and recruit him at that time."

"Good work," said John. "I think this is going to be a very valuable operation. By the way, Kim, I don't think we have gone over the tradecraft you are using in your meetings with FLAG. Tell me what you are doing."

Kim replied that they were not meeting clandestinely, but they were using 'social cover' instead.

"That's not good enough," remarked John. "You need to move this out of the public eye and meet clandestinely. I think we have a recently acquired safehouse that has not been assigned to any other operation. Check with Tim when he gets back this afternoon. This new safehouse is essentially an apartment rented by a DOD[16] contractor who travels outside Riyadh most of the time. I think he is here only on weekends, so you shouldn't have any conflicts if your meetings are during the week between Sunday and Thursday[17]. Given the involvement of ISIS, this operation has the potential to become quite dangerous. So, I don't want any mistakes that could lead to you or your asset being put in danger. Before your next meeting, I want you to give me a detailed meeting plan with safety signals, SDRs, cover for meetings, and some form of plausible denial."

"Okay, John, I'll do that," said Kim. "But soon, I will need another safehouse for an-Nassar."

John agreed with him and said he wanted Kim to get as much information about an-Nassar's daily routine as possible in order to make meeting arrangements around an-Nassar's usual lifestyle and habits.

Within a couple of days, Hqs sent a message regarding the intelligence supplied by Amal. They congratulated the station for providing the critical information. Most of the names listed as the recipients of funds were known to be organizers of radical groups. However, there were three individuals named who were only suspected of being involved in radical or terrorist activities. There were individuals on the list in Cairo, Algiers, Rabat, Tunis, Kabul, and Islamabad. The Agency had strong relationships with the local intelligence services in each of these countries, and Hqs was contemplating sharing some of the information with these local services. That was the best way to take action against those who were receiving funds and undoubtedly using the funds to sow discord in their respective countries.

However, the sharing of information would not be done unless the Riyadh station was in agreement. There was a recurring problem with information on

16 DOD: Department of Defense
17 In Saudi Arabia, Friday and Saturday constitute the weekend.

counter-terrorism. In order to effectively put counter-terrorism intelligence to use, it had to be acted upon. But acting on intelligence always put the reporting agent in jeopardy. So, the station producing the information was always given the opportunity to have a say in how that information was shared. Lastly, Hqs informed that it had approved the resettlement of Amal in case she was put in a dangerous position because of her work for the Agency.

John responded to Washington saying, in effect, that the Riyadh Station, in theory, supported the sharing of MONEY'S intelligence with local intelligence services. John said in his message that he realized collecting such information and then sitting on it was not an option. However, he wanted to be in a position to approve the passage of the information and the form in which it would be shared on a case-by-case basis. He wanted to protect Riyadh's asset, and by doing so, Riyadh would be in a position to receive updated information on these radicals and terrorists.

As for passing on this information to local intelligence services, John said that he believed that the information could be framed in such a way that it would appear as if it had originated from a bank – a bank that had questioned the transfer and reported it to the Fed[18] in New York. Of course, that would only apply to those transfers that passed through New York. For those that did not pass through New York, John asked Hqs to devise a plan that made it appear that a correspondent bank had reported the transfer to local authorities in its home country.

Then there was the question of what to do about Prince al-Talal. In response to Hqs' suggestion, John said that it would be counterproductive to raise the issue with Saudi intelligence. The Saudi royal family tended to protect its members and was very tolerant of family members supporting radicals outside the Kingdom. Indeed, Saudi princes and other rich Saudis had supported radical movements throughout the Middle East with impunity.

A prime example of this was the near civil war that took place in Algeria shortly after the war in Afghanistan with the Soviets had ended. Saudi support for former Afghan jihadis of Algerian nationality was well known. These returning jihadis committed many atrocities, particularly in rural areas

---

[18] "The Fed" is the common term for the Federal Reserve System, which is the US' central bank.

of Algeria, and for a while, they had threatened the very existence of the Algerian government.

Moreover, going to the Saudis with the information about Prince Talal was not an option because it would most likely expose MONEY. John said that they would work with MONEY to try to come up with a plan to bankrupt Prince Talal and, perhaps, frame him for fermenting plans against the Saudi regime. It was one thing to support radicals outside of the Kingdom, but supporting them inside the Kingdom could bring swift retribution.

John sat in his office, immersed in thought about how to bring down Prince Talal. The Prince was single-handedly the driving force behind a dozen radical organizations in the Middle East. Neutralizing him would almost cripple some of these terrorist organizations and cause the demise of those that were in their infancy. One of the first things that needed to be done was to determine how much of the transferred funds remained in the recipients' accounts. If a great deal of the funds was still in an account, perhaps they could be seized. Secondly, an effort had to be made to determine how much money, if any, the heads of these various organizations had siphoned off for their personal use. Such information could be used to discredit the individuals and dampen any desire of others to contribute to their cause. John knew that while many of these radicals preached a good sermon, all too often, they were more corrupt than any of the Middle Eastern politicians, and most of those had a well-deserved reputation for corruption. Working with local intelligence organizations, it should not be too difficult to lure some of these radicals into a prostitute's lair and get pictures taken of the radicals lolling about with naked women. Of course, empty bottles of Johnny Walker Blue scattered around would only enhance the image of debauchery. Perhaps, they could arrange for similar pictures of Prince Talal, either real or photo shopped. John suddenly realized that they knew practically nothing about Prince Talal. That would have to change. Still thinking about Talal, John asked JoAnn to signal George Willis to meet him in the bubble.

When the two got together, John told George that they needed to develop a complete picture of Prince Talal. "We are working in the dark now because we know so little about this guy. Do you think we can use Amal to get close to him and see what makes him tick?"

George said that he had not given any thought to that possibility but would raise the subject with her. "To be honest, I don't think she will be amenable to getting very close to Talal."

John said, "I believe you told me that she is a real beauty, isn't that right? And if so, would she really object to doing just a bit of flirting to get a closer look at Talal?"

"Indeed, she is quite beautiful, but because of her antipathy toward Saudi men, she might not be the best candidate for this job."

"Okay, maybe she isn't. Why don't you ask her? You can preface your request with the fact that we know very little about the Prince and want to bring him down. She might find it a challenge."

George pondered the suggestion and said, "I just don't want to leave her with the impression that we are trying to pimp her out just to get info."

"I can understand that," replied John. "Just use your judgment on how to go about it, but do float the proposal in front of her in some fashion." John left the bubble hoping that George was not allowing his emotions to get in the way of making sound operational decisions.

On the other hand, George left the meeting thinking that he did not favor the idea of Amal flirting with Talal in order to assess him. He didn't know if his objection was emotional or if he had a solid reason for not being in favor of this approach. The more he thought about it, he had to conclude that emotion was clouding his judgment. He also thought that Amal might conclude that he was trying to pimp her out and that could turn her against him and the very foundation of their relationship. He decided that he had to raise the issue with her, but he was going to have to be very careful about how he phrased this proposal so as not to offend her sensibilities. On the other hand, George was pleased to have a reason to signal her for an unscheduled meeting so soon – his sexual desire for her was becoming overwhelming.

Having signaled Amal to meet him that evening, George went through his SDR plan and took considerable precautions to ensure that the meeting was secure. As he arrived, he noted that the drapes were open, so he quickly entered the home like the last time. This time, she was waiting for him, and to his surprise, she was wearing something out of Victoria's Secret that got his heart beating very quickly. Seeing his reaction, she smiled and said, "It appears I have achieved the desired effect."

"If you mean reducing me to my animal instincts, then yes. You have *certainly* achieved your desired effect," George replied. "But first, let's get business out of the way so we can enjoy each other fully."

John told her that the information she had provided was highly appreciated and a decision had been made to undermine the efforts of Prince Talal. However, the Agency did not have much information about this Prince. Apparently, he had been operating under the radar. So, it would be necessary to learn more about him in order to formulate a plan to reverse his achievements and emasculate his endeavors. George then asked her if she could provide a good assessment of Prince Talal.

Amal told George, as she had done previously, that the Prince hardly spent any time at the charity, and when he was there, he was very aloof.

George said, "Look, Amal, if you can reduce me to a bumbling idiot just by looking at me, surely you can get this Prince to reveal a bit about himself."

"What exactly are you asking me to do?"

"I know what you're thinking, and that is not what I want. I just want you to be friendly enough with him to gain some insight into what kind of a person he is and what he does with his time. Nothing else."

Amal said she would give it a try, but it would not be anytime soon. She said that the end of the year was looming and she had plans to visit Beirut for several weeks. She told John that her family was really into celebrating the New Year and she had promised her parents that she would be there this year. Besides, she had several weeks of paid vacation coming up that she would lose if she didn't take it by the end of the year. "I wanted to give you a special present before I left, and that is why I am so provocatively dressed," Amal said. She noted the instant disappointment on George's face and attempted to assure him that she would work twice as hard for him after her return. With a sly look on her face, she said, "I am going to make sure you leave here tonight with memories that will hold you over till next year."

George thought he should make the best of the situation. He said he had noted that the information she had provided contained the names of several recipients from Lebanon. "Do you know these individuals, and if not, can you get to know them?" George asked.

Amal had to explain that she did not know any of them personally and it had been made clear to her when she was first hired that she was not to contact any of the recipients. She had never questioned this order, but she thought it best to heed that rule. George sighed. *I'm not making much progress this evening. I might as well start having fun.* The two of them began a long night of vigorous sex, which left both of them completely exhausted.

On his way home that evening, George began to realize that he really liked this woman. In addition to her very imaginative sexual prowess, she was funny, sweet, bright, and beautiful. He could not help but compare her to Amy. Actually, there *was* no comparison. Amy was dull, both intellectually and sexually. As he thought about it, it dawned on him that he had not had sex with Amy since he had started a sexual relationship with Amal. *There is no good ending to this relationship*, he thought. He wondered how it would end but knew that he didn't want it to end any time soon.

CHAPTER X

With Amal leaving the Kingdom for a few weeks, George decided to focus more on Mohammed al-Masri, his Egyptian developmental. He had only seen al-Masri a few times since he reviewed this case with his COS. Each time he saw Mohammed the latter appeared eager to be friendly with George. George had told Mohammed that being an outsider, that is, a non-Arab, he often misunderstood political nuances and he was relying on Mohammed to guide him in the right political direction.

"Firstly," Mohammed said, "I am an Egyptian, not an Arab. We Egyptians are descendants of the Pharaohs, not Semites. In fact, in terms of culture and history, Egypt is closer to Turkey than Arab countries. The Ottomans founded modern Egypt and ruled there from 1517 until well into the 19th century. But some of our more recent leaders, like Abd-an-Nassar and Sadat, brought us into the Arab World. Indeed, Nassar renamed our country the 'United Arab Republic' only so he could dominate Arab countries. The UAR didn't last very long, only from 1958 to 1961. That was because it was supposed to be a union with Syria but Nassar dominated it politically, and eventually, the Syrians withdrew from it. Later, Anwar Sadat renamed Egypt the 'Arab Republic of Egypt,' So, no wonder the world considers us Arabs. I suppose that by the modern definition of an Arab country – a country that speaks Arabic – we are Arabs. In any event, my friend, I can be your political guide through these messy

Arab waters. You can trust me to provide the correct interpretation of Arab events and fully explain these matters to you."

George told Mohammed that he was very grateful for his friendship and assistance but he could not allow Mohammed to give so much without he, George, giving something back. "What can I do for you, Mohammed", asked George.

Mohammed, who had received a bottle of Johnny Walker Black each time they met, told George that his friendship was all that mattered and he needed nothing else.

These Egyptians are real bullshitters, George thought to himself, *but I'll play along.* Indeed, Mohammed had a firm grasp of political events not only in Saudi Arabia but throughout the Middle East. Although he had not provided George with any classified information, his explanation of political events was very helpful to George. George knew that it was time to move this relationship along to a more professional level, which meant turning Mohammed into a spy. But, of course, he would never use that word in front of Mohammed.

George discussed his relationship and meetings with Mohammed in detail with his COS. John's experience with Arabs in general, and Egyptians in particular, was invaluable in leading Mohammed down the path to his recruitment. John instructed George to keep Cairo station informed about every step he took and every meeting he had with Mohammed. Historically, the Egyptian General Intelligence Service, better known as the GI, had been quite good at uncovering CIA recruitments of Egyptian nationals. In fact, the GI would, on occasion, "dangle" a prospective Egyptian agent and allow him or her to be recruited by an American. Then, they would patiently wait to discover who the American case officer was. After making such discoveries, they would put the American case officer under intense surveillance in order to identify any other Egyptian agents he might be handling. The Egyptians were quite good at intense surveillance because of the multitude of paid sources they had. There was a street vendor on most corners in Cairo, and chances were that every one of those street vendors received 5 or 10 Egyptian pounds, which was about $2–$4, per week from the GI to report any unusual activity that they may witness. John had remarked that while they had cameras in the West to observe activity, the Egyptians had street vendors, taxi drivers, hotel doormen, and others to observe. The big difference was that one had to query the camera to get information, while the "man on the street" in Cairo, knowing he would get a reward if his information was valuable, provided the information without prodding.

John advised George to wait until Mohammed provided him with information about something that was generally not known, specifically something that could be considered confidential. "Once that happens," said John, "give him $1000. Don't give anything to him for his interpretation of an event, but wait until he tells you something you would not otherwise know. He will probably refuse at first, but you can explain to him that if you had to hire a research or some other kind of firm to obtain such information, they would charge you more. So, you want your *friend* to benefit rather than some company. If he is venal enough, he will take it. The first time may be difficult for him, but if he takes it once, he will be expecting it in the future."

The next time George saw Mohammed, the latter insisted that they retire to a quiet place to have a serious chat. At the time they were at a national day reception at the Polish Embassy. George suggested that after the reception they move to his house, which was not far.

"OK," said Mohammed, "I'll wait until I see that you have left and then I will follow about 5 minutes later. George agreed and thought Mohammed was taking the first steps toward a clandestine relationship.

When Mohammed arrived at George's home about a half hour later, he appeared to be rather agitated and at loose ends. "What's wrong?" asked George.

"Nothing," replied Mohammed, "it's just....I hope I was not seen coming here, not tonight anyway."

"But you are here now," said George, "settle down and tell me what's bothering you."

Mohammed confessed that he was privy to some very confidential information that he was going to share with George. However, he said that it was crucial that it never came to light that he had provided this information.

He said, "I feel a little guilty for what I am about to do, and that is why I'm... unsettled."

"Listen Mohammed," said George, "I would never want you to put yourself in an untenable situation. It must be important if you are this shaken."

"The thing is," said Mohammed, "I am one of very few who knows about this information and for me to be coming directly to you afterwards might lead some to the correct conclusion."

Taking a chance he might blow the potential recruitment, George said, "Mohammed if you are fearful that associating with me will bring some harm to you, perhaps you should leave now. I don't want anything untoward to happen to you."

Mohammed brushed aside the concern and said that he thought he was doing the right thing. "So here it is," said Mohammed. "The Saudis are leading a campaign to ostracize Qatar from other Arab countries. I *don't know* where this will lead, but the Saudis have asked us to review the damage the Qatari regime has done to Egypt. They have suggested that we have high-level talks to discuss what action should be taken against Qatar. I can tell you that this will be music to our President's ears. He believes that Qatar played a key role in promoting the Muslim Brotherhood's overthrow of Mubarak and its rise to the Presidency in Egypt. If high-level talks between our two countries lead to a meeting of the minds, the Saudis then plan to enlist many other countries, including the rest of the GCC[19] countries, to break diplomatic relations with Qatar."

George told Mohammed that the information he just gave him was explosive. "Mohammed, this information is certainly key to U.S. involvement in the area. We have important relationships with both Egypt and Saudi Arabia. And complicating matters is the fact that the U.S. air base in Qatar is the most active against ISIS. We will have to carefully plan our course of action in response to action you and the Saudis take. Can I rely on you to keep me up to date on any actions Egypt and Saudi Arabia plan to take?"

Mohammed said he had every intention of keeping George informed. Then he said that he could probably do a better job of it by traveling back and forth to Cairo in order to get a first-hand impression of Egypt's reaction

[19] GCC: Gulf Cooperation Council

to the Saudi initiative. "However," said Mohammed, "my limited budget will not bear the cost of travel back and forth on a regular basis."

"Mohammed, this is too important to worry about the costs. I'll provide you with an ample budget so that you have the best insights into what is happening on this important subject."

When George reported this meeting to John, the latter told him, "You have all but recruited this guy. Let's get the necessary approvals so you can formalize the relationship at the next meeting. I guess he already suspects that you work for the CIA and wants to be put on the payroll. Let me remind you though that this would not be the first time Egyptian intelligence dangles someone in front of us for the sole reason of identifying our officers. We are not going to be sure of Mohammed until we get some verifiable information from him that is clearly damaging to Egypt, that is, something that Egypt *certainly* would not want us to have. Actually, his report about Qatar may already meet that criterion. In any event, you will eventually have to put Mohammed on the 'box'. If he passes the polygraph, we can have significantly more confidence in him.

"So, once you get the approval from Hqs to proceed, tell Mohammed that you cannot expect him to be spending all this time ferreting out information for you without compensation. Tell him that you are going to put him on a retainer of $2,000 per month. He will probably balk, but that will just be bullshit. Keep insisting on the payment, and he will accept. Also, there is no need to break cover at this point. He suspects that you are CIA. Don't deny that, but don't confirm it unless he asks. Once you get him to accept payments on a regular basis, you can break cover and tell him that he is working for the CIA. Eventually, you will want him to meet a Cairo Station officer in Cairo. That will be a *major* step. Accepting money from you and meeting you here in Riyadh is one thing, but the meeting in Cairo will have to be conducted clandestinely. That will *really* test his mettle, and the thought of it will scare the shit out of him."

In a couple of days Hqs came back with a POA approving the recruitment of Mohammed and providing him with the crypt CHANCE. With his POA in hand, George arranged for a meeting with Mohammed for the following night. He was hesitant to offer the $2,000/month salary to Mohammed, thinking the latter was going to be offended and have a negative reaction. So he slow-walked his way into that part of the recruitment by saying, "Mohammed, I am asking a lot of you and it would not be fair to expect so much from you without some compensation. Therefore, I am prepared to put you on a retainer of $2,000 per month for all your efforts."

Mohammed replied, "I think that is fair compensation, when do I start getting it? Also, my travel expenses will be rather hefty. Am I correct in assuming that you will reimburse me for travel, in addition to the retainer?"

George was taken aback, but masked his surprise, he simply said, "I have the first installment here in my pocket, just sign this receipt and, yes, travel expenses will be paid separately."

"What, sign a receipt?" cried Mohammed. "I don't want to make a written record of the fact that you are paying me."

George told him that he could use an alias if he wished. "But," he said, "the guys with the green shades back at his office will hound me for a receipt. You don't have to sign your real name – any name will do." He was prepared to drop this request if Mohammed continued to object, but the latter quickly came up with the alias "John Smith" and signed the receipt accordingly. CHANCE was now signed, sealed, and delivered! George wondered if all Egyptians were this predictable. His COS had given him a script, and Mohammed had acted as if he had read it too.

Cairo Station was very pleased when they saw George's report of his recruitment of CHANCE and they said as much in their return message. However, they were cautious about having a Cairo Station officer meet him when the latter visits Cairo. Cairo Station said Mohammed would have to be fully vetted before they would meet with him. They further explained that fully vetted meant verifying all of the information he provides AND successfully passing the polygraph. George knew from his COS that Cairo Station was going to insist on "boxing" Mohammed, but he knew Mohammed was going to vigorously object to it. John had advised George to have Mohammed on the payroll for several months before addressing the polygraph. The idea was to get him used to the regular payments before the veiled threat of discontinuing them should he not acquiesce.

CHAPTER XI

As John arrived early in the morning to his office he found, as usual, that JoAnn was already at her desk. She greeted him and said there was an interesting message from Washington. It was a joint Headquarters/ JSOC After Action Report and a Damage Assessment. John got right to it, as he had been expecting it and wanted to see if Washington's assessment coincided with his. Typical of the military, their portion of the report was exhaustive. It covered every detail from the inception to conclusion.

The bottom line, however, was that both the CIA and the JSOC agreed that the operation had failed because the Saudi agent had been a double. They left open the possibility of the whole operation being compromised from the beginning, but the consensus was that a high-level AQAP meeting really had been planned and it was scrubbed after the Saudi agent reported back to AQAP. The report speculated about two other possible causes behind AQAP knowing about or anticipating the raid. First, AQAP may have sighted some of the recon drones that the U.S. had sent over the area and assumed that the drones were doing a recon for the raid. Second, some human sources of the U.S. could have had asked too many questions about a possible meeting in Yuwan, making AQAP suspect that the meeting had been compromised. The theory was that the information about the meeting in Yuwan was probably a closely-kept secret in AQAP, and by evaluating those who were privy to it, they had probably discovered that the Saudi agent was the only one traveling outside of Yemen. This, of course, assumed that the Saudis were meeting their agent in Saudi Arabia.

When John finished it, he could not help but think that as exhaustive as the report was, it did not answer all his doubts. Actually, the report admitted there were doubts in Washington about its conclusions. One of the recommendations was that the Station attempt to learn the identity of the Saudi agent. If the agent's identity is revealed, said the report, his movements and activities might be pin pointed. Indeed, identifying the agent could answer many questions.

John thought that the best way to identify the agent was to ask Prince Mohammed directly. John knew that protecting the identity of agents was sacrosanct in the intelligence business. The names of agents were almost never shared between intelligence services. John thought that Prince Mohammed might make an exception in this case since the agent was no longer active and could even be dead. Under the circumstances, the Saudis would want to know what had happened to their agent even more than the Americans did. So, if the Americans could learn what had happened to the agent, the Saudis would be grateful, and it would do them no harm. With that in mind, John made arrangements to meet Prince Mohammed the following evening.

At the meeting the following day, John began by asking about Captain al-Sudari's well-being. Prince Mohammed reported that al-Sudari was recovering nicely. In addition to the wound that broke his right arm, he had several broken ribs. His armored vest had stopped at least one round from hitting him in the chest, but the blow was so severe it broke two ribs. The Prince said, "Truth be known, Hasan is wearing his wounds like a badge of honor. It's not many Saudi officers who have engaged terrorists and have lived to tell about it. From what you have told me, Hasan proved to be courageous under fire and for that reason we are giving him a medal."

John said, "That medal is well deserved. I can tell you, all of the Americans were impressed with Hasan's response after he was hit. But let me address my real purpose for requesting this meeting today. I would like to ask some questions about the agent who initially reported that there was going to be a meeting. Have you been able to re-contact him?"

"We have not, John, and it's not because of a lack of effort. My officers have tried everything but it's as if he disappeared off the face of this earth."

John took this opportunity to ask the Prince to reveal the agent's identity. He said, "I know this is *almost never* done, but we want you to identify the agent – what's his name, where did he live, where was he employed and what was his relationship to AQAP. If we can get those facts, we may be able to track him down, if he is alive. If he is not alive, we may be able to determine what happened to him."

Prince Mohammed said that he was glad that John had raised the issue because he did want the Americans' help in finding out what had happened to their agent. The Prince identified the agent as Abd-al-Aziz Numari who was a Yemeni truck driver transporting fruits and vegetables between Yemen and Saudi Arabia. He said that AQAP had recruited Abd-al-Aziz to report on security on the Saudi side of the border with Yemen. Abd-al-Aziz had worked in Riyadh a few years back, and he knew that he was risking his livelihood by reporting to AQAP. So, shortly after AQAP had recruited him, he had sought out Saudi authorities during one of his routine trips. Abd-al-Aziz, as it turned out, was originally from Yuwan and knew Ahmad al-Tuwayjari well. It was Tuwayjari who had told him about the plans for the meeting.

"Do you know how old he is … or was?" asked John.

The Prince called in an underling who informed him that Abd-al-Aziz was 34. Prince Mohammed said, "You know, John, most of these Yemenis do not have an allegiance to a country. Their allegiance is to a tribe. It is not unusual for a Yemeni to be looking out for himself when in circumstances like that of Abd-al-Aziz because neither Saudi Arabia nor Yemen conjures up loyalty in his book. He was just trying to earn a living and keep himself alive."

John thanked the Prince for the information and upon returning to his office he conveyed to Washington the details of his meeting with Prince Mohammed. He asked that the Agency do its best to learn what happened to Abd-al-Aziz. Terrorist organizations often times do not do things that might be expected. For instance, if they caught a double agent and decided to kill him, one might think that the act of murdering one of your own might be something to you would not want to advertise. However, these organizations want to send a message in such situations and so they let it be known what happens to someone who double crosses them. If the word is out that Abd-al-Aziz was murdered, chances are the Agency will learn of it.

About that time Tim Haggerty walked into John's office and announced, "We just received a message telling me to return to Hqs to sit on a promotion panel."

John thought about this for a moment and said, "I really don't see a problem with that Tim. Things are slowing down here since the failed raid in Yemen. Also, I think that sitting on a promotion panel might help you to get a good perspective on writing fitness reports. I know that I write better reports now after sitting on a couple of panels. While on the panel you will learn what they are looking for when making recommendations for promotion. Perhaps just as importantly, you learn what kind of fitness report can sink someone's chances for promotion. These can be subtle differences and once you know them, you can achieve your desired objective when writing one for an employee. I have had some officers think that I was giving them a glowing report when in actual fact I meant to bury them, and *did*. On the other hand, I can recall one good officer complaining to me that he would never get promoted given the fitness report I wrote for him. I refused to change the report and he agreed with me several months later when he received his promotion."

Tim asked how long these panels typically met and John said he thought Tim should plan on being away for about a month to six weeks. Given that situation, said Tim, "I think I will take my wife Denise with me."

"Good idea", said John. "Both of you probably need some time away from this sandbox."

I don't know about this guy, John thought to himself. *He is smart and thoughtful, but I think he needs to get out and meet more people.* John thought that the promotion panel might do Tim a world of good. *He will see that officers who are out trying to recruit new agents are the ones who get promoted. Those who are content with "handling" existing agents typically don't get past the journeyman level.* The Agency was not part of the Civil Service system, but the law allowed the Director to adopt the Civil Service pay scale to compensate employees, and that was what had happened. Tim was a GS-15, which was about the equivalent of a Colonel in the military. The fact that he had reached that high in the Clandestine Service for someone who was not particularly a people person was unusual, but it was clear to John that he wasn't going any further.

The Agency was somewhat like the military when it came to promoting its officers. In the military, the best way to become a general officer was to have success in combat. Likewise, in the Agency, the best way to make it to the "super grades" was to be successful in generating new operations, which generally meant recruiting new agents. However, many officers both in the military and the Agency got to the Colonel level by specializing, and apparently, that is what Tim had done up to this point. He had been a counterintelligence specialist, which required a sort of dogged pursuit of facts and figures. Tim was a born researcher, and that made him quite a good CI officer. But now that he was in a station, he needed to broaden his skill set.

CHAPTER XII

Hussein al-Biladi returned from meeting his cousin Rifat in Baghdad and signaled for a meeting with Kim Malloy. During Hussein's absence Kim had arranged for the use of a safehouse, per his COS' instructions. His standing meeting arrangements with Hussein was to meet him in a coffee house. This time Kim waited until he was sure Hussein was in the coffee house and then he entered. He sat with Hussein only long enough to pass him a sheet of paper on which he had written the address of the safehouse and had drawn a map of its location. He told Hussein to meet him there in one half hour. Kim left first without telling Hussein that he would be counter surveilled by 3 other Station officers, just to make sure he was clean before going to the safehouse. As it turned out, there was no surveillance on Hussein.

Upon entering the safehouse Kim gave Hussein the traditional embrace men do in the Middle East. This came natural to Kim who grew up in Egypt but most other officers found it a difficult practice to adopt. Kim addressed Hussein as 'brother Hussein' and immediately after making arrangements for the next meeting, asked Hussein if he had encountered any danger and if he considered himself safe.

Hussein responded, "all went well, my brother, I faced no difficulty. I didn't notice that anyone paid any unusual attention to me. I'm really not sure we need all this cloak and dagger stuff here in Riyadh."

"Just do what I ask, if for no other reason, just to amuse me," said Kim. "It may be a bit time consuming to go through some security procedures, but you never know when those procedures will keep you safe. Anyway, let me know about your trip to Baghdad."

"I met with Rifat every day I was in Baghdad and secured his cooperation. Rifat had heard of Prince Talal and was more than happy to cooperate with him. He was particularly happy about receiving a monthly stipend from Talal. As a starter, he gave me a list containing the names of all the ISIS members in his cell and the names of the ISIS leaders to whom he reports. The list is rather extensive and it is in Arabic but you should have no trouble reading it."

"More importantly, Rifat told me that the morale of ISIS members in Syria is at an all-time low. Their numbers are decreasing daily as is the territory they hold. Many ISIS members, according to Rifat, assume that their days are numbered. Rifat said he could not remember the last time they had had an influx of new members from abroad. He contrasted that to a couple of years ago when new members were arriving from all over the world on a daily basis. He also said that there was considerable talk among the leadership of ISIS about regrouping into smaller cells and foregoing territorial claims. Many of the ISIS leaders are now favoring a more secretive organization that hits the West with large-scale attacks that kill many, rather than the attacks that have occurred more recently in which only a few people have been killed.

"Interestingly, Rifat said that the only leader who was not in favor of a major realignment was Abu Bakr al-Baghdadi, the head of ISIS. Al-Baghdadi wants to hold on to territory and continues to see himself as a 'caliph' and you can't be a caliph without territory."

Kim told Hussein that this information was very valuable. "But", he said, "What we are really after is information on any new terrorist plans. Were you able to convince Rifat, without raising his suspicion, that Talal's main interest is future terrorist attacks?"

Hussein responded that he had told Rifat that Prince Talal wanted to direct his funds where they would do the most good. "I told him," said Hussein, "that Talal would increase the funds available to a given group if he knew that group was about to conduct a new operation. I told him that Talal realizes that successful operations require planning and money and he did not want an operation to fail because the group lacked sufficient funds. Rifat completely bought into that argument and told me that he would make every effort to get me details on any pending terrorist attack. However, Rifat said that at the moment, he was unaware of any impending plans."

Kim told Hussein he was very pleased with his accomplishments. He asked, "Brother Hussein, what arrangements did you make with Rifat for him to contact you in the event he learns anything of value?"

Hussein said that he and Rifat had worked out signals that Rifat would use in text messages to alert him about important information. " If he has important information and the timing is not critical, Rifat will text me that our aunt is sick and we should be by her side. Meaning, there would be sufficient time for us to meet in Baghdad before the operation's planned launch date.

"However, if time *is* critical, the location of the impending attack will be identified by its dialing code in the text. The numbers have to be sequential but can be separated by text. All numbers in one sentence will identify the location. Let's say, Rifat's text says 'come 2 auntie's as soon as you can for 0 reasons other than to be with her for at least 1 day before she goes.' The numbers are 201, which equates to Cairo, Egypt – 20 being the country code for Egypt, and 1 being the designated city code for Cairo. Likewise, a message saying '41 people came to Esham's 22nd birthday' would mean that an attack is pending in Geneva, Switzerland – 41 being the country code for Switzerland, while 22 is the city code for Geneva. Further, the day of the proposed attack would be designated by a number in the sentence following the one identifying the site of the attack. Again, it will be a number that will identify the day with Sunday being 1 and Saturday being 7. For instance, the sentence following the one about Esham's 22nd birthday could be a sentence saying 'he only received 2 presents,' which would indicate that the attack is scheduled for Monday."

Kim said, "Don't you think those signals are a bit cumbersome? Are you sure that you and your cousin can pull it off."

"Not at all. Rifat and I played very complicated word games as children and we will not find this challenging."

"Okay, but my preference in all cases is for you to meet Rifat in person before a planned attack. Ideally we want as many details as possible before the attack so we can come up with the best plan to counter it. If we have enough time to plan, it might be possible to circumvent the attack, apprehend the terrorists and make it appear as if we did not have advanced knowledge of it. In that way, we can protect you and Rifat."

"I'll try to do that, brother, but I wouldn't count on it. Most likely my usefulness to you will be over once a terrorist operation I report on is foiled."

"Hussein, you don't know how resourceful we can be when it comes to protecting our friends", replied Kim. But he thought to himself that Hussein was probably right.

The next day Kim was anxious to brief his boss the developments with Hussein and his cousin Rifat. Kim asked John to meet him in the bubble to go over the results of last night's meeting. John told him he would be there in about 5 minutes and said that he wanted Tim in the meeting too. It was Tim's last day before returning to Washington and John wanted Tim to be in a position to relate details of their new operations to the desk officers back in Washington.

The three of them sat in the bubble for about 45 minutes going over the details of the FLAG operation. All three officers thought Hussein was a first rate recruit, as he followed direction extremely well but also was imaginative, as demonstrated by his development of a reporting system via text messages.

Kim also briefed them on his latest developments with Hisham an-Nassar. He said Hqs had given the approval to move forward with the recruitment of an-Nassar and they encrypted him GREASE. Kim said his relationship with an-Nassar continued to develop along predictable lines. At every meeting an-Nassar was providing interesting information about Saudi petroleum policies and activities. Additionally, he continued to complain about the Royal Family's treatment of its citizens, particularly women.

Haggerty commented that it was quite unusual for a Saudi man to find a common cause with female issues, and he asked Kim why he thought Nassar felt that way. Kim explained that an-Nassar and his wife had lived in the U.S. for many years and the wife was very strong-willed. Since her return from the U.S., she had been quite unhappy with the restrictive nature of her life. Hisham, her husband, was very sympathetic to her feelings, as indeed he needed to be if he wanted to maintain peace at home. Kim said that Hisham had told him that his wife was very unhappy here and wanted to leave. Hisham himself would like to leave, but the salary and benefits he received from the Saudi government were simply much better than what he could earn outside the Kingdom. An-Nassar had said that he wanted to build a nest egg over a few years and, then, perhaps return to the U.S. Tim remarked that given an-Nassar's plan, the offer of a salary from Kim might be more meaningful to him than it would be to most Saudis. They all agreed with Tim.

The meeting with Kim was coming to an end when Tim said, "For a variety of reasons, I haven't gotten an update from George on his all developmentals for more than a month. I haven't had the chance to go back and read all the operational communications I missed. He did give me a short brief on CHANCE yesterday, but I understand he has an even better recruitment. I would like to get that update today before I leave."

John agreed that it was important for Tim to get a firsthand briefing from George and added that George had had some real successes in the past couple of months. So, John asked JoAnn to signal George to come to the bubble for a meeting. When George arrived, they explained to him that Tim was in the dark about his accomplishments during the past couple of months and because Tim was going back to Hqs, a briefing from George was essential.

George apologized and asked if it would be possible to delay the briefing until later in the day. He said, "An American teenager, the son of a U.S. Congressman, has just been arrested on drug charges, and I have been asked to help him. The penalties can be severe, but early intervention by the Embassy may save this kid from receiving some very painful lashes."

"Okay, George," said John, "you should go take care of it. But be sure to brief Tim as soon as you return."

However, the briefing never took place. Early in the afternoon, Tim received a call from Saudia – the Saudi airline – advising him that a severe sandstorm was due to hit the Kingdom that evening. No flights were expected to leave Riyadh late that evening, and therefore, Saudia was rescheduling the departure of his flight. The new departure time was 5 PM rather than midnight. So, Tim had to hurry home and finish packing, particularly since his wife Denise was yet to locate all of their warm clothing.

Given that Tim would not be receiving the briefing from George Willis, he would not be able to give the Saudi desk officer back home a detailed briefing on George's operations. With that in mind, John decided to write a six-month review of the station's accomplishments dating back to his arrival last August. He thought that they had some major accomplishments, and he wanted to put them on display. He also wanted to share some of his thoughts about the one major failure – the disaster at Yuwan. So, John wrote the following cable:

SECRET

TO: *Director*
SUBJECT: *Review of Riyadh's Operational Activities*
REF: *None*

Since COS' arrival last August, the station has witnessed some very meaningful accomplishments. This contrasts sharply with the year prior to the COS' arrival when there were no recruitments and the only contributions that the station had been making to counter-terrorism came from Saudi Liaison. By contrast, in the past six months, the station has made three solid recruitments, and a fourth is almost in the bag. Here is a summary of those recruitments:

MONEY is the manager of a Saudi charity that is funding radical and terrorist organizations throughout the Middle East. Thus far, this operation has provided valuable information on the identities of the donor and recipients of funds. We anticipate that future intelligence from this operation will allow us to cripple the activities of these groups and dry up the source of their funding.

CHANCE is an Egyptian diplomat who has provided very important information on the foreign policy plans and intentions of a number of countries in the Middle East. We anticipate that this sources' reporting will increase dramatically once he returns to his home country. In Egypt, he has access to information at the highest levels of government.

FLAG is a visiting worker in Saudi Arabia who is related to a high-level ISIS official. The agent made a false flag recruitment of that ISIS official. The operation has already produced valuable information about ISIS, and we anticipate that it will provide actionable information on counter-terrorism.

GREASE is not yet considered a full recruitment, but the individual involved, a Saudi National working in the petroleum sector has already provided some information on Saudi Petroleum plans. It is expected that this individual will be fully recruited within the next few months.

While the above provides a brief look at some of our successes, we have had one major flap, and that is the failed CAPTURE operation in Yemen. The consensus of all involved – the Saudis, JSOC, Hqs, and the Station – is that the operation was "blown" by the Saudi agent. Most believe that the Saudi Agent was either doubled after first reporting on the proposed meeting or had been under the direction of AQAP from the very beginning. COS Riyadh has some reservations about the conclusion, but at the moment, we do not have a solid alternative theory. The Saudis have identified their agent, and we are hopeful that by identifying him, we will be able to determine precisely what had happened to him. Those results should allow us to have a better understanding of what went wrong with this operation.

DCOS Riyadh will be arriving in Hqs shortly, and he can amplify the information provided above.

END

SECRET

CHAPTER XIII

Faisal al-Awad, commonly known as Abu Iyad since his firstborn son was named Iyad, was in charge of all ISIS cells in Saudi Arabia. Abu Iyad's family was originally from Syria and had immigrated to Saudi Arabia in 1982. His father was a member of the Muslim Brotherhood that had opposed the rule of Hafiz al-Assad, the father of the current Syrian ruler, Bashar al-Assad. Abu Iyad's family had lived in Hama, Syria, and most of them had been killed in February 1982 when the Syrian army had killed tens of thousands of Hama's citizens. His immediate family members had been the lucky ones who were able to flee to Saudi Arabia.

While the Saudis had allowed the Awad family to immigrate, they were never allowed to become citizens or given the many opportunities granted to Saudis. Hatred for the Assad regime in Syria had been drummed into Abu Iyad from an early age, and it was followed closely by a constant diatribe against the ruling al-Saud family in Saudi Arabia. As Abu Iyad absorbed propaganda from ISIS, he developed a new hatred – America.

Abu Iyad had received a good education and eventually landed a middle-income level job at the Saudi Ministry of Communications and Information Technology. However, his hatred for the al-Assad regime continued to boil just below the surface. So, when ISIS began to gain notoriety in 2013, Abu Iyad decided to return to Syria and join the fight against Assad. He received paramilitary training in Syria, but ISIS leaders quickly decided that he could be more valuable to them back in Saudi Arabia rather than on the front lines in Syria and Iraq. They wanted him to return to Saudi Arabia and start to quietly build and organize ISIS there, as they considered it the next country that was to be conquered.

Abu Iyad had always been shorter and smaller than his classmates. Early adolescence had brught about intense acne that had left him with deep scars that covered his face. As a self-conscious kid, he also tended to overeat. The result was that he was short, fat, and ugly, which led to him being constantly bullied. This had created a very flawed individual with a violent mean streak. Indeed, some of his underlings said he was a psychopath.

Abu Iyad was a very disciplined person and knew how to discipline others. In fact, he tended to go overboard. His father was more than just a strict disciplinarian – he had abused both his children and his wife. Abu Iyad had grown up in fear of corporal punishment for the slightest of infractions, so it was not surprising to find that he ruled ISIS in Saudi Arabia as a tyrant. He had killed more than one subordinate for minor infractions. In fact, he derived great joy out of killing people. He was one fucked up individual.

In early 2017, an ISIS courier hand-delivered an encrypted message from Syria to Abu Iyad. The message was from ISIS caliph Abu Bakr al-Baghdadi. Abu Iyad had never received a message from the head of ISIS before. Indeed, he had never spoken to or seen al-Baghdadi. Knowing that it was from the Caliphate, Abu Iyad's hands shook as he began to decrypt the message.

Dear Brother, I have excellent news for you and instructions that you must follow carefully. Our brothers have succeeded in penetrating the evil CIA, alhamdulillah[20]. They have identified the sons of dogs who are working for the evil enemy and the American dogs to whom they report.

Here are the names of the traitors and their American puppet masters, yikrib baythum[21].

Hussein al-Biladi *– He is working at ARAMCO.*

Mohammed al-Masri *– He is an Egyptian diplomat working at the Egyptian Embassy in Riyadh.*

---

[20] This is an Arabic phrase meaning "Praise Allah."
[21] This can be translated as "May Allah destroy their homes."

George Willis – This son of a dog is a spy working from the American Embassy.

Kim Malloy – This is another American spy working from his Embassy. Inshallah[22], you will find each of these individuals and discover where they live and what they do. Then, you will formulate a plan to kill all these dogs. Share the details of your plans by return message only to me.

Allah ma'ak[23]

Abu Bakr al-Baghdadi

After reading the message from the caliph, Abu Iyad was in a joyous mood – he was either going to kill traitors and spies or arrange for someone to do the job. That night, he signaled four of his underlings to meet him. Once they were together, he shared them with the names included in the message. He told the group that he wanted them to work together to identify where each of these individuals lived and determine if they had any set patterns or routines that they followed. He cautioned them to be extremely discreet. His beady eyes burned holes through them as he said, "If you are discovered in your inquiries or surveillance, you will have destroyed important business of the Caliphate, and then, I will be forced to kill you. Do not fail in your assignment!" He deliberately refrained from telling them that the ultimate goal of this operation was the assassination of all four.

Over the next several weeks, the ISIS team was easily able to identify and surveil CHANCE since the Egyptians were not particularly security conscious. One of the team members simply went to the Egyptian Embassy and asked to speak to CHANCE. He was asked his name but was not required to show identification, something the team already knew. CHANCE came to the small meeting room in the lobby of the Egyptian embassy to see his visitor. The surveillant told CHANCE that he had once worked in Cairo and grown to love Egyptians and he wondered if CHANCE might have a job for him. CHANCE was annoyed that the receptionist had not screened the individual, and he quickly dismissed the ISIS team member by telling him that this was not an employment agency. However, from that brief encounter,

---

[22] This means "If Allah wills it."

[23] It can be translated as "May Allah be with you," but in reality mean farewell or goodbye.

ISIS was able to acquire a physical description of CHANCE and put him under surveillance.

It took them much longer to find FLAG because he was frequently in Dammam, not Riyadh. Identifying the two Americans was also somewhat of a challenge. There were many Americans working in the Embassy, and the Embassy was located in the diplomatic quarter, known locally as the 'DQ." In the DQ, there were armed guards on every block. Anyone who did not look like a diplomat or seemed to not be actively at work drew immediate attention. So, casual surveillance was not an option. When one of the surveillants went to the outer receptionist at the American Embassy, he tried to pull off a ruse similar to the one that had worked at the Egyptian embassy. The outer reception was located in a small, separate building just in front of the Embassy building. However, this time, he was closely questioned and asked for identification, which he did not have in the name of the alias he was using. When it became apparent that he was suspect, he panicked and left abruptly.

So, they decided to concentrate on CHANCE. Once CHANCE left the DQ, he was under intense surveillance. The team discovered very quickly that CHANCE was a creature of habit. He rarely changed his routine except for evenings when he typically attended a diplomatic reception or dinner. He left his home every morning just after 9 AM and went directly to the Egyptian Embassy. He left the Embassy shortly after 1 PM and then went to have lunch with one or more diplomats from the Riyadh diplomatic community. Then, he stayed at home for a couple of hours before starting his evening social event. He slept late on Fridays and then went to the mosque to pray. This was followed by a late and leisurely lunch, often alone but occasionally with a fellow diplomat. Finally, in the early evenings of Fridays, he visited Riyadh's Souk al-Zal. CHANCE was a born haggler. He would go to the souk even if he needed nothing, but he always bought something. He just wanted to negotiate the price of some item, and if he succeeded in the negotiations, he purchased the item regardless of his need for it.

After surveilling CHANCE for several weeks, the team reported the details of their observations to Abu Iyad. He told the group, "We are going to kill this son of a dog. From what you have told me, I believe it is best if we hit him as he enters the souk on Friday evening. It will be crowded, and with enough of you there, one can do the execution while the others 'accidentally' block anyone attempting to pursue our executioner. Are we in agreement on how to do this?"

Ghaith, one of the team members, said, "Why are we killing a brother believer? We should be killing the foreign devils."

Abu Iyad flew into a rage. His face turned red, and he was trembling as he grabbed a brass coffee pot that was still hot and smashed Ghaith in the face. "You are *not* to question orders!" Abu Iyad screamed. "You will kill *whoever* I tell you to and *when* I tell you. Do you understand?"

With blood oozing out of his forehead and running down his face, Ghaith pleaded for forgiveness and swore that he was prepared to follow any order Abu Iyad issued. Two of the other team members were as fearful as Ghaith. They quickly let it be known that they would never question orders from Abu Iyad. The fourth team member, Ali, simply gave Abu Iyad a cold, mean stare. Ali was similar to Abu Iyad in that he had a psychotic desire to hurt people, but the major difference was that Ali was a big, brawny man. He had been hurting people his whole life.

Abu Iyad sensed that he had little control over Ali, and truth be known, he was afraid of him. Abu Iyad instinctively knew he had to tread lightly with Ali, but at the same time, he knew it would be a mistake to show weakness or fear.

He glowered at Ghaith. "To prove you can follow orders, you will be the trigger man on this operation." Pointing at the two fearful members, he said, "Ali and you two will block anyone from chasing after Ghaith." Showing some deference to Ali, Abu Iyad continued, "Ali can probably accomplish this on his own, but you two should watch and learn from him."

The following Friday, the ISIS team lingered around the entrance to Riyadh's Souk al-Zal in the early evening. It didn't take long before they saw CHANCE approaching the souk.

CHANCE was very pleased with the situation that had developed with his American friend George. He told himself that he was doing the right thing. America was helping all the friendly countries in the area, and it was only right that it should be aware of all significant political activities. He had to admit that his country and most of the others in the area were riddled with corruption. The people here did not have a strong sense of nationalism, but rather their allegiance was mostly to family and tribes. He thought that Egypt probably had more of a sense of nationalism than any other country in the area. Most of the other countries had been constituted by colonial powers during the last century, and the citizens were more closely tied to a tribe rather than a national government. Besides, their leaders had only one political objective: *stay in power*. He rationalized that by helping America, he was also helping Egypt and other Middle Eastern countries.

Then, of course, there were the other advantages. Now that he had some extra spending money, he was able to buy his son small presents on a regular basis. Indeed, that is what he was about to do as he walked to Souk al-Zal. *Life is good*, he thought. Suddenly, he sensed that there was someone behind him. Just as he was about to turn and look, everything went blank. Ghaith had approached him from behind and fired his 22 caliber revolver into the back of CHANCE's head from only a distance of about three inches. A very small hole was created in the back of CHANCE's head but his face was nearly blown off with blood and brain matter splattered around the area.

Ali threw himself in the direction of CHANCE as if to come to his aid. In the process, he knocked over three observers. In no time at all, the scene turned chaotic. With people scattered on the ground, it was difficult to determine if anyone was seriously injured. One of those who had been knocked to the ground later told the police that he had indeed seen a nondescript man come up behind CHANCE and fire a single shot to the back of his head. This man said that he had immediately been knocked to the ground by someone attempting either to help the victim or protect himself. By the time the man had regained his composure, the assassin was long gone.

CHANCE had apparently made a trip to Cairo, and he had telephoned George to tell him that he was back in Riyadh. CHANCE had said he was anxious to meet George, so they made arrangements to meet a couple of days later. Besides wishing to collect any intel that CHANCE had obtained in Cairo, George was anxious to brief Mohammed about the security precautions to be taken before meetings. He had intended to have CHANCE institute a routine of using SDRs before coming to meetings.

Around the same time, George Willis had started on an SDR run. A surveillance team composed of Norm Halderman and two support officers were positioned at various points along the SDR route. It was a detailed, 2-hour SDR with multiple stops. After the last stop, the surveillance team leader, Norm Halderman, radioed to George that he was clear and could go to the safehouse. George went to the safehouse and waited, and waited, and waited – Mohammed was a no-show. George returned to the Embassy and reported it to John who was waiting impatiently for news of the meetings. John said, "I'll arrange for someone in the political section to pay a visit to Mohammed tomorrow, just to make sure he is well."

There was no need for John to make those arrangements. The following morning, headlines in the local *Al-Riyadh*, the semi-official Arabic language newspaper, read, "Egyptian Diplomat Gunned Down." The article went on to say that Mohammed al-Masri, a diplomat assigned to the Egyptian Embassy in Riyadh, had been shot and killed just outside Souk al-Zal. The souk was located in the old al-Dirah neighborhood whose narrow streets were typically crowded in the early evening. The newspaper said that the call to prayer had just been announced from the muezzin and shops were being shuttered with people hurrying to the mosque to pray when a lone gunman had approached al-Masri from behind and shot him in the back of the head. In the confusion that had followed, the gunman had disappeared down the crowded, narrow streets. "Saudi police," the article continued, "have conflicting descriptions of the killer, and no motive is currently known."

John called a meeting of the entire station, including the operational, admin, and clerical staff. He said, "One of our agents was murdered last night, and we are assuming that the murder was ordered by a terrorist group. Furthermore, we have to assume that this terrorist group somehow or another discovered that our agent was a spy. We don't know if this terrorist group knows any more information that is harmful to us, but we must operate on the assumption that they do. I think we need a bit of a cooling-off period during which we will stand down on all operational activity. I may be overreacting here, but I want to proceed with an overabundance of caution. So, until you hear otherwise, don't do anything risky, and pay attention to your surroundings. Take the usual precautions of not following routines, and look for surveillance at all times. If you need to go downtown, it's probably best that you have another station member accompany you. Does anyone have any questions?"

One of the admin assistants asked, "Do you have any thoughts on how the bad guys could have learned that the fellow who was killed was an agent?"

John said, "First of all, I'm not sure he was killed *because* he was one of our agents. We are simply proceeding on that assumption to be on the safe side. But if he *was* killed for that reason, I can only assume he hadn't kept his mouth shut about what he was doing for us. He may have confided in the wrong person that he was helping the CIA, and the word probably got back to the terrorists."

After a couple of weeks of inactivity, John decided that they should test the waters. John told his officers, "Let's have George schedule a meeting with Amal first, and if that goes well, Kim can meet FLAG. I believe it's possible that somehow, the bad guys have made you, George, and that is how they got on to CHANCE. So, we will cover you like a blanket just in case you have been made."

The station formulated an intense SDR for George, calling for five stops over a two-hour period. Six other officers, including Sam Butterfield, Norman Halderman, and a couple of the ex-JSOC operators would be on the street looking for surveillance. If there was going to be any trouble that night, these fellows were up to the task of handling it. At the end of his SDR, it was clear that George was clean, so he went directly to Amal's home. She was anxious to see him and had obviously expected that they would be intimate immediately. George told Amal that there had been some security concerns and they would have only limited time together. He told her that there was a team of Americans watching his every move that evening, so prolonged sex was off the table.

He got no argument from her, although she did ask, "Am I in any kind of danger, George, and if so, what should I be doing about it."

"I truly believed that you are not, but just in case, the American counter-surveillance team is going to remain near your home for the remainder of the evening. These guys are highly trained and they will protect you if any kind of dangerous situation develops."

Those comments only served to heighten her fear. "What about tomorrow? Or the following day? How long can this team stay with me?"

"If there is no suspicious activity around here tonight, then we can be fairly certain that you are in the clear."

He asked her if she could make another trip abroad anytime soon so they might meet in a more secure locale. She told him that for the past few months she has been putting off a trip to Geneva to meet their bankers.

"I can go to Geneva almost immediately without drawing any suspicion," she said.

George told her to arrange a trip to Geneva and meet him in two days in front of the coffee shop they had first gone to. He told her to write down the dates of her travel on a piece of paper, and he suggested that she make reservations at either the Beau Rivage or Le Richemond hotel. She should indicate on the sheet of paper the name of her hotel. When they would pass each other in front of the coffee shop, she would give him this sheet of paper in a brush pass. He had her practice a brush pass with him several times until she appeared to be competent at it. He told her that he would be at her service 24/7 while in Geneva.

Eyeing him coyly, she said, "Well, I can't wait! But for now, can you at least hold me?" George enveloped her in a warm embrace, but their passions rose immediately, and the embrace turned into much more. Soon, they were passionately tugging and pulling at each other. George had thought that his security concerns would be such that sex would be off the table. He had underestimated the intensity of the passion they had for one another.

After quickly reaching satisfaction, George kissed her tenderly and said, "I can't wait until we have extended and uninterrupted time together to make love that lasts for hours."

Amal said, "That will be heaven, but this quickie was pretty good too." They both laughed, and George headed out the door.

George cautiously left her home, waiting for the unexpected to happen. Just as he reached the corner, he heard a roar from a car, and he hit the deck, unholstering his 9 mm Beretta in the process. As he looked up, he saw a young Saudi in a Lamborghini racing through a street about a block away. This was not an uncommon occurrence in Riyadh. *I must look like a fool,*

George thought, *but better a breathing fool than a dead hero.* The surveillance team members had smiles on their faces, but they all thought to themselves that they would have done the same thing under those circumstances. Part of the team remained near Amal's home, while the remainder stayed with George until he reached the Embassy. John was quite nervous about this first meeting after CHANCE's murder, and he was waiting for George at the Embassy. George told him that the meeting with MONEY had taken place without any incidents and he planned to meet her in Geneva soon for a thorough debriefing. John's relief was apparent on his face.

CHAPTER XIV

Given the trouble-free meeting with MONEY, John told his ops officers that they should resume operational activity but asked that they review such activity with him beforehand. *Perhaps*, he thought, *the murder of CHANCE had nothing to do with the fact that he was a CIA agent.*

On the following Sunday, FLAG received a text message from his cousin Rifat, which read, "Hope you can come 4 auntie's birthday on the 9th, as she will be 69. Flights are 5 times a week, so you should be able to come." FLAG nervously decrypted the message to read that an attack would take place in Frankfurt, Germany (49 being the country code for Germany and 69 the city code for Frankfurt) on Thursday (the number 5 indicating Thursday).

FLAG immediately signaled for a meeting that evening with his case officer, Kim Malloy. At the last meeting, Kim had instructed him to start using two-hour SDRs before coming to meetings just to be sure that he was not being followed. So, on that evening, he headed out an hour before 8 PM, which was when the meeting was scheduled, to ensure that he was not under surveillance. In fact, he was late, so his SDR lasted only about 45 minutes, but he promised himself that in the future, it would be at least an hour long. He drove to a nearby mall and quickly walked through the various shops, looking at the windows for reflections of anyone following him. FLAG was more than a bit obvious in his movements, as this was his first attempt at following an SDR. He spent 20 minutes in the mall and detected no one of interest. He returned to his car and drove for another 10 minutes, making unexpected last-minute turns. He saw no surveillance. Satisfied that he was clean, FLAG discreetly parked on a side street about a two-minute walk away from the safehouse.

At the time, he was thinking to himself that his relationship with American intelligence had given his life new importance and meaning. He had put himself in a position to right some of the wrongs that Arabs were committing, and in the process, he was enjoying the danger associated with clandestine meetings. Of course, the added riyals to his wallet each month were a sweet bonus. Still preoccupied with these thoughts, he exited his car, and as he did, he noticed a Toyota Land Cruiser, a type of vehicle that was ubiquitous in Riyadh, approaching quickly. The Toyota came roaring down the road, and before he could even finish the thought that it was coming too close to him, it hit him in full force. Hussein never had another thought. The Land Cruiser never slowed down and certainly did not stop. Later, it was confirmed that Hussein had died instantly at the scene of the hit-and-run.

Meanwhile, Kim had been making his way to the meeting, and he too conducted an SDR with the help of two other station officers. But in contrast to his agent's SDR, his was for two full hours. On his third stop on the SDR, which was at a small *bakaal* or grocery store, he purchased a pack of gum and made his exit. Suddenly, the mic in his ear began to chirp. "You have company. Return to the *bakaal*."

Kim did as he was instructed. The two officers who were part of the SDR had noticed a white Land Cruiser at the previous stop along the SDR route. Now, the same Land Cruiser had circled the block and positioned itself along the street in such a way that it could intercept Kim when he left the *bakaal*.

Both station officers were armed, so they decided to investigate by approaching the vehicle and asking for directions from the occupants of the Land Cruiser. They could, thereby, establish who were the occupants of the vehicle and whether they appeared to be hostile. The two officers approached the vehicle on foot from different directions, but when they were about 10 meters away from the Land Cruiser, it left the area at high speed. The officers returned to their vehicles and instructed Kim, "Stay put until we give you the all-clear." One of the officers had a police scanner in his vehicle that had already been turned on. No sooner had he returned to his vehicle than he heard a report over the scanner that there had been a hit-and-run about five minutes away with a pedestrian casualty. The sharp-witted officer decided that it was time to abort the potential meeting. He thought it best to retrieve Kim directly from the *bakaal*, as Kim could be in real danger. But first, he radioed his companion surveillant Sam Butterfield and asked him to check out the hit-and-run situation that had been broadcasted on the police scanner.

With Kim now in a station vehicle, he was briefed about what the other two officers had seen and about the nearby hit-and-run. Kim said, "Let's drive by the scene of the hit-and-run and see if that tells us anything."

Meanwhile, the other surveillant, Sam Butterfield, was trying to get near the hit-and-run scene, but traffic had been stalled by all the first responder vehicles in the area. Up ahead of him, he noticed the white Toyota that had been tailing Malloy. He knew he could do nothing of significance by himself, what with all the cops and other officials in the area. So, he did the next best thing. He quickly parked his vehicle, jumped out, and walked quickly to the Toyota ahead of him. As he got closer to the Toyota, he noticed two occupants shouting with their heads out of the windows.

Ali was at the wheel of the Land Cruiser, and he was threatening all those within earshot. He was trying to tell whoever would listen to get out of his way or he would run them over. He contended that they had an emergency and needed to move. However, there was nothing anyone could do for them – they were all stuck. Ali was at the point of flying off the handle, and someone was likely to get hurt.

Sam was fortunate to have with him a "quick-plant" beacon. This was a small beacon attached to a strong magnet so that it could be quickly – thus "quick-plant" – placed on any vehicle. So, while the two occupants were shouting like banshees, Sam discreetly walked behind their vehicle, dropped something on the road, bent down to pick it up, and at the same time, attached the beacon to the underside of the vehicle. It wasn't an ideal placement, but it was the best he could do under the circumstances.

The police were directing traffic in the area and not allowing vehicles to come close to the scene of the accident. With the abundant police presence, Kim decided that it was safe for him to exit his vehicle and walk past the accident. Sam was out of his vehicle, which housed the radio system's transmitter, and, therefore, could not advise his colleagues that the suspected surveillants were held up in the traffic. So, Kim was walking into real danger. As he approached the area, he saw the first responders trying to resuscitate the injured man on the ground. When he got closer, the blood drained from his face. The victim was his agent FLAG. Kim lingered in the area for another few minutes, long enough to see that the first responders had decided it was fruitless to continue their efforts. As they pulled a blanket over Hussein's face, the realization that his agent was dead hit Kim hard.

The occupants of the white Toyota noticed Kim near the crime scene. They thought about leaving the Toyota in the middle of the street – it wasn't going anywhere in any case – and finishing the job they had been unable to complete earlier. But just as they were about to exit the vehicle, they noticed Sam Butterfield, obviously an American, standing near them with his hand inside his jacket. Ali could not be held back. He wanted to hurt someone very badly, and this big American didn't scare him. Ali exited the vehicle with a tire iron in his hand and quickly approached Butterfield. He intended to severely hurt this guy, hopefully crushing his skull.

Sam watched nonchalantly as Ali furiously approached him. When Ali got within striking distance, Sam's hand flew out of his pocket, and with knuckles, he jabbed Ali in his Adam's apple, following immediately with a punch to his solar plexus. Ali fell to the ground in excruciating pain as Sam casually walked away. The ISIS team members who had observed the confrontation sat with smiles on their faces. They had all been subjected to Ali's earlier threats. *This is payback*, they thought. There were also smiles on the faces of all those who were sitting in stalled traffic and who had been subjected to curses and insults from Ali.

Kim returned to the Embassy immediately after seeing his agent pronounced dead. He asked the Marine Guard to call the COS and request him to come to the Embassy. By the time John got there, several other officers from the station were already there. John asked the Marine to call in all of the members of the station.

Once all members were present, John asked Kim and his surveillance team to give them a detailed report on the evening's events. After the report,

John said that it was clear to him that the FLAG operation had been compromised, and ISIS had targeted FLAG and Kim. He told them, "From here on out, all officers should be armed any time you are outside your homes or the Embassy. No operational meetings will be held until I get a better handle on things and advise you otherwise. In other words, stand down on all ops until further notice. Also, I don't want anyone out on the streets by themselves. Lay low as much as possible until we figure this out, and if you do have to go out, take a team of at least two others from the station with you. Plan your movements in advance, and make sure you keep an eye out for any surveillance. Be sure to not follow a routine of any sort. If you normally come to work at 8:30 every day, stop doing that. Pick a different time to come to work every day. Never follow the same route when you come to work, go to pick your kids up from school, or whatever. Take a different route to all your regular destinations. Lastly, if you have to leave your vehicle outside of a protected compound, don't start your vehicles without first checking the undercarriage for possible bombs."

Some of the faces in the room had turned white. John said, "I don't want to overly alarm you, but the procedures I've just outlined are ones that I use always. Terrorists will always choose the easy target or target of opportunity. If a terrorist group has been told to strike an American target, let's not make it easy for them. If you don't make it easy for them, they will go after someone else. Does anyone have any questions?"

One person on the admin staff asked, "Exactly where and what should we be looking for under our vehicles?"

"I'm glad you asked that, Jerry," said John. "What you should do today is get down on your hands and knees and closely examine the undercarriage of your vehicle until you become familiar with it. In fact, get your phone out, and take a picture of it. Then, when your vehicle has been parked in an unprotected area, closely compare how it looks then to what it should look like. Use the picture if you are not sure. Oh, and one more thing about vehicles –this is pretty elementary – make sure you lock your vehicle every time you leave it."

Next, John asked the Marine on duty to call the Ambassador and ask him to come to the Embassy. When Fred arrived, John briefed him about what had happened earlier that evening. "Fred, it appears that ISIS is targeting Kim Malloy and possibly others in the station. It is not unreasonable to assume that they do not have a good fix on who all are the Station officers. They may mistakenly target one of your guys believing that he is one of mine. You know best who among your officers might be a target. But I think a couple of your officers who are out and about the city a lot could very well be mistaken to be with the CIA."

"I fully agree with you, John. I'm going to call in the DCM[24], the Political and Econ section chiefs, and the Defense Attaché. I want you to stick around and brief them about tonight's events. Tell them what you think they should be doing to protect themselves and their underlings."

John told the Ambassador that he was happy to oblige but recommended that he include the RSO in the group. "I think the security officer may have some specific recommendations for keeping your people safe, and that's why I think he should be here."

Fred agreed and had his secretary, who he had called in, round up all the desired officials. It turned out to be a long night for John. He had to write a detailed report on the evening's activities and the station's reaction to them. But first, he had to see Sam Butterfield who had been trying to get his attention.

Finally, Sam was able to get his chief alone and tell him that he had placed a beacon on the vehicle of those surveilling them earlier in the evening. Sam said, "This certainly isn't the vehicle that killed FLAG. But most likely, it belonged to the same group of killers."

John thought for a moment and then told Sam that they would have to act boldly and swiftly. He said, "Sam, get several of your ex-JSOC guys together and try to find that vehicle. We have a TECHNICAL SERVICES tech visiting the station. Take him with you, and if he has any audio transmitters with him, tell him to bring one along."

Sam quickly rounded up three PM officers and the tech officer, Mick Dreggar. Mick and John were old friends. Mick had been an instructor in the PM course when John had undergone training. At the time, his area of expertise had been sabotage – he was very good at blowing things to kingdom

---

[24] DCM: DCM is the Deputy Chief of Mission, while the Ambassador is the Chief of Mission.

come. The bomb people were sort of the stepchild of the TECHNICAL SERVICES, as some techs thought that they were more akin to the PM knuckle draggers. That being said, Mick was an ambitious guy, and he had soon learned enough about all the other disciplines in the TECHNICAL SERVICES to become one of their top officers. He did have one annoying habit, particularly to the women in the Agency. Mick was forever scratching his balls. When he was deep in thought, he would give them a real yank.

In response to Sam's question, Mick explained that the beacon's signal could only transmit for about two miles, and depending on the area, it could be only a block or two. A tall building, for instance, could block the signal and, thus, limit the range. Fortunately, Riyadh was not a city with an over-abundance of skyscrapers. The Capital Market Authority Tower was the tallest building with 77 floors, followed by Burj Rafal and the Kingdom Center with its sky bridge being some 300 meters high in the air. Therefore, the signal might be easier to find than in a skyscraper-rich city. But it was still going to be time-consuming, given that they had no clue where to start.

There was also the question of the battery life of the beacon. Ideally, beacons were attached to the host vehicle's battery when time and circumstances permitted. In this case, there was only a small battery within the beacon, and it might not last more than two days. So, when it was first suggested that they start searching the first thing the following morning, Sam said that had they better clear that with the boss first. When they told John, his reaction was negative.

"I want you guys to start *right now*," John asserted. "We have two things that dictate immediate action. The first is the limited battery life of the beacon. We only have two days, so we must go after it immediately. Secondly, that beacon will be more difficult to find if it's moving about the city, constantly changing locations. You will have a much better chance of locating it if it is stationary, and most likely, that will be in the middle of the night. I know all of you are pretty tired, but we have no choice but to start now."

They had two receivers in the station that could pick up the beacon's signal. So, they took two separate vehicles, and around midnight, they began patrolling the city from opposite ends. By 7 AM, neither vehicle had received the slightest blip on their receivers. Frustrated and discouraged. they decided to call it quits until nighttime.

Before starting again around 10 PM the following night, the two teams reviewed the areas they had covered the previous night on a large map. They were surprised to note that over half of the city had been covered. On the one hand, this gave them some sense of relief in that they could certainly cover the remainder of the city that night. But on the other hand, there was the nagging feeling that the vehicle was not in Riyadh and they would never find it.

Their fears proved to be unjustified. Around 3 AM, Sam and Mick heard a squeal from the receiver that made their hearts pound. They knew that the vehicle was close by. They were in the Batha area of Riyadh, which was mostly inhabited by Asians and people from the subcontinent. More specifically, all guest workers – Filipinos, Pakistanis, Indians, Sri Lankans, and Bangladeshis – resided there. This was certainly not the tony area of Riyadh. They were at the intersection of the Abu Ayyub Al-Ansari and Al Ras streets when they heard the signal. When they drove from Al Ras Street onto the narrow Amir Ibn Awf Street, the signal was loud and clear. Mick said to Sam, "Do they ever clean the streets in this area? And does anyone eat anything but curry? The smell is making me gag!"

Just then, they spotted a white Toyota parked on the street. Sam checked his notes from the previous night. He had recorded the plate number of the Land Cruiser that was intent on hitting Malloy. Sure enough, this was their target vehicle. They didn't know what to do about it now. They had assumed that they would find it parked in front of a single residence, but there were only shoddy apartment buildings in this area. It would be difficult to tell which building housed their targets. So, they alerted the other team by radio to stand down and then decided to sit tight for a while hoping that they would get lucky.

As the early morning light began to brighten the littered street, people began to appear. The team's vehicle received close attention from everyone who passed by. They were clearly out of place even though their vehicle did not have diplomatic plates. They were Westerners in an area that had none. Sam was worried that if they were made by their targets, the latter would leave the area permanently, and they would never find them again. It was time to regroup.

The team returned to the Embassy, and everyone but Sam headed for bed. Sam waited for John to arrive, but he didn't have to wait long. At 7 AM, John hurried into the Embassy. Sam caught up to him immediately and briefed him about their success. John said, "That's great! I really appreciate your efforts. Now, I have to figure out our next move. From what you've said, we cannot surveil the area with station officers. That means we must use the station's local surveillance team."

The local surveillance team comprised two Pakistanis and three Yemenis. They were paid well and had been working for the station for several years. They could be trusted but only up to a point.

John told Sam that he would order the local surveillance team to sit on the area, identify the owners of the vehicle, and then discover exactly where they lived. They would be strictly advised to do nothing else.

This situation was favorable for the station's local surveillance team. Sometimes, they stood out when trying to surveil a rich Saudi, but in the Batha area, no one gave them a second look. They descended on the area with three different vehicles: a Chinese-made motor scooter, a Rube Goldberg motorbike, and a 1997 Toyota Corolla. Men sitting around on the street doing nothing or hanging out in coffee houses doing nothing was the norm here. So, without much effort or need to disguise their real task, the surveillance team focused on the Toyota Land Cruiser.

The Land Cruiser sat idle until shortly after 2 PM when four men from the apartment building across the target vehicle straggled out, entered the Toyota, and drove off. They didn't go far – only a few miles to the Ghubairah area where there were many auto repair facilities. The Toyota pulled up in front of what looked like an auto repair garage. The garage was locked up tight, requiring the one who appeared to be the leader of the group to use three different keys to open all the locks on the doors. Clearly, this garage was not open for the public's business. The leader of the CIA's local surveillance team, Abu Ayub, sent his man on the motorbike to the garage with orders to learn what he could without being overly inquisitive. As soon as the motorbike pulled up close to the garage, a husky, dark, Arab-looking man came out. "What the fuck are you doing here?" Ali barked.

The skinny Pakistani surveillant explained that his motorbike needed tuning and he was looking for a shop that could do the job.

"Get your ass out of here!" yelled Ali. "We are not open for business."
Ali was still smarting from the blows delivered by Butterflied, and he wanted

revenge. In his mind, physically punishing any other human would help satisfy his desire. But this little Pakistani sensed the danger and quickly began
to leave.

As he was leaving, the Pakistani was able to glance over the unwelcoming
Ali and into the garage. He spied another white Land Cruiser with a front end
that was damaged on the right. The Pakistani reported his unpleasant encounter to Abu Ayub and added that he could not see a thing inside the garage
except for the damaged Land Cruiser. The windows of the garage were all covered with some kind of black material, and the door had remained closed except for the brief moment when he was being verbally assaulted.

"Okay. Let's see if we can identify which apartment these guys live in,"
said Abu Ayub. He then instructed the man on the motor scooter to hang
around the area and notify him by text if the targets left the garage. "A simple 'departed' is all you need to say in the text," Abu Ayub instructed.

Ali, Ghaith, and the two other ISIS members remained closed up in the
garage for about three more hours before they left. As soon as he received
the text that they had left the garage, Abu Ayub put one of his men on the
top floor of the apartment building and another out walking on the street
nearby. The surveillant on the street was to follow the targets into the building. Between the one that was to follow the targets into the building and the
one pre-positioned on the top floor, Abu Ayub was confident that they would
be able to identify the apartment belonging to the targets. They had ascer-
tained that an occupant of one of the apartments in that building was a
widow, Mrs. Ghanim. They had observed her leave in a taxi shortly before
the incoming text. So, if any of the surveillants were asked what they were
doing in the area, they were to say that they were looking for Mrs. Ghanim.

The targets must have stopped to get something to eat because even after
a couple of hours, they had not returned to the apartment. Abu Ayub was
beginning to fear that Mrs. Ghanim would return before the targets and their
"cover for action" would have evaporated. But he was lucky. The targets all
returned and proceeded to enter their apartment. Both the pre-positioned
and the tailing surveillant were able to watch them enter apartment 4C.

Each floor of the building had four apartments, and the ground floor
was not considered the first floor in Middle East parlance – it was the ground

floor. The first floor, that is the floor on which apartments 1A through 1D were located, was actually on the second level, and the floor containing apartments 4A through 4D was actually on the fifth level. Abu Ayub made this very clear in his notes because during an operation years ago, he had given an incorrect floor number – that is, incorrect as far as the Americans were concerned – to a CIA entry team that had tried to enter an office on the third floor while the target office was one flight up.

Abu Ayub gave his report that night to Sam Butterfield who was in charge of directing the team. Sam described his encounter with Ali and asked if any of the four fit Ali's description. Abu Ayub checked with the motorbike man, and the latter said that the description precisely fit the Arab man he had encountered at the garage. Sam checked the Embassy and found that John was there. He immediately reported the findings of the surveillance team to John.

John rose to his feet. "We have to find out what those guys are doing in that garage. I want to think about this overnight and should have a plan of action by morning. Get in touch with Mick Dragger, and both of you should meet me first thing tomorrow morning." Given the identification of a white Toyota Land Cruiser with a damaged front end, John was convinced that they had in their sights the killers of FLAG as well as the terrorists planning to hit Kim Malloy.

CHAPTER XV

John thought long and hard about what could and should be done about the bad guys. He couldn't go to the Saudis because that could potentially blow his officer, Kim Malloy. But it was clear to him that he had to learn what these guys were planning. They were obviously targeting Malloy, so something had to be done. He decided that he would have the tech attempt to put a transmitter in the target apartment. If the targets were undisciplined in security, they might talk freely about their activities and plans.

So, when Sam and Mick came into the station the following morning, John told them what he wanted to achieve. Mick balked at the idea of trying to bug the apartment without a thorough casing of the place. Mick said that they would need to case the apartment if John wanted a professional placement of the transmitter, and they would need the casing report to get Hqs' approval for an audio op. John said, "We don't have time for that bullshit, Mick. Lives are at stake, and time is of the essence. We have to get into that place today and start listening to what these guys are saying."

After taking a long pull on his balls, Mick said, "Okay, but don't come back to me later and point at me when this all turns to shit."

"It's *not* going to turn to shit, Mick, and the reason it won't is that we have one of the best and most resourceful techs on the job."

"If you think sweet-talking me is going to get you somewhere, you are wrong, John." Mick smirked. "It will get you *everywhere*. Okay, I'll improvise and do what I can, but when Chief TS wants to kick my butt, I expect you to stand up for me."

"Don't worry about the Chief TS. When you are in Riyadh, you take orders from me. You may voice your objections, which you have, but now you have your orders, and that is what I'll tell C TS if it ever comes up. Now, let's get the surveillance team back out there. You will stand out like a sore thumb, so you must stay out of the area until the surveillance team alerts you to the targets' departure. Then, both of you will enter the target apartment and install the transmitter as quickly as you can. Meanwhile, I'm going to have a member of the surveillance team try to rent a nearby apartment that we can use as a listening post. How close does the LP have to be in order to pick up the signal from the transmitter?

Mick said, "It's hard to say precisely what the maximum distance is because so much depends on the environment and other signals in the area. But to be on the safe side, we should stay within two blocks of the target. In other words, not more than half a mile."

"Fine. Sam, you instruct the surveillance team to get in position and report when the targets leave their apartment. Let's make sure we use encrypted radios for comms between all parties. Also, have one of the Pakistanis on the team rent an apartment as close to the target as possible. Get him some fake docs, a passport, a credit card, and pocket litter. Tell him to rent a place by the month if possible. If we have to, we'll rent the place for a whole year."

The local surveillance team took their positions as they had done the previous day. They blended into the neighborhood like vermouth with gin. Just as the last time, the targets did not emerge from their apartment until approximately 2 PM. Abu Ayub quickly notified Sam and Mick that the targets were on the move.

Mick said, "Let's get the show on the road, Sam." The two set off for the apartment building on Amir bin Awf Street. Mick had little difficulty picking the lock of the target apartment. They carefully looked for traps before moving into the filthy room. Mick said, "It will be hard to find traps among all this clutter, but given the state of this place, I doubt there *are* any."

Mick quickly surveyed the only sitting room in the apartment, looking for the ideal place to plant his transmitter. He noticed an electric wall outlet that was a couple of feet above the baseboard unlike most of the others that were closer to the floor. Although this outlet was situated behind a chair, its elevated position would probably help receive better audio than those closer to the ground. Mick said, "I'm going to place my transmitter in the wall behind that electrical outlet, and I'm going to use the existing electrical current to power the transmitter instead of a battery. That way, we won't have to worry about a battery dying on us."

Mick removed the faceplate from the wall and began examining the small electrical box that was fitted into the wall opening. The box had a bunch of wires running through it, so he decided that he had to drill a small hole into the box to fit the transmitter. This would require some noise and mess. The walls, unlike those in the U.S. and some other parts of the world, were made of cinder blocks covered with actual plaster.

No sooner had Mick started to drill with plaster and dirt flying around the area than they heard Abu Ayub's excited voice over their radios. He reported that one of the targets was returning to the area and, most likely, to the apartment. "You have about five minutes to get out of there!" shouted Abu Ayub.

"Damn," cursed Mick. "Murphy's law strikes again. Let's try to clean up a bit before we bug out." The two quickly scooped up as much plaster as they could and taped the wall plate back onto the wall. Then, they pushed the chair back against it to cover the obvious destruction around the wall plate. It was by no means a clean job, but they had to take the risk, hoping that the target would not notice the altered wall. They had to move quickly because Mick had to lock the door with his picks, which was not as difficult as opening the lock but still a task that could take time. As Mick inserted his picks outside the apartment, they heard the door to the building open below them.

"Put a move on," whispered Sam.

Mick did not even bother to give him a reply. He had to concentrate on getting that door locked *now*. Just as they heard footsteps on the stairs two floors below, the bolt slid into place, and the door was locked. The two Americans gathered their gear and crept up the stairs to the sixth floor.

Sam put his mouth near Mick's ear and said, "Let's just stay here in hopes that he forgot something and will retrieve it and leave immediately."

Mick replied, "But what if he finds the mess around the wall plate and alerts his buddies? We may not be able to get out of here before they come with an army of guys looking for us."

Before they could decide what to do, the target entered the apartment below them and almost immediately came back out, locked the door, and left.

As soon as they heard the building's entry door close, Sam got on the radio and asked Abu Ayub to monitor the target's movements and give him an assessment of his mood. "I want to know if he appears agitated or in an extreme hurry," said Sam.

Several minutes went by before Abu Ayub reported that the target was on his way back to the garage and that it seemed as if he didn't have a care in the world.

Both Sam and Mick breathed a sigh of relief and re-entered the apartment to complete the installation of the transmitter. Mick did a great job of restoring the wall and electrical outlet to appear as if they had not been touched. They wanted to test the installation before leaving the apartment, so they asked Abu Ayub to turn on the receiver they had left in his car. As they spoke in soft voices, Abu Ayub reported by radio that he was hearing them loud and clear.

The bug was in place, and the LP had been rented by the Pakistani surveillant. Now, they just had to wait and see if the targets would discuss their plans and intentions. The Pakistani LP keeper did not speak Arabic, so he had to record all the conversations of the target. This was not a problem because the recorder was voice-activated and the Pakistani did not have to be present to turn the recorder off and on. But that was unimportant because as soon as the targets returned to their apartment that evening, they started a lively conversation about an operation.

Back at the station the following morning, Sam delivered the first audio disc from the previous evening's operation. John called in Kim Malloy who was by far the best Arabist in the station besides being the officer who the bad guys were after. John asked Kim to listen to the recording as soon as possible.

A couple of hours later, Kim reported back to John. He said that it was clear that the targets were building a bomb in the garage and it was almost ready. "They did not say what the target is," said Kim. "However, they did repeat several times that they were going to teach the Americans a good lesson. The only other good piece of intel I got from the recording is that they are going to detonate the bomb using the electrical current from a cell phone – when the cell phone rings, the bomb would detonate. They were testing this in the apartment where they had the cell phone connected to a light, and they were simulating the light as a bomb. When they called the cell phone, apparently the light lit, and they hollered that they could imagine the infidels being blown apart. The good news is that they said the telephone number out loud, and I have it.

"The other issue I noted is that these fellows are obviously foot soldiers, not high up in the chain of command. They mentioned ISIS leader Abu Bakr al-Baghdadi several times, so I assume they are affiliated with ISIS. They also mentioned several times Sahibna Abu Iyad or Raisna Abu Iyad, meaning their immediate boss is someone named Abu Iyad."

John was now totally focused. "The bottom line here is that we have to stop this attack even if that means blowing your cover to the Saudis. I would rather not do that, but it may happen. In the meantime, we need full coverage of these jihadis by the local surveillance team, backed up by our own guys. That means I want our fully armed PM team out on the streets just behind our local surveillance team. If the surveillance team reports that a terrorist op seems to be eminent, our PM guys may have to step in and eliminate them. Hopefully, we will have time to learn more about what they're planning so that we can foil that plan discreetly. I'll have to get Washington's approval to have our guys intervene with deadly force."

John called a meeting of all station officers and briefed them about the terrorist threat that may have Kim Malloy as its target. As he was wrapping up the briefing, JoAnn interrupted the briefing to tell John that the surveillance team was on the radio and they wanted to talk to him or Sam *immediately*.

John went to the commo room and connected with Abu Ayub. Abu Ayub reported, "The targets are on the move. This is the first time they have headed out in the morning. They went to the garage but spent only about 10 minutes there. I fear that they are operational and an attack is about to happen."

John asked, "Are all four guys in their car?"

"Actually, they have added a fifth member. A teenage boy is with them now. I think we should take them out *now* if we can."

John said, "Give me a minute, please." He knew that he had to make a decision. Was the young boy in the car the son of one of the members? Would he be killing an innocent person if he ordered their execution? His stomach churned as he decided what to do.

Just then, Abu Ayub interrupted, "I think we have to make a decision *soon*, John. They are out of the Batha area and seem to be heading toward the diplomatic quarter."

John called JoAnn and said, "Get Kim up here." He held the radio mic in his hand like he was hanging on to a rope from the 20th story of a tall building with sweat pouring from his brow.

As soon as Kim appeared, John said, "Give me that telephone number you got from the recording yesterday." Then, he turned on the mic and asked Abu Ayub, "Where are you now?"

"We are on the South Ring Road heading northwest."

"What's the traffic like?"

"We see a moderate amount of traffic now. In my experience, traffic will diminish considerably once we pass the Al Shabiah Mall, which should be in about five minutes."

"Can you tell if they are doing anything in the car, or are they just riding along?"

There was a brief pause. "I can't see any movement in their car. They are cruising along normally."

"Okay, Abu Ayub, let me know when the traffic thins out."

John began to think this through again. Was he getting ready to kill innocent people, particularly a child? He reasoned that if he called the number Kim had given him and the bomb was in the car, already rigged for detonation, he would kill all the occupants. But that would also mean that there were no innocents in that car – they were ISIS members who were prepared to kill one or more innocent persons. If, on the other hand, they were not intending to detonate the bomb, someone would answer the ring, no bomb would detonate, and there would be no deaths. This line of thinking helped him make a decision. He decided to call the number.

"How does it look out there?" John asked over the radio.

"If you mean the traffic, it is very thin. We had to drop back a good ways from them in order not to be made."

With a shaking hand, John picked up the phone and dialed the number. As soon as it rang, Abu Ayub shouted over the radio, "Holy shit! The target vehicle was just blown to smithereens."

John's only response was, "Make yourself scarce. Get the hell out of there before the cops show up."

John was stunned by what he had just done even though he thought it was the only justifiable action he could have taken. He then began to think about how his decision would be viewed at Hqs. Certainly, he should have sought authorization before deciding to kill people. The more he thought about it, the more conflicted he felt about his actions. Time had been of the essence, and if he had not acted when he did, American lives could have been lost. He told himself that he was prepared to righteously defend himself if he came under criticism. *If our government leaders choose to sacrifice me, so be it. If that is their position, I don't want to work for them anyway.* But on the other hand, his decision weighed on him. *I just killed five people. Can I ever forgive myself?* he wondered.

Enough second-guessing, John decided. He could do that later. At the moment, he had to take some action. He got Mick and Sam on the secure radio and asked how far they were from the bugged apartment. Mick and Sam were only a short distance behind Abu Ayub on the Ring Road, and they estimated that they were about half an hour away from the apartment.

John said, "Get back to that apartment now and retrieve that transmitter. Did you use gloves when you entered the apartment?"

Mick replied that they had. "In that case," said John, "don't wipe all the prints away. We don't want to give the appearance that there has been a hostile entry. Just get that transmitter out of there quickly and return the wall to its original condition. I assume it will take the cops a couple of hours to determine the identity of those guys and a bit longer to identify their address. So, you have some time to make the retrieval, but the quicker you get it done, the better."

It was too early in the morning for Paul Brant to be in his Washington office, so a secure phone call was out of the question. Therefore, John decided to write a short "eyes only" Flash cable to Paul in which he provided a summary of what had happened and what had led him to make the monumental decision.

A few hours later, he received a Flash cable from Paul, which was "eyes only." The cable only said that Paul understood the situation and would be briefing the Director soon and the Director would, in turn, brief the President as soon as possible. Paul went on to say, "Until advised to the contrary, do not brief anyone outside the station, not even the Ambassador. Let's keep this within the company for the time being. I'll get back to you later with more instructions."

In the hours that followed, many theories were thrown around about how ISIS had been able to compromise the FLAG operation. Most believed that Prince Talal had already had a connection with Rifat's cell or, perhaps, Rifat directly. From the information that Amal had provided, it did not appear that Rifat's group was receiving funds from Talal. That had led the station to believe that there was no relationship between Rifat and Talal. However, in the aftermath of Hussein's death, they began to rethink that assumption. On the positive side, the fact that no money transfers had been directed to Rifat from Amal's fund was likely to protect her from being suspected by ISIS.

Some doubted the generally accepted theory that Rifat was the instigator of his cousin's assassination. If that was the case, wouldn't it have been much easier and safer to have had Hussein killed in Baghdad, which was still kind of like the Wild West? The risks associated with an assassination were much higher in Riyadh than in Baghdad. However, there was some sound reasoning suggesting that an assassination in Baghdad would not have been optimal. For one, Rifat was there and might have been suspected immediately. Secondly, and perhaps more importantly, ISIS seemed to have wished to direct its retribution not only at Hussein but also at the CIA, leading to the attempt on Kim Malloy's life. This led to the question of how ISIS knew that Kim was Hussein's case officer. No one seemed to have a good answer to that.

It was impossible to raise the subject of Hussein's assassination with liaison without drawing attention to the fact that he was an Agency asset. The local newspapers had covered the killing as a hit-and-run accident, something that would not be of concern to intelligence agencies. John was hoping that one of the Saudi services would come to the conclusion that it was not an accident but a terrorism-related assassination and that they would then raise the subject with him. Alas, that was not to be! John would have loved to see the Saudi investigative report. He decided to have the RSO check the plates of the white Land Cruiser. The team that had been helping Kim with his SDR had recorded the plate numbers that evening, but the station could not share that with the Saudi Liaison without blowing Kim's cover.

The RSO had regular contact with the Saudi police, and he routinely reported suspicious vehicles to the police. So, that seemed to John to be a natural route. After being briefed by John, the RSO went to the police with the plate number and the description of the vehicle. Interestingly, the police told the RSO that the vehicle surely belonged to a terrorist organization. They said that four ISIS members along with the son of one of the members had been carrying a bomb in that Land Cruiser when they had accidentally detonated it. Naturally, everyone in the vehicle had been killed. The police had identified the individuals that had been killed, and they had turned that information over to the intelligence services for further investigation. The police suggested that the RSO follow up through the normal channels of the Embassy and with the Ministry of Interior.

John kept a lid on operations for the time being. He assumed that with the police and intelligence services actively investigating the group, its leader and foot soldiers were laying low and may have already left the Kingdom.

No station had witnessed the kind of disasters that had been visited upon the Riyadh station this past year. John felt a personal responsibility for those who had lost their lives, and he began to question his competence and judgment. On top of that, he had just killed five people, including a teenaged boy. With a feeling of despair, he wondered if it was time to leave this business and allow younger and, perhaps, brighter minds to take over. It certainly would not take much for someone to do a better job than he had since coming to Riyadh. Tim Haggerty, who had just returned from sitting on a promotion panel in Washington, came into his office to commiserate with him. John said, "Tim, I must have lost my touch for running operations. This station is in utter chaos."

"I know how you are feeling, John, but these setbacks cannot be attributed to you," said Tim.

"Setbacks? These are fucking disasters, Tim, not setbacks!" exclaimed John. Tim suggested that they calmly review all operational activity and try to determine what, if anything, they had done wrong. He said that most likely, they had simply been hit with a major dose of bad luck. John disagreed with his statement regarding bad luck but did agree with his suggestion of conducting a major review of all operational activity in an effort to discover the problem. Tim was the intellectual type who was well suited to conduct such a review. However, before doing anything, John wanted to confer with his boss back in Washington. So, he told Tim that he wanted him to undertake the task of reviewing all station ops eventually, but for the moment, he wanted everyone to stand down.

John made a secure phone call to D/NCS Paul Brant in which he relayed the latest calamity to hit the station. He revealed to Paul his self-doubts and told Paul that he understood if Paul had lost confidence in him.

"Let's not jump to any conclusions before we examine all the facts, John," Paul responded, "I've known you for a long time, and I can't imagine that you have changed overnight. If you have caused some major blunders, you will have to pay the price, but my gut tells me Riyadh's reversals were caused by elements that have nothing to do with your judgment and decisions. For starters, sit down and bring all the facts together in one document and send that to me 'eyes only.' I'll share it with the Director, and then, we will share our thoughts with you. In the meantime, put a freeze on all activity in Riyadh, and that includes the review you are planning to have Tim undertake."

John said that he had already ordered a freeze, but a meeting with MONEY had been scheduled outside of the Kingdom and it would be difficult to cancel it because the agent had already left the country.

Hearing that the meeting was scheduled to take place in Geneva, Paul said the Agency was well-positioned to protect their case officer and agent in Geneva. He asked John if MONEY might be able to provide any information on the assassinations of the two agents.

John said that it was possible but he doubted that she could. He gave Paul a quick review of her access and operational utility.

Paul said, "Well, she is connected to the terrorist world, and we have had a successful meeting with her since at least one of the compromises. Have your case officer meet her in Geneva. We'll make sure both are well protected, and hopefully, she will give us some clue as to what happened. I still haven't been able to get the Director alone to brief him about the killing of the five terrorists. He has been testifying before Congress all day. As soon as he gets back. I'll brief him. I just don't know what his reaction is going to be."

After the secure call, John called for a meeting with all the ops officers. At the meeting in the bubble, John told everyone to stand down on all operational activity. He told Tim to hold off on conducting the review until he heard back from Hqs. The one exception was that George could meet MONEY in Geneva. George said that it was good news, as the message he had received in the brush pass from her two days earlier had indicated that she had been planning to leave for Geneva the previous day. She was going to make a stop in Beirut for a day and then go to Geneva where she would stay at Hotel Beau Rivage. "What am I missing here? I don't know who MONEY is," said Tim. After a short discussion that was embarrassing for Tim, it turned out that he had been absent anytime there had been a discussion about MONEY, and because of the hectic events, he had not reviewed operational messages about her.

John told Tim not to concern himself with that oversight, as there would be plenty of time for Tim to catch up. John said, "I want everyone to stick to non-operational tasks for the immediate future. Don't go out alone, and make sure you conduct a thorough check of your vehicle before using it. And above all, do not follow any given routine – change your schedules and routes for all events."

John returned to his office and wrote the following message:

SECRET

TO: Director, EYES ONLY D/NCS
SUBJECT: FLAG/CHANCE – Terrorist Actions Against Station Assets
REF: Riyadh 70298

As you are aware, the station had made four substantial recruitments against the terrorist target in the last 8 months. Specifically, both MONEY AND CHANCE were recruitments made by George Willis who subsequently handled the agents. MONEY is the manager of a charity that is funding terrorist organizations. This asset is still active. CHANCE was not primarily recruited to report on terrorist activity, but he did report on the periphery of the subject. He was killed by a lone assassin in a Riyadh souk.

FLAG was recruited by Kim Malloy who directed his agent to false flag recruit his cousin, encrypted COUSIN, a high-ranking ISIS member. FLAG was killed while on his way to meet Malloy, and immediately thereafter, Malloy was targeted for assassination.

Because the assassinations were against agents who were handled by different case officers, we believe that this is not a case of the opposition "making" one officer and discovering other agents through him. We should also mention the failed CAPTURE operation that had been compromised – it had no apparent relationship with the compromised agent operations. We are coming to the conclusion that one factor has led to the compromise of all the operations. Unfortunately, we cannot identify that factor at this point.

It is clear that case officer Malloy is known and being targeted by ISIS. We believe he is in serious danger and request that he is reassigned outside of the Arab world immediately.

We will be examining all of the factors in these cases over the coming days and hope to provide Hqs with some substantive conclusions. In the meantime, we request that Hqs create a task force for the sole purpose of examining the major compromises here in Riyadh and attempting to identify the cause. Hopefully, MONEY, who will be met in Geneva shortly, will add to our limited understanding of the cause behind our setbacks. END

SECRET

CHAPTER XVI

The following day, John received a cryptic message from Paul telling him to return to Hqs ASAP. The message also instructed John to reemphasize to his subordinates that there was to be no operational activity while he was gone except for the meeting in Geneva.

The following day, both John and George left Riyadh but on separate flights. At 1 AM John was scheduled to board the British Airways flight to London from where he would take a connecting American Airlines flight to Dulles Airport near Washington, DC. George booked himself on a direct Saudia flight to Geneva, which left at a more civilized hour of 9 AM.

When George arrived in Aéroport de Genéve and passed through immigration control, he was approached by a Geneva station officer who introduced himself as Stan Wolsky. Wolsky said, "This looks like a first-class op you have going here, George. I have seen your asset, and I can imagine you are having a hard time keeping your hands off her. Anyway, I'm envious of your op, particularly for a first-tour officer. That wouldn't happen here in Europe!"

Wolsky continued, "You will be counter surveilled to the Beau Rivage. We have conducted a thorough security check of Beau-Rivage and found that no Middle Easterners were staying there, and as of an hour ago, there were none in the lobby or the hotel's restaurant. What is your operational plan, George?"

"I intend to meet my agent in either my room or hers. Neither of us will leave the hotel until we are ready to leave Geneva."

"That's fine, George, but to be on the safe side, neither you nor that hot babe should eat at the restaurant. If you are content with staying in your rooms, that would be best. Although it wouldn't hurt if you left the hotel to pick up some take-out, she should *definitely* stay put. Part of the problem is that any woman that looks like her is going to draw attention and, most certainly, will be remembered."

Wolsky then provided George with his contact information and told George to contact him if he needed any assistance. George said, "I anticipate the need to send an ops message or two and perhaps an intel report. So, I want to be able to get in touch with you on short notice."

"Fine," said Wolsky. "Just give me a call, and I'll pick up your messages. Also, give me advance notice of when you plan to leave Geneva so we can prepare a surveillance team to cover your route to the airport. We will have some security people in and out of the hotel the whole time you are here. If we see anything or anybody suspicious, I'll contact you directly."

Then, the officer provided George with a cell phone containing a local SIM card and told him not to use any other phone during his stay in Geneva. "One last thing," said Wolsky, "your agent is in room number 412. It's probably best if you do not contact her via the hotel's internal phone system."

George left the airport by taxi for the short ride to the Beau Rivage. The driver asked, "Bonjour, où allez-vous?"

George told him to drive him to the Beau Rivage Hotel. Next the driver asked, "Êtes-vous un Américain?"

George, who was quite competent in French, said, "parle pas français." George was in luck. This was one of the few taxi drivers in Geneva who did not speak English, which resulted in a much desirable silent ride to the hotel. George had made a conscious habit of not getting into casual conversations with service personnel. Too often, they worked for a local or other intelligence service, and casual remarks made to them could be regrettable at some point in the future.

As he entered the hotel, George did a quick visual sweep of the lobby. He saw nobody that looked like an Arab, nor did he see anyone who stood out as an American security type. *This is good*, he thought. As luck would have it, he too was booked into a room on the fourth floor. After registering, a bell boy took his bag and led him to his room. Exiting the elevator, he noted with satisfaction that room 412, Amal's room, was between his room and the elevator. If there was anyone in the hallway when he would make his way to her room, he would simply proceed to the elevator.

Ten minutes later, he lightly rapped on the door of room 412. Amal opened the door immediately and said, "I saw your taxi arrive, so I was anticipating your knock." They immediately wrapped their arms around each other in a warm embrace. Then Amal said, "We have to contain ourselves for a few minutes. I have some interesting information that I have picked up since our last meeting." George made himself comfortable on the couch as Amal closed the curtains.

She began, "First of all, Prince Talal made one of his infrequent visits to the office the day before I left. He said he had heard I was going to be away for a while and asked where I was going. I told him that my mother was in Beirut and was feeling ill, so I wanted to be with her. At first, I thought he was annoyed that I was leaving, but it was just the opposite. He said my trip was fortuitous, as he wanted me to deliver a message to one of our recipients in Beirut – a message that could not be relayed by phone or email. Then, he gave me the name and phone number of Ahmad Dijani. He said that I was to tell Dijani to discontinue his activities until he was advised otherwise. I asked Talal what activities he was talking about, but he simply said that Ahmad would know. I tried to engage him in conversation, but this cold fish talked to me and treated me like a servant! It's clear that I won't be able to get much out of him."

Amal went on to say that she had contacted Ahmad Dijani shortly after her arrival in Beirut and delivered the Prince's message in person. She said she had been surprised when Ahmad had assumed that she was aware of his activities and had proceeded to speak freely with her. "To begin with," she continued, "he said it was unfortunate that he was required to halt operations. He said they recently added 'a Lebanese brother' who had a U.S. Green Card[25] and the 'brother' was prepared to carry out his orders in the U.S. He

---

[25] A "Green Card" is an informal name for the identification card issued to Permanent Resident Aliens. The original identification cards were green; hence the name "Green Card." Green card holders are allowed to permanently reside and work in the U.S.

said that this brother had just returned from Atlanta, Georgia where he had chosen several targets that he thought were suitable for a bombing operation. And the brother was ready to undertake these operations himself.

"What is also interesting is that Ahmad said he was not surprised by the order from the Prince to halt operations. The reason he gave was that he had heard that an American in intelligence was working for ISIS and, therefore, ISIS was being cautious until they were able to learn more about America's efforts against them."

George's immediately asked, "How long do you plan to stay in Geneva?"

"I can probably stay for a few days without having anyone ask questions."

George thought about this and told her, "I think it would be best that you do not return to either Beirut or Riyadh until I let you know that it is safe."

Amal's heart skipped a beat. "What's going on?" she asked.

George said, "I'm *really* not sure at the moment, but so much has happened in the past month or so that I don't want you to take any chances until I'm confident that you'll be safe. The situation is confusing at the moment, but I'm sure we will have it figured out shortly. Anyway, I'm going to stay with you here as long as I can."

"Well, if *you're* going to be here, I'm happy to stay. But you know the prices at this hotel are *way* beyond my means."

George told her not to worry about the costs. "I'll cover all your costs, Amal."

Amal nodded and then moved in close to him. "We have a *lot* to make up for."

"Yeah…but as much as I would like that, we have to wait. What you told me needs to be reported immediately. I'm going to go back to my room and draft some messages. When I'm done, I'll come back, and we can spend the rest of the day in your room… making up."

"I suspected as much," said Amal. "Go back to your room, and do your thing. I want you back here as soon as possible."

George went back to his room and called Wolsky on the phone that the latter had provided. "I will have something for you to pick up in about 45 minutes," said George. Wolsky told him that he would knock on George's door in approximately one hour. Then, George sat down to write his mes-

sages. Essentially, he wrote an intel report about an ISIS operative casing Atlanta. He included a code word in the heading that would prevent the report
from being automatically disseminated to the Washington intelligence community. He wanted the report to be reviewed in Hqs before dissemination
to the intelligence community so that distribution could be limited to only
those who had a need to know.

Moreover, George wanted Hqs to have an opportunity to identify the
possible ISIS member. He had no idea how many Green Card holders of Lebanese descent had recently returned to Beirut from Atlanta, but he assumed
it was not a large number. So, in a second operational message that refer-
enced his intel report, George alerted Hqs to the fact that the ISIS member
had been in Atlanta until a few days back and had then returned to Beirut.
George requested Hqs to have the immigration and airline records checked
to determine the names of all Lebanese Green Card holders who had departed Atlanta for Beirut within the past 10 days.

Then, in a separate operational message addressed "Eyes Only COS Riyadh; D/NCS; and CNE," George relayed the information Amal had provided
about an American "in intelligence" having been recruited by ISIS and the circumstances under which she had obtained that information. He addressed the
message such that it would be delivered to John Thorne in Washington, making sure it was not delivered to Riyadh or any other location outside the U.S.
George was not sure how he should handle a message with such damaging information, so he limited the distribution to only those few individuals. He assumed that they would come back to him with a million questions, the answers
to which he did not have. He would press Amal later for any more info, but
his impression was that she had nothing else to report.

Stan Wolsky appeared at George's room about an hour later. George had
not quite finished his three reports, but he was almost there. Wolsky relaxed
on the sofa while George completed the last report. He put the eyes only message in a separate envelope and marked it "private." He told Wolsky, "This envelope contains an 'Eyes Only' message that you should give directly to your
COS for him to sign and release. The other messages can be handled routinely."

As soon as Wolsky left, George hopped into the shower, changed his
clothes, and then headed to Amal's room. She answered after the first knock,

and they quickly embraced. But before they started to get too far along, George said he wanted to ask her a few questions while his mind was still functioning. He asked her to repeat what Ahmad had told her in his exact words.

She said that there was nothing more to tell. "As I recall, Ahmad said he wasn't surprised that the Prince had asked him to stop all activity because Ahmad had heard that an American working in intelligence has been cooperating with ISIS. I believe those were his exact words."

"Did he say where he had heard this information?" John asked.

Amal said that he had not. She went on to explain that she had not grilled him on that point or any other for that matter. She had assumed that he should not have been telling her this information, and she did not want to appear too aggressive by being over-inquisitive. Just as George had suspected, there was nothing else she knew about this subject.

Shortly thereafter, George and Amal were enjoying each other's bodies and minds. While their sex was intense, their intimacy was that of a couple that had been together for years. George was not sure why this was happening, but their comfort level was well beyond anything he had previously experienced. He had to admit that the ease with which they discussed almost any topic was incredible. *This is a real relationship*, he thought.

With a glass of wine, they sat together looking out the hotel window. It was a beautiful evening, and the traffic was humming along the Quai du Mont-Blanc just in front of the hotel. Beyond it was Lake Geneva itself with Jet d'Eau, the large fountain in the middle, spewing water almost 500 feet in the air. George told her that it was unfortunate that they had to remain in the hotel. He said, "There is a wonderful Lebanese restaurant just a short walk up the Quai, but I'm sure it's filled with Arabs. We cannot risk being seen there. I might walk to that restaurant tomorrow to pick up some takeout for dinner." He also spoke of a great Italian restaurant in Cologny, which was on the opposite side of Lake Geneva. "The next time we come back here," he told her, "we will see all the sites of this beautiful city."

CHAPTER XVII

April 2017, Langley, Virginia

When John finished reviewing the events of the past eight or nine months, he was feeling really weary. He had come to Hqs directly from Dulles Airport, so he had been traveling for almost 24 hours. It was almost 5 PM in Langley but almost 1 in the morning of the following day in Riyadh. "I know you are tired," Paul said, "but I have an update for you from George Willis. I thought it best that you give us the review before seeing this, but what I'm about to show you changes everything." Paul gave John a copy of the "eyes only" message sent by George.

When John finished reading it, Paul asked, "Do you believe she is telling us the truth?"

"I have my doubts, but they are not based on anything concrete," said John.

Paul sighed. "I've been giving this a lot of thought, John, and I have asked myself *why is it* that your two other non-Saudi recruits get rolled up but not the one that is apparently working for ISIS and other radical groups. Does it not bother you that MONEY has not faced any problems? In fact, it seems that she has ISIS spilling their guts to her!"

John told Paul that he had been having similar thoughts and, quite frankly, his gut was telling him that perhaps his case officer, George Willis, had lost some objectivity when it came to MONEY. "I'm pretty sure that George is mesmerized by this woman," said John.

"What's your recommendation?" Paul asked.

"I think we should get a polygraph operator down to Geneva tomorrow and put her on the box. We really need to know for sure if she has been doubled against us or if she is being truthful."

"I agree," said Paul, "and I'll order that up now. We have to get a polygraph operator from Frankfurt down to Geneva first thing in the morning."

Paul called in one of his special assistants and told him to send out a FLASH message to Frankfurt instructing a polygraph operator to go to Geneva on the first available flight. "Include COS Geneva on that message, and tell him to contact Willis first thing in the morning to let him know we want MONEY polygraphed and an operator is on his way to do just that."

Then, Paul said, "But if she's telling the truth, that means we have a mole in the Agency, and most fingers will point to your station. Any thoughts on that"?

"As much as I abhor the thought that someone in my station is a sellout to ISIS or some other terrorist group, I have to seriously consider that possibility. Too many ops have been blown and lives lost. We certainly owe it to Bill Lucas and his family to investigate every possible angle. I can tell you, Paul, that I've been having some heartache about my secretary ever since my arrival. She is in the office from morning to night, and by night, I mean midnight. Not only does she see all my correspondence but everyone else's as well. She stays and reads all operational and intel messages that come into the station. Besides, she is the station's IT person in that she backs up the computer system and has access to the hard drive. I don't have any other reason to suspect her, but I have never been exposed to any other clerical or admin employee who puts in so many hours. Other than that, I don't have the slightest suspicion about anyone at the station."

Paul said, "Okay, let's get the polygraph done so we know where we stand with MONEY. If she fabricates and dissembles, we will know where our problem lies. If she is being truthful, we have to look inward.

"Before I let you get some rest, I have to tell you about the Director's and the President's reaction to you blowing up those jihadis without seeking or receiving permission from Washington."

"Oh, oh, here it comes," said John.

"Yes, here it comes. Both the Director and the President were pleased. The President, in particular, said that it's great to see someone in government take initiative without covering his ass. He told the Director to bring you over to the White House so he can 'shake your hand.' That being said, John, *please* try to alert me in advance if something like this happens again."

"You know I had no choice this time, Paul. Quite frankly, I hope I am never in such a situation again. Just before I left Riyadh, I picked up a local newspaper that had a sensational article on the incident. Most prominently displayed with the article was a picture of the 13-year-old boy who was in that car. I'm having a hard time getting that picture out of my head, especially when I try to fall asleep at night."

"Not very many of our officers have had to make a decision like that, John. I believe there was only one correct decision, and you made it. If you were not losing some sleep over killing five people, I would be disappointed. And if you had been callous about the situation, I'm not sure I would be comfortable having you in a position to make those kinds of decisions."

CHAPTER XVIII

The FLASH message arrived in Geneva and Frankfurt around midnight CET. The polygraph operators stationed in Frankfurt were used to getting short-fused messages at all hours instructing them to travel. This was going to be an easy one, as Geneva was only an hour's flight away. A quick glance at the Lufthansa's schedule revealed that a 7:25 AM flight was the first one available and it would get the operator to Geneva at 8:30. The next operator in the rotation was Mike O'Leary, so he was advised to book himself a seat on the 0725 flight to Geneva. Frankfurt then sent a FLASH message to Geneva with a copy to Washington in which Geneva was informed that O'Leary would be arriving at 0830, and it requested that someone from Geneva Station met him at the airport.

It was close to 2 AM, and COS Geneva decided that it was best to contact George Willis immediately and let him know that Hqs expected his agent to be "boxed" in the morning. So, Stan Wolsky was called into the U.S. Mission and told to let George know that Hqs wanted to have MONEY polygraphed the next day. Stan in turn telephoned George and simply said, "I'm coming over to talk with you."

George had been asleep with his right leg stretched over Amal's right hip when Stan phoned him. They were both groggy when George managed to tell her that he had to get back to his room for an important message. He said that he would stay in his room for the rest of the night so as not to disturb her. She rolled over to face him, and with a coy smile, she said, "You better get back here as soon as you can. My butt gets cold without you cozying up to me. So, regardless of the time, come *back*." George promised her that he would.

George hustled back to his room and ruffled his bed to make it appear as if he had slept in it. Soon, Stan Wolsky was at his door. Stan informed him that Hqs was insisting that his agent be boxed immediately. "A poly operator will be arriving at 0830, and he will be ready to put her on the box shortly thereafter."

George said, "This is going to come as a shock to her. Give me a few hours to break the news to her and get her prepared for the examination. Let's shoot to have it done here in my room at 11 AM. If there is a problem or I need more time, I'll let you know."

Stan said, "The operator will want about an hour with you alone beforehand to decide on a list of test questions."

George was surprised to learn that Hqs had not supplied a list of questions. He thought that they probably did not want to believe anything she had said and were waiting for the poly to prove that she was a *double*. George and Stan agreed that Stan would bring the operator, Mike O'Leary, back to George's room at 10 AM.

After Stan left, George went back to Amal's room. He slipped into bed next to her and said, "I have some news that you are not going to like. The powers to be in Washington have decided that they need to be absolutely certain about your information, so they want to subject you to a polygraph test."

Amal said, "I have no problem with that. Bring it on." She was a bit surprised when George told her that the test will be administered in just a matter of hours. She said, "You guys don't mess around, do you?"

George told her that the suggestion of an Agency employee being doubled by ISIS or some other radical organization was unthinkable to him and his bosses. "That is really mindblowing," he said. "Even I am having a hard time coming to terms with that possibility, and I have *complete* faith in you. To the guys in Washington, you are just a name on a paper, so you can imagine their incredulity." George was relieved that Amal did not seem to be bothered by the fact that her credibility was being questioned. She seemed to understand that it should be and wanted to prove herself.

At 10 AM, Stan Wolsky brought Mike O'Leary to George's room. After introductions, Stan said that there was no reason for him to stay around for the entire session and asked George to give him a call when Mike was ready to leave. With Stan gone, Mike sat down and said, "I've been given to understand that your agent has provided information indicating that an 'American working in intelligence' is helping ISIS. In other words, a 'double.' We are to use the polygraph to determine the veracity of her report. Is that it in a nutshell?" asked Mike.

"That's it," said George.

"Okay, this should be relatively easy," said Mike. "I want to start with a list of 'baseline' questions, and for that, I need your input. What her name is, where she was born, what her nationality is, in what city she lives – those will be the basis for my baseline questions, so I need you to give me the answers now. I will ask those baseline questions first to get her comfortable and get a read on the chart when she is being truthful. I might come back and repeat some of these questions if I believe she is unnerved and needs to be calmed. Next, I will ask if she is a supporter of ISIS. Then, I will ask if she had learned from this guy – please give me his name – that an American is working for ISIS. Lastly, I'll ask if she has told anyone that she is cooperating with U.S. intelligence. Does that make sense to you, George?"

"It sounds good to me, Mike."

Mike said, "If I see no deception, I will turn the machine off and tell her that there seems to be a problem with a couple of her answers and I need to review them with her. I'll then hit her kind of hard on the questions we are most interested in. If she sticks to her guns, I'll turn the machine back on, and we'll go over the questions again. If she continues to show no signs of deception, we can be fairly confident that she is telling the truth. Often, things are not that clear-cut, and some readings can be inconclusive. If that is the case, I will go over those areas again and again to try to sort out the basis for the uncertainty. This could last 20 minutes or it could last hours. So, let's prepare the list."

They worked together to come up with the following questions:

1. Is your name Amal Ansari?
2. Were you born in Beirut, Lebanon?
3. Are you of Palestinian descent?
4. Do you live in Riyadh, Saudi Arabia?
5. Do you know someone by the name of Ahmad Dijani?
6. Are you a supporter of ISIS?
7. Did Ahmad Dijani tell you that an American working in intelligence is cooperating with ISIS?
8. Did you tell anyone that you are affiliated with the Americans?
9. Did you tell anyone that you are cooperating with George Willis?
10. Did you convey to Ahmad Dijani that he must temporarily refrain from operational activities?

George said that he liked the list and when Mike was ready, he would get Amal. Mike was ready, so George walked down to Amal's room and brought her back to his. Although Mike usually had a very comforting effect on people, Amal was already calm and needed no soothing. Mike smiled broadly and told her that she had nothing to fear from him or the machine. In fact, he was going to give her the questions before he switched on the machine. Then, he went over each question with her and asked if any of the questions were a problem. When she indicated that she was not bothered by any of them, Mike hooked her up to the machine with a blood pressure cup on her arm, metal plates on her fingers to measure her electrodermal response, and a belt across her chest to measure her heart rate and breathing patterns.

Mike went through the questions one by one.

1. Is your name Amal Ansari? Answer: Yes
2. Were you born in Beirut, Lebanon? Answer: Yes
3. Are you of Palestinian descent? Answer: Yes
4. Do you live in Riyadh, Saudi Arabia? Answer: Yes
5. Do you know someone by the name of Ahmad Dijani? Answer: Yes
6. Are you a supporter of ISIS? Answer: No
7. Did Ahmad Dijani tell you that an American working in intelligence is cooperating with ISIS? Answer: Yes

8. Did you tell anyone that you are affiliated with the Americans? Answer: No

9. Did you tell anyone that you are cooperating with George Willis? Answer: No

10. Did you convey to Ahmad Dijani that he must temporarily refrain from operational activities? Answer: Yes

Mike switched off the machine and told her that she was having trouble with three questions and they should talk about them. He said, "Question number 6 – are you a supporter of ISIS – is a real problem. Why do you think you are having a problem with that question?"

Amal responded that she should have clarified the question before they started. "Technically, I do support ISIS because that is my job. I funnel money to them, but I don't believe in their cause. And, to be honest, I didn't even know it was ISIS until I met Ahmad Dijani."

Mike said he understood and he should have made that question clearer. He said he would rephrase the question in three ways. He told her that there was also a problem with her affirmative response to the question about whether Ahmad Dijani had told her that someone working in U.S. intelligence was cooperating with ISIS. In reality, the machine had not detected any issue with her answer, but Mike wanted to make her concentrate on this most important question.

Amal said she did not understand why there would be an issue with that question, as she was very certain about it. Lastly, Mike told her there was an issue with question 9, which was about whether she had told anyone that she was cooperating with George Willis. Amal said that she was thinking about that question because she did tell her mother that she had met an American man with whom she had developed a close relationship. Mike asked her if she had revealed George's name to her mother or if she had revealed that this American worked in intelligence. She said that she had not. She had only mentioned an American to her mother and nothing about intelligence.

Mike said, "Okay, I have drawn up a new set of questions and have one repeat question. These questions should clarify your previous answers. Here they are:

1. Were you aware of the fact that you were channeling money to ISIS before you met Ahmad Dijani?
2. As a part of your employment, are you required to transfer funds to accounts of people or organizations unknown to you?
3. Do you believe in the basic tenets proclaimed by ISIS?
4. Did Ahmad Dijani tell you that an American working in intelligence is cooperating with ISIS?
5. Did you reveal George Willis' name to your mother?
6. Did you tell your mother that your American friend is working in intelligence?

Mike hooked her back up to the machine and started asking the questions. She responded negatively to questions 1, 3 5, and 6. She answered "yes" to questions 2 and 4. When they finished, Mike said that he was satisfied with the results and told Amal that he would like to talk to George alone for a few minutes.

With Amal back in her room, Mike told George that there was no hint of deception on her part. "She's being truthful, George. If this guy Dijani knows what he's talking about, we have a mole in the Agency." Mike said that he would go back to the station and put out a report about the results of the poly.

George told him that the report should be highly restrictive. "Make it 'Eyes Only' for the D/NCS and COS Riyadh. Don't send a copy to your people in Frankfurt. We need to keep this very limited." Mike said that he understood and would do as George asked.

When Mike left, George went to Amal's room and told her that she had passed this polygraph with "flying colors."

"That's a relief!" she said. "Even though I knew I was telling the truth, it was still unsettling, and I was beginning to doubt myself."

"That's a typical reaction, Amal, but you handled it exceedingly well. I'm proud of you. We – not you and I, I mean the Agency – have a real problem now. We have to ferret out who it is that Dijani was referring to. I'm going to sit down and put my thoughts to paper for my boss, and then, I'll come back later this afternoon. You don't mind spending some time alone, do you?"

Amal told him that she was perfectly capable of looking after herself. "One last thing," said George. "Who, if anyone, did you tell that you were traveling to Geneva?"

"Initially, I told people in the office that I was planning to come here to Geneva to talk to our bankers, but I later changed that to say that I was going to Beirut to see my ailing mother. After that, I didn't tell anyone I was going to Geneva, not even my mother."

Back in his room, George sat and contemplated the situation for a while. He kept wondering how it was that two other agents, FLAG and CHANCE, had been compromised, while Amal had been allowed to continue to operate. If there was a mole in the Agency, it was most likely that it was in the Riyadh station. *But if there is a mole in Riyadh, why was Amal allowed to carry on?*

He conveyed his thoughts and questions back to John and D/NCS Paul Brant in an "eyes only" message. When George's message arrived, it was early in the morning at Hqs and John was already at the office. He also received the results of the polygraph exam, leading him to ask himself the same questions George had. It dawned on John that they did not yet know why MONEY had not been targeted, but he felt confident that it was a mistake on ISIS' part that they have probably rectified since. Most likely, she had an X on her back now. It was imperative that she did not return to Riyadh until this was sorted out. He also thought that George could be a target, so he too should refrain from returning to Riyadh. In fact, if there was a mole in his station, the fact that MONEY was in Geneva was probably known to ISIS by now. John conveyed his thoughts to Paul Brant who fully agreed with him.

Paul said, "I can arrange to get them out of Geneva on an Agency plane, and I think we should do that now. We'll get them down to Frankfurt where we have major capabilities, and we will limit the knowledge of their whereabouts to just those few people who need to know." So, Paul notified people in Geneva and Frankfurt about their plans on a need-to-know basis and started the process of having an Agency exfiltration plane collect Amal and George from Geneva.

At about that same time, the security team assigned to protect Amal and George in Geneva began to notice the presence of several individuals of seemingly Middle Eastern origin in and around the Beau Rivage Hotel. First, there were two or three of them, but shortly thereafter, their numbers gradually increased to about 10. It was clear to the security team that these Middle Easterners were actively looking for someone. As people would enter or leave the hotel, these potential bad guys would refer to a book they were carrying. Clearly, the book concealed pictures of Amal and, possibly, George Willis. The security team reported back to the Geneva station and asked for guidance.

Gregory Whitehead, COS Geneva, reported these observations via FLASH message back to Washington and then got on a secure phone call with D/NCS Paul Brant. John joined Paul on the call with Whitehead, and the three of them discussed the options available to them. "The logical choice," John said, " is to bring in the Swiss liaison, the Federal Intelligence Service."

"We can do that," said Greg, "but the Swiss are going to have their noses out of joint because we did not tell them in advance we were meeting someone with ISIS connections in their country. If there is another way out of this, I would rather we follow that route."

Paul said, "Let's not get the Swiss involved at this point. Most likely, it will get messy if we do. I want a solution that allows us to walk away as if nothing has happened in Geneva instead of having a shootout on Quai Mont-Blanc."

John joined in. "How about if we disguise both MONEY and Willis and get them out of there without the bad guys knowing?"

"That was my idea," said Paul.

"We must have some disguise techs available in Frankfurt," John said.

"Right," said Paul. "I'm going to arrange for a disguise tech to travel to Geneva on the same Agency plane that is meant to evacuate MONEY and Willis. That plane is in Frankfurt now. I'll get a disguise tech on it, and you, Greg, should have someone at the airport to get that tech to the hotel ASAP."

Gabriella Saint-John had worked as a makeup artist in Hollywood for about 15 years. Now, she was stationed in Frankfurt as a disguise tech for the CIA. She loved her job. Sometimes, she was required to drastically alter people's appearances, and her failure to do the job properly could be a matter of life or death. She was given to understand that this was one of those times. That got her adrenalin flowing. She immediately asked for a description of both MONEY and Willis. Details were available for Willis, but only a general description was available for MONEY. That was, however, enough for her to work with. She put together various hairpieces, a lot of makeup, various shoes and boots, contact lenses, nose and chin adjustors, mustaches, beards, etc. She was ready to go within 20 minutes. An hour later, she landed at Genève Aéroport. She was approached by Stan Wolsky who told her that reservations had been made for her at the Beau Rivage Hotel. Stan gave her a quick briefing on the situation at the hotel and told her that it was probably best if she traveled to the hotel alone by taxi.

Once checked into the Beau Rivage on the fifth floor, Gabriella took the stairs down one flight to Willis' room. George had been expecting her, and after a quick introduction, he asked how they should proceed. Gabriella said, "It's best if you bring your agent to my room since all of my equipment and disguises are there."

Having just a quick look at George, she pretty much knew what she was going to do with him. Now, she wanted to get a look at Amal. George told her that Amal was waiting and he could bring her up to Gabriella's room in about five minutes.

Meanwhile, Amal was feeling the tension of all that had transpired and decided that she needed a stiff drink. Fortunately, she had a bottle of Johnny Walker Blue in her room, and all she needed was some ice. So, she dashed down to the end of the hall where there was an ice machine. One of the ISIS thugs had wandered up to the fourth floor, and he couldn't believe his luck when he saw the Arab beauty coming toward him at the end of the hall. He kept his head down until Amal entered the area that housed the ice machine. He quickly followed her into the small alcove, and approaching her from behind, he covered her mouth with his left hand and put a knife to her throat with his right hand.

Calling her a *sharmoota*[26], he told her that if she made one sound, his sharp knife would slice through her carotid artery. Swiftly deciding that she was not long for this world if this brute was to take her to his safe haven, Amal attempted to jab her captor with her elbow, instantly resulting in a blow to her head with the large handle of the knife. Amal did not completely lose consciousness, but she could barely stand on her own. The ISIS

---

[26] This means "whore."

thug was intent on dragging Amal to the staircase, which was close to the ice machine, and bringing her down to the third floor where ISIS had secured a room.

He put his hands under her armpits and pulled her back toward the door that led to the stairs. He let go of her with one hand and reached back to open the door to the staircase. Behind the door stood Dick Kane, one of the station's security officers, who was just about to enter the fourth floor. Dick, a former bodybuilder with massive arms, immediately grasped the nature of the situation and took action. He wrapped his right arm around the thug's neck in a vice grip to cut off any airflow. The ISIS brute thrashed about in an attempt to escape, but he was no match for Dick's superior strength. In less than 10 seconds, he was unconscious. Dick said to Amal, "Get back to your room *now*." Amal took off, trying to run to her room but stumbled most of the way. When she reached her room, she slammed the door behind her, put on the deadbolt, and secured the chain in place.

Meanwhile, Dick injected the hapless goon with a sedative and then dragged him back into the ice machine room. There was just enough room behind the machine to fit a body, but Dick had to struggle to squeeze him into the space such that he would not be seen by an uninterested ice seeker. Dick then radioed to his supervisor, informing him about what had taken place. He emphasized that the ISIS brute had come across Amal by chance and that Dick had instructed Amal not to leave her room again without an escort.

George was apprised of the attempt on Amal's life, and he rushed to her room. He had to spend some time calming her, as her encounter with the ISIS attacker had left her very distraught. Once she calmed down a little bit, he briefed her about the plan and said, "We have to move quickly, as the sedative given to that thug will only last for about an hour." He then brought her up to Gabriella's room where Dick and another security officer were on guard. Once Amal and George were in Gabriella's room, the disguise tech conducted a quick assessment of Amal's appearance. Then, she asked, "Amal, do you have any long slacks with you on this trip?" Amal said she did and was requested to go back and get them with Dick as an escort. While she was gone, Gabriella began work on George. It didn't take long to make him appear about 25 years older and slightly taller with lifts in his shoes, and she gave him a pale complexion as opposed to his typically tanned appearance. The lifts in his shoes were of different sizes, which gave him a small limp when he walked. She topped it off with some grey in his hair and a greying mustache.

When Gabriella was finished, Amal looked at George and gasped. "Wow, even *I* would not recognize you."

Next, it was Amal's turn. She had put on her slacks, which were fitted just above the waistline. Gabriella asked her if she could pull them down to her hips so that they dragged on the floor. With the slacks pulled down, Gabriella fitted her with a pair of boots, and instantly, she went from 5'4" to 5'8". Then, Gabriella applied makeup to change Amal's complexion from an earthy Mediterranean look to a Northern European's fair complexion. Blue tinted contact lenses, a sandy-colored wig, and brushed-on coloring on the eyebrows along with fake eyelashes completed the transformation of an Arab woman in her late 20s to a fair, Northern European in her mid-40s. In less than two hours, Gabriella was able to make George and Amal appear to be completely different people. Because of the time it had taken to disguise George and Amal, Dick was required to return to the ice machine room and inject another sedative into the now compliant ISIS thug.

The plan now was for Amal and George to take whatever possessions they could fit into a purse or briefcase and leave the hotel separately – George alone and Amal with a security guard who was in his early 50s. Amal and the security guard would appear to be a middle-aged couple.

Before they could return to their rooms to take whatever possessions they could, Stan Wolsky appeared at Gabriella's door, breathless and anxious. He told the group that one of the apparent ISIS operatives in the hotel had just been seen passing some funds to a front desk clerk. It could only be assumed that he was now in possession of Amal's room number and, perhaps, George's too. Thus, neither of them could return to their rooms. Whatever they had with them now was all that they would be allowed to take. A security officer would later pack up their bags and check them out of the hotel but not until they were airborne.

Amal left Gabriella's room first, accompanied by the 50-something security officer. For all the world, they appeared to be a cosmopolitan European couple. Amal was fluent in French, so she chatted away with her companion in French. The security officer's French was practically negligible, so he had to be a docile husband by simply mumbling "oui," "bien," or "d'accord" to whatever she said. They marched through the lobby, passing at least six of the ISIS types. The latter did not even give them a second glance. The couple entered a black Mercedes that was waiting for them and were whisked off to the airport. A few minutes later, George limped through the lobby, and he too did not receive a second look from the terrorists. Stan was waiting for George in his vehicle at the front of the hotel, and as soon as George exited the hotel, he jumped inside Stan's car for the quick ride to the airport.

The security procedures at the private side of Genève Aéroport were very relaxed, particularly for an inter-European flight. So, Amal quickly passed through immigration without even having her passport stamped. A few minutes later, George followed, and they were airborne within minutes. A security officer told them that their possessions were being retrieved now and would be available to them later in the day. Meanwhile, the ISIS operatives had been watching Amal's room, and they began to follow the security officer who had retrieved her belongings. The American security officer noted the surveillance and relayed his predicament to his colleagues who then began to surveil the ISIS types. Within a few minutes, the ISIS operatives were outnumbered by about two to one.

While all this was going on, a second security officer was retrieving Willis' belongings from his room, and he did not receive any attention from ISIS. The security officer in possession of Amal's suitcase had checked her out of the hotel in advance and had a receipt that allowed him to leave the hotel with the suitcase without being questioned by the doorman. Once he exited the front door, other security officers stepped in the way of the ISIS group and prevented them from exiting the hotel. They flashed forged badges of the Swiss police and told the ISIS operatives that a VIP government official would be passing by in a few minutes and the police did not want spectators crowding the Quai. They said, "Please remain here for just a few minutes, and then you can be on your way." Being outnumbered and outsized and in a hostile environment, the ISIS operatives did the smart thing, which was *nothing*. Meanwhile, the Geneva station's liaison officer was meeting Swiss intelligence to tell them that several suspected ISIS operatives were in and around the Beau Rivage.

CHAPTER XIX

With their case officer and his agent out of harm's way, the Agency directed its attention toward uncovering the mole in their midst. Paul Brant asked that secure video conferencing be established in Frankfurt so that he, John Thorne, and Willis could put their heads together and try to come up with some answers. Once they were in communication and before they began a general review of what had gone wrong in the past nine months, Paul said that he had just received intelligence that impacted their case. From both human sources and intercepts, it was now certain that Abd-al-Aziz Numari, the Saudi agent who had first reported on the meeting that was to be held in Yuwan, had been detained and killed by AQAP shortly after his return to Yemen. This fact assured them that their assumption about the existence of a mole inside the Agency was correct.

John told George about his unease regarding his secretary's long hours and her complete knowledge of all that had transpired.

George said, "I too thought that it was strange that JoAnn spends so much time in the office, but I think she has no other life and that is why she is there. We know that she had access to all our plans and intentions, and given that situation, why didn't the opposition know that we had increased the size of the raiding force in Yemen? Also, why didn't they know about MONEY until the start of this trip to Geneva?"

John thought about what George had said and quickly came to the conclusion that he was right. It was not very logical that JoAnn was the mole. John said, "The person we are looking for must have had only sporadic access to all the information. Could it be that not all the other officers in the station were aware of your recruitment of MONEY and her subsequent reporting, George?"

George replied that he and all the other officers had sat around the bubble discussing George's recruitment pitch to MONEY in detail. "They were all fully aware of almost every detail surrounding the recruitment," said George. "It was important for them to learn what had worked in the pitch to her so they could refine their own recruitments when the time comes."

"How about someone on the support staff?" asked Paul. "Did they have access to all this information?" Both John and George thought about this, and John replied that the station did not generally conceal information from the support staff, but to his knowledge, none of them showed any undue attention to operational details. "It's possible," John said, "but I don't see it."

George was then hit with a fact he had all but forgotten. He said, "John, do you remember? At one of our last meetings in Riyadh shortly after Tim had returned from serving on a promotion panel, he was surprised to learn about MONEY."

John was shaken to the core as alarm bells went off in his head. He immediately remembered that Tim had been in Najran when MONEY was first recruited. Then, he had missed getting a briefing about her because his Saudia flight had left early. And what was even more damning was that Tim had not known about the increase in the size of the Yemen raiding party until he was in Najran. If he was the mole and was reporting to someone in ISIS, his ISIS contact would have been in Riyadh. That meant he would, most likely, have been unable to inform them about the more robust raiding party. John then revealed his thoughts to Paul and George.

Paul said, "If it turns out to be Tim, we are going to have a real black eye. How could he have been an officer for so long with no one ever suspecting him of giving away secrets? We must tread carefully now."

John agreed and said, "I'd simply never would have thought of Tim as a mole. It just seems... improbable."

"The first step is to inform the Director about our suspicion," said Paul. "Secondly, we must bring the Bureau into the investigation. We suspect an officer, a U.S. citizen, of committing a major crime, and that takes it out of our jurisdiction. The FBI must take the lead role. I'm going to set up a small task force of people in the Counter Intelligence staff, put them in a separate area from the rest of the CI staff, and have them concentrate on this subject. The Bureau will be able to task them at will, but we too can share our thoughts and facts. So, let's take a break now so that I can brief our Director and, then, the Director of the FBI. I'll let them know what we suspect, why we suspect it, and what we have done about it up to this point. Afterward, we must look to the Bureau for direction."

Paul Brant immediately briefed the Director of the CIA about all the details. The Director was not pleased but said, "Okay, we have to get at the truth of this. Get the Bureau involved fast. In the meantime, I'll brief the President, and I can tell you we might all be looking for a job after that."

Paul then called the Director of the FBI and made an appointment to see him as soon as he could make it to the Bureau's Building across the Potomac river in Washington. He took the private elevator down to the Agency's garage where chauffeured limos were waiting for the top brass. The limo sped out of Hqs and made the 20-minute trip to the FBI building in downtown DC. As Paul began to brief the FBI Director, the latter said, "I see where this is going, and I believe I should get a few more people in here so we can all hear what you have to say." He called in his executive director for National Security and two of his underlings, the Director of the Counterterrorism Division and the Director of the Counter Intelligence Division.

When all were assembled, Paul briefed them about what had transpired in the last nine months, who they suspected, and why. Paul was asked if they had any hard evidence to prove that Haggerty was doubled. Paul admitted that they did not. It was only circumstantial, and by a process of elimination, the finger had been pointed toward Haggerty. He went on to say that all of Haggerty's colleagues thought highly of him, at least in terms of his patriotism, and no one had suspected him up to this point.

The FBI officials then began a discussion on subjects that Paul did not routinely get exposure to. Mainly, they discussed probable cause and the basis for a FISA warrant[27]. Paul knew that getting a FISA warrant would be the first step in proceeding with an investigation, but he was not steeped in the intricacies of the warrant process. However, it did not take long for the FBI officials to determine that a FISA warrant was needed and that there should be no difficulty in getting the FISA court to issue one. They told Paul that they would start working on the application for the warrant immediately and would have the Attorney General sign off on it before the end of the day.

Anticipating that the warrant would be in hand shortly, they asked for special clearance for investigators to get CIA badges and join the task force that Paul had established. The joint task force would ensure that the FBI had access to all of the information available to the CIA. They also anticipated the need to have some agents in Riyadh, and they asked Paul how they might accomplish that without giving notice to the entire Embassy that there was an FBI investigative team present. Paul told them to work that out with COS Riyadh who happened to be in Washington. Paul said that he probably should have brought John Thorne with him but John would be available to them tomorrow.

The FBI indicated that their first objectives would be to delve into Tim Haggerty's financials. They would also wish to copy the hard drives of all his computers, and finally, they would like to put discreet surveillance on him in the hopes of observing a meeting between him and his ISIS handler. There was always the possibility that the handler was another U.S. citizen recruited by ISIS to act as a mediator between them and Haggerty. Paul said that conducting surveillance would be easy with Saudi Intelligence Service's assistance, but he was not going to brief the Saudis about this until they were absolutely certain that Haggerty was the mole.

Then, they broke for the day with the FBI officials stating that they would have a team at the Agency's Hqs the following morning. If John Thorne was available, they would certainly like to meet him. As Paul was leaving, the Executive Director remarked, "This has shades of Ames and Hanson[28], a history that both our organization would like to forget."

---

[27] FISA warrants are those warrants issued by the secretive Foreign Intelligence Surveillance Court.
[28] Aldridge Ames is a former CIA officer who was convicted of spying for the Russians, while Robert Hanson is a former FBI agent who was similarly convicted.

The next day, a joint task force was officially established, and they were housed in a vaulted room within the Agency's Hqs. Only those with a "need to know" would be allowed inside the vault. Two of those from the FBI were destined to operate in Riyadh, and the lead agent, Dominic Santorelli, was anxious to talk to John Thorne about how they could go about their investigation in Riyadh without attracting attention.

John gave this some thought and recalled that there had been a few intel reports indicating that a radical group was threatening to kill the U.S. Ambassador. The threats were not taken very seriously, but it wouldn't surprise anyone if the State Department decided to add a couple of security officers solely for the protection of the Ambassador. He said that he would clear this with the Ambassador as soon as he returned to post but would also clear it with State's Assistant Secretary for Diplomatic Security there in Washington.

John asked Paul about CIA's elite surreptitious entry team, a group of highly trained technicians who were capable of entering almost any building or room without detection. These guys were sort of the antithesis of Houdini. Whereas Houdini could get out of anything, these fellows could get inside anything. John wanted to know if they could be made available to him for entry into Haggerty's home and copying of his hard drives, phones, and any documents he had that might incriminate him.

"Tim is a trained ops officer," said John. "I wouldn't be surprised if he has set several traps in his home and office. So, we need the best there is to overcome any traps."

Paul assured him that the team would be available to him as soon as he required their services. "Let's allow the Bureau to decide when that step is to be taken," said Paul. John wanted to get back to Riyadh soon. He and Paul decided on a cover story for Haggerty that would provide a false narrative regarding the CIA's thinking about the recent 'flaps' – something that would disguise their interest in him. They decided that they would claim that Diplomatic Security had detected some radio signals emanating from the Embassy, and it was feared that someone had planted a bug somewhere in the station. This would suggest that ISIS had obtained information about CHANCE and FLAG via electronic surveillance. The surreptitious entry team would come to Riyadh and claim that they were a "sweep team" looking for bugs in the station.

As John was preparing for his return to Riyadh, he began to question his ability to conceal from Tim the fact that he was now the prime suspect. John wondered if he could look Tim in the eye without revealing his suspicions. He knew that he *had* to pull that off. For one thing, if they were wrong and Tim was not doubled, he did not want Tim to know that he had been suspected. And if Tim was the guilty party, it was even more important that he did not make Tim cautious until solid proof was obtained. John hoped that he had not falsely accused Tim. John was still coming to terms with the real possibility that Tim was their mole, and it was hard for him to accept it.

The joint task force began their work in earnest. They began by pulling all of Haggerty's fitness reports, assignment details, and every document he had written over the years. They were not sure what they were looking for, but they were confident that they would know it when they saw it. Early on in the investigation, there was the question of Tim's wife Denise. Was she involved in this? Did she know what her husband was doing? If Tim was the mole, what was his motivation? Had he ever been thought of as anything other than a patriot, and if so, by whom and why?

CHAPTER XX

That evening, John boarded a United Airlines flight and headed to Frankfurt where he would switch to Lufthansa for the remaining part of his journey to Riyadh. He doubted that he would be able to sleep on the flight – something he normally did without difficulty. In fact, he usually had to force himself to stay awake through take-off. But tonight, his mind was whirling with thoughts about Tim Haggerty and how this would all end. He thought about the tragic ending for the two agents and the effective compromise of a third, MONEY. Had those three agents remained active and reported up to their potential, his station would have been well on its way to achieving the results he had sought when he had first arrived in Riyadh. More importantly, there were four deaths he had to account for. The two Americans lost in Yemen had dedicated their lives to the cause of their country. Similarly, the two foreign agents had risked and lost their lives trying to help the U.S. They had put their trust in the Agency. *But we failed them*, John thought. In addition to that, he still could not get the picture of the 13-year-old boy out of his mind – the boy that he had effectively killed by detonating a bomb.

He also worried about whether he was going to sound convincing when he told Tim that the consensus in Hqs was that there was a bug somewhere in the station. The more he thought about that, the more he believed that it would not be a problem. First of all, he remembered the FBI telling him that their experience with traitors had told them that the mole always assumed he was much smarter than everyone else and had done nothing that would lead to his detection. Secondly, it dawned on John that he would not have to explain this to Tim. The standard practice in the Agency was to never discuss an upcoming sweep. The theory was that if you were being bugged, those who were listening to you would learn that a sweep team was coming, and they would take measures to prevent the discovery of the bug. Most often, that simply meant remotely turning the transmitter off. So, in a station that was expecting a sweep team, a note was passed to all explaining what was happening and cautioning all not to verbalize anything about the sweep.

Thus, John decided that he would write a note to Tim telling him that there was a potential bug in the station and a sweep would be conducted soon to detect the bug. There would be no break in his voice, no tell-tale flickering of his eyes. He won't have to say a word. John was somewhat calmed upon reaching a satisfactory solution to this dilemma, and now, he could possibly catch some sleep. *If only the picture of the boy would disappear,* John thought and grimaced.

Once he was back home, John was delighted to see his wife. Whenever he was stressed about work, being with her brought him great relief. They sat next to the audio system, turned up the volume, and he gave her a summary of what had transpired and what conclusions had been drawn. John had not allowed his emotions to cloud his thinking and reactions to all that had happened. He had to remain emotionally detached from the events to maintain some degree of objectivity. He had found that if he remained detached, he was able to think clearly and not allow emotions to distort his conclusions. But Alice was a different story altogether. She had no reason to hold back her emotions. She was seething with anger when he told her that most likely, Tim was the Judas among them. Seeing her reaction, he cautioned her to stay away from both Tim and Denise if she could not control her emotions.

Alice said, "That son-of-a-bitch killed four people, one of whom was a member of the station. No, I *can't* control my emotions. In fact, I want to smash that fucker in the face. But knowing Denise... I can't believe she was part of this..."

John smiled. This was classic Alice. She wore her emotions on her sleeve and did not believe in diplomatic niceties – she was honest as the day was long. However, he now regretted telling her. He would just have to make sure she was not in the same room with Tim. She asked, "What about you? Do you think Denise is in on it?"

John said, "That is still an open question, but thus far, there is nothing to indicate that she is complicit in any of Tim's nefarious activities."

The next morning, John was still groggy from his trip, as jet lag was a real problem after an 8-hour time change. However, he still reached the office at 7 AM. JoAnn was already there, and she greeted him with a big smile and a hot cup of coffee. She had developed a real fondness for her boss. When he was around, there was energy in the air and things seemed to get done. While he was away, it had seemed like all the action was elsewhere and Riyadh had retreated to its old sleepy self.

John had decided to include the entire station in the deception about there being a bug in the station. Until they discovered proof that Tim was the rat, he had to proceed on the assumption that others could be involved as well.

So, he wrote a note to JoAnn giving her the cover story about a bug in the station and the impending visit of a sweep team. She wrote back, "I don't believe it. They will be wasting their time. I practically live here, and if someone planted a transmitter, I would know about it."

John wrote back, "I hope you are right, but if you are, we have a problem somewhere else."

"I'd be looking somewhere else right *now* if I were you," she wrote with a determined look on her face.

John then asked her, in writing, if she knew something she should be telling him. She said that she did not, but her instincts told her that their problems had not been instigated by a bug. John ended the correspondence by writing, "If you have any suspicions or facts that may be relevant to all that has happened here, let me know."

JoAnn picked up her pen and wrote, "I have no concrete proof, but I see and hear almost everything that goes on here. If I were you, I would look within the Agency. Your deputy has been working against your best efforts ever since you arrived. I don't like it, but I don't know if his behind-the-scenes activities rise to the level of treachery."

John thought to himself that he should have had more trust in this lady and sought her opinion much earlier.

John went into his office and typed a note for all station employees. In it, he discussed the potential listening device in the station offices and the sweep team that was coming to look for it. When Tim came into the office, he warmly greeted John and said that he was delighted to have the boss back. John immediately signaled Tim over to his desk, picked up the note, and showed it to him. Tim nodded knowingly, then took a pad and wrote, "I thought something like a bug was our problem. Let's hope the sweep team finds it."

What a duplicitous son-of-a-bitch! John thought to himself. *First, he denigrates me while I'm gone, and then, he gives me that bullshit about being delighted to have me back. Under the circumstances, the last thing a professional would point toward is a bug. The station has limited access at all times. The char force that cleans at night is always escorted the entire time they are in the station's offices. And they are never allowed in the sensitive areas of the station. Besides, all sensitive discussions are held in the bubble, and it is certainly not bugged. No, a bug would not be my first conclusion. Maybe it would be my last.*

An "eyes only" message had been sent to the Ambassador that gave him a broad outline of the problem but did not identify a suspect. John thought that he owed it to the Ambassador to share with him the assumptions about Tim. So, he went to the Ambassador's office and told him he had a very sensitive subject he wanted to discuss with him and asked the Ambassador to join him in the bubble for this discussion. Fred Wagner found this to be highly unusual. *But if John is making this request, it must be something very sensitive,* he decided.

In the bubble, John quickly reviewed what had taken place in Geneva and the conclusions that they had drawn about Tim. He also explained that the Bureau was the lead agency in the investigation and some FBI investigators were going to be assigned to the mission under the cover of the Ambassador's personal security guards.

Frank simply listened to John until the latter ended his review. Then he said, "This must be a real blow to you, John. I truly sympathize. Whatever I can do to help, I'm ready. Just ask."

John was very appreciative of Frank's sensitivity to the issue and his willingness to help, and he conveyed the same to the Ambassador.

Over the next few days, the FBI investigators arrived. They met John, and it was agreed that the lead agent, Dominic Santorelli, and he would meet in the bubble every morning at 7 AM, well before Tim's typical arrival at around 8:30. They told John that the joint team had reviewed tons of information and nothing had yet confirmed that Tim had been 'turned.' They told John that after he had left Washington, it had been decided that a robust surveillance team would be needed if they were to observe Tim "in the act." So a six-man FBI team had been dispatched to Riyadh, and they had been ostensibly assigned to one of the U.S. military units in the area. They would not come to the Embassy but would take direction from Santorelli via secure communications.

Santorelli told John, "These guys are good at what they do. You can be sure that they will not be made, and if there is anything to see, they will see it." They agreed to coordinate the knowledge of Tim's movements by comparing what Haggerty was supposed to be doing to what he actually did as seen by the surveillance team. John said that he thought it important to get at Tim's computers, phones, other kinds of devices, and documents as soon as possible. The FBI agents agreed, so John sent a message to Hqs telling them that the station was ready for the sweep team, that is, Hqs should send out the elite surreptitious entry team.

Within a couple of days, the surreptitious entry team had arrived in Riyadh. They had taken a crash course in detecting electronic emissions and, therefore, were well prepared to pull off the ruse of being a sweep team. Shortly after their arrival, John announced that he was hosting a station farewell party for the station's logistics officer whose tour in Riyadh was coming to an end. This was sort of a "command performance" for those members of the station. Thus, Tim and Denise Haggerty needed to attend.

This set in motion the plan for the entry team to get into Tim's house and copy his devices and documents. Beforehand, John informed Alice about the plan and told her that she had to keep an eye on Denise at all times during the party. If Denise left for any reason, Alice was to alert John immediately. Likewise, John took it upon himself to keep his eyes glued to Tim. As soon as the Haggertys entered the Thorne residence, John sent a signal via text to the entry team, giving them the "OK" to proceed.

The entry team already knew what kind of locks there were on the Haggerty house, but they had to be watchful of traps on the doors, computers, cabinets, etc. So, they quickly picked the lock on the front door, but as they went about their business, they found that traps had been set in many places: the entryway to Tim's study, several cabinets in his study, and the keyboard of his computer. The traps at the doorway and cabinets were relatively simple: strands of hair taped across entryways. The computer keyboard, however, had a soft coating that would leave a tell-tale impression if touched. The team had come across this previously, and they knew it was difficult to defeat unless it could be replaced. Unfortunately, they did not have a replacement and decided not to disturb the keyboard. A quick examination of the computer tower revealed that it was free from any traps. Having encountered similar situations in the past, the team instantly knew what to do. They opened the tower, removed the hard drive, and copied it using the unique equipment they had with them that would leave no sign of the intrusion. Given the protection afforded to the computer, they were fairly certain that it would reveal significant and damning data.

Next, they concentrated on the cabinets beset with traps. An initial search revealed nothing of interest, but the team leader was convinced that something was to be found there. The leader told his team to search for false compartments within the cabinets. Sure enough, they discovered several hidden compartments, disguised by false bottoms in the cabinets. They contained cash, a false passport, a cell phone, and a ream of documents. They photographed everything, quickly copied the data from the cell phone, and put it all back where it was found. They were out of the house in less than two hours.

Tim was suspicious that evening. It would be more than a month before the logistics officer would leave his post, so he wondered why the COS was having the party so early. However, he was fairly unperturbed because he had laid a number of traps in his house, and if anyone attempted a search, he would know. So, when he returned home after the party, he immediately checked his computer keyboard and the cabinets. He concluded that nothing had been touched.

At 7 AM the next morning, the Bureau's lead investigator, the head of the entry team, and John met in the bubble. Jay McGovern, the head of the entry team, informed the others that they believed they had a treasure trove of information. What it all meant, however, was not known. Per agreement with the joint task force, all documents and data were to be transmitted by secure communication back to the joint task force in Washington. Jay did tell them that given the traps that had been set, he had little doubt that the information would be damning.

The FBI agent said that his surveillance team had been watching Haggerty closely when he returned home the previous evening. The team reported that Haggerty had immediately headed for his study, but they had been unable to observe him while he was in there. They did note that he had turned off all the lights and used a device that had cast a blue light. The blue light had only been on for only a few moments. Jay then mentioned the coating they had found on the computer's keyboard and stated that the blue light had been used to detect any impressions on the keyboard.

CHAPTER XXI

Back at Langley, the joint task force was going through the data and documents they had just received. One of the first things they discovered from the data on the hard drive was that Haggerty's computer had been hacked. Some very sophisticated hackers had done a number on him. Their examination revealed that Tim was a compulsive online gambler, and the hackers had manipulated him into losing over $2 Million. Tim had hocked his home back in the States and almost everything else he owned. He was in serious financial debt and at the mercy of those who had set him up. The task force was able to determine that at one point, his debt had been approximately $3 Million and he had been able to pay off almost $1 Million by accepting payment from the terrorists.

The elaborate scheme that had been put in place was a giant hoax. The gambling site was false and rigged, and the apparent reduction in debt of $1 Million was a complete ruse since the gambling site Tim had used was non-existent. Tim seemed to believe that part of his debt had been paid by those with whom he was now cooperating. The task force concluded that the bottom line was that Haggerty had been set up to lose vast sums and he had never questioned the authenticity of the scheme. It was clear that whoever had recruited him had agreed to pay off his debt in exchange for information on the CIA's efforts against ISIS.

That conclusion was reached by the fact that $400,000 had been removed from his debt around the time the station had learned of the meeting in Yemen and begun planning to raid that meeting. Another $300,000 had been removed immediately after the false flag recruitment of COUSIN. Finally, another $300,000 had been removed directly after the recruitment of CHANCE. What Haggerty had not understood was that this had simply been a paper exercise. No actual dollars had changed hands. There was just the appearance of a reduction in debt since there never was a real debt. But how, when, and who had made the actual recruitment was unclear and, perhaps, never would be.

Among the documents recovered, there was a list of all the ops officers in Riyadh and copied photos of them. There was a map of Yemen with Yuwan circled. There were copies of the SDR routes that George Willis and Kim Malloy had drafted in preparation for their agent meetings. Clearly, Haggerty had been sharing sensitive operational information with someone and, in the process, undermining almost everything that the Riyadh station was doing. However, the smoking gun was not there. In other words, while it could be plainly deduced that Haggerty was working for some foreign entity, evidence that could be used to convict him in a court of law was lacking.

They had the data that had been collected from Haggerty's home, but this was not evidence. And even if it was evidence, there was the problem of "chain of custody." Jay McGovern was not a law enforcement officer. This meant that at trial, a defense attorney could ask that everything that had been taken from Tim's home be excluded, and a judge was very likely to agree to such a motion. Likewise, the identity of the people Haggerty was working for was also uncertain. The task force concluded that the Agency's cyber section would eventually be able to determine who was behind this whole charade, but identifying them was going to take time.

The joint task force's findings were communicated to John through "eyes only" messages. John in turn shared the findings with Dominic Santorelli, the lead FBI agent. "It's going to be up to your surveillance team to catch him in the act, Dom," a weary John said.

"We can do that, but how long will it take for him to contact those who are directing him?"

In response to Dominic's question, John went into a trance-like thought process and then began expressing his thoughts out loud. "Well, a terrorist

group appears to have benefitted from his treachery, right? So, we must manufacture an operational scenario that is convincing and has all the appearances of being *extremely damaging* to a terrorist group. We had two ops
against ISIS that he helped ruin, so I want to manufacture a third op against
ISIS, something *so* enticing that he will be *compelled* to report it to his handler. I think we need to get a hidden camera in his office in case he wants to
photograph a document, and then, if he attempts to pass the document to a
foreign operative, we will have proof of his treachery."

"I like that," said Dominic, "but I'm worried about the takedown." John
asked what Dom meant by this. Dominic then explained that if they were in
U.S. territory, there would be no problem, but in Saudi Arabia, they had no
police force or powers to arrest Tim. "What are we going to do if we witness
Tim passing damaging info or documents?" Dominic asked.

John said that he had given this some thought and agreed that it was a
dilemma. "My initial thought," he said, "was to bring Prince Mohammed,
the Interior Minister, into the equation. He has been most helpful in ops
against terrorism, and I have developed a strong relationship with him. The
problem is that I have not been able to get an appointment with him recently,
and this city is abuzz with rumors predicting his removal from office. That
leads me to conclude that we have to handle this op unilaterally all the way.
I think we should have a counter-terrorism team ready to capture Tim's handler and make him available to any court proceedings. We'll have to get the
Agency's lawyers and the DOJ[29] involved to make sure that whatever we do
does not jeopardize a criminal conviction. In fact, we should proceed in a
way that will enhance the chances of getting a criminal conviction. If it works
out that way, I will have to take some serious flak from the Saudis for not
bringing them into the picture, but I have broad shoulders. Anyway, let me
send something back to the task force and let them know about our plan.
I'll ask them to bring in the lawyers from the Agency and the DOJ for the
operation in order to get a ruling on our plan."

It didn't take long for Hqs to completely debunk their plan. Firstly,
Washington did not want there to be any legal questions about the apprehension of a third party in a friendly country. Secondly, Hqs believed that

[29] DOJ: Department of Justice

because the Saudi side had taken the blame for the failed op in Yemen and offered an apology directly from the King, the U.S. side needed to show good faith by bringing them into the operation. "However," Hqs said, "the Saudis should not be told about Haggerty until we have something more concrete against him. Let's be sure we are on the right track before we identify one of our own as a traitor." Hqs went on to say that if the station could capture Tim clandestinely photographing a sensitive document on video, that would be considered concrete enough, and at that point, the station should bring in the Saudis.

John got hold of Jay McGovern and asked if his team had the equipment and expertise to mount a hidden video camera in Tim's office. Jay said that it should be easy for them but he would like to have a good look at Tim's office before making any commitments. John told Jay that he could do that in the evening. He said he would write a note to JoAnn telling her she had to be out of the office that evening due to the tests Jay was going to run to find any bugs. So, on that evening, Jay and his team planted a video camera in one of the ceiling lamps of Haggerty's office. They tested it and put the receiving equipment in John's desk, which he kept locked. Since John's office was adjacent to Tim's, the video signal would be strong and easy to capture.

Next, they needed to develop an operation that would tempt Tim. This presented several difficulties. First, they were not prepared at this time to include anyone else from the station in their plan, and they could not claim it was a liaison operation because Haggerty was in contact with the liaison team. So, they decided to falsify a would-be unilateral paramilitary operation into Yemen. The scenario would be that they would receive a TOP SECRET message from Hqs claiming that a meeting site for senior elements of ISIS had been discovered just outside of Sana'a, Yemen and Hqs wanted Riyadh Station to develop a plan to "take out" this site and its inhabitants. The message would include attachments with drawings and maps, and it would state that whether the op called for a missile strike using aircraft or a special ops team that would be inserted into Yemen was something that Hqs wanted Riyadh to examine.

This is ideal, thought John. He did not have to inform others from the station about the ruse. Thus, John had Hqs send the TOP SECRET message, which he shared with Tim and Norm Halderman, the station's military specialist. He told the two of them that he wanted them to develop a plan for an attack on the purported meeting site in Yemen.

Soon, his ruse paid dividends. That afternoon, Tim closed the door to his office and locked it. He sat there staring at the wall for the longest time. He thought to himself, *how the hell did I get myself into this situation? Here I am acting as a traitor to my own country and for the worst of reasons – money. There was no information that this Station was producing when I first got into this jam. So it was easy for me to agree to pass them information in exchange for cancelling my debts – we had no information. Then came John Thorn and all that changed. I may not like my boss that much but I have to admit that I admire his accomplishments, even though those accomplishments got me in deeper trouble. I just wish I could somehow go back in time and never started gambling.*

John was watching the whole thing on the small monitor and video recorder he had kept in his desk drawer. He began to think, *have we reached the wrong conclusions about Tim? No, that can't be as we have too much information that tells us otherwise. So what is he doing?*

At that point Tim breathed a sigh of resignation and pulled out a miniature camera, and copied the message from Washington along with all the attachments. This was the proof John and the FBI wanted. He immediately sent a message to the task force informing them of Tim's actions. He indicated that he would immediately seek an appointment with Liaison in order to bring them into the picture and have them join the Bureau's surveillance team. Now that solid proof of Haggerty's duplicity had erased any doubts that John had had about him, his suppressed emotions began to surface. *I want to string that bastard up!* he said to himself.

John phoned the Ministry of Interior and spoke with Prince Mohammed's special assistant who told him that the Prince was "indisposed." John told the aide that it was absolutely crucial that he met the Prince immediately, as it was a matter of grave importance. The aide told him to "hang on" and put John on hold.

After several moments, Prince Mohammed came on the line and said, "Is this really necessary, John?" John told him that it was and it was extremely important that he met the Prince immediately. A reluctant Prince Mohammed finally agreed and told John to come to his palace instead of the office. John let Dominic know what he was about to do and then rushed out the door.

Upon arrival, John was immediately ushered into the Prince's private office. "This *better* be good, John," said the Prince.

John began by telling him that they had both been wrong about Abd-al-Aziz Numari, the Saudi agent. "We now have confirmation that he was killed by AQAP almost immediately after he returned to Yemen from Saudi Arabia. And just an hour ago, we have confirmed who the real double is. Unfortunately for me, it's one of mine. To be precise, it's Tim Haggerty. We have had our suspicions for several weeks now, but legally, we were prohibited from sharing that with you until we had some proof, which we obtained a short while ago. We have a video of Tim photographing a TOP SECRET document that contains contrived information about a paramilitary operation in Yemen. We assume that Tim will be contacting his handler shortly in order to pass on to him the contrived document. We have an FBI surveillance team here that is prepared to arrest Tim, as he has diplomatic immunity that prevents your people from detaining him. However, his handler is *all yours*."

"This is startling news," said the Prince. "We will help you in any way we can, but unfortunately, for reasons that you will soon learn, you must coordinate this with the Deputy Minister. I'll set the wheels in motion for instant coordination, but after today, it's my Deputy you will be dealing with." The Prince then called in one of his aides and issued orders for a Saudi surveillance team to be made available within the hour to meet John and an American team at the Ministry of Interior.

"By the time you get to the Ministry, our team will be ready. When you get there, ask for General Abd-al-Rahman al-Rubayan. In the meantime, I will inform the King and others about the situation."

John said, "Obviously, we are very embarrassed about the fact that one of our officers committed this treason and undermined the operational lead you gave us. From the Director on down, we all ask for your understanding."

The Prince told John that as he had been in the same position a few months back, he sympathized with him. He told John that the important thing was to apprehend all those involved, and that might mean a delay in the arrest of those they would immediately identify. The Prince explained that they would want to determine who Haggerty's handler is and to whom the handler reports. "If the handler is known to us," said the Prince, "we agree that the arrest should be made immediately. But if not, give us some time to determine who he is working for."

John told him that he wasn't sure he could delay the arrest of Haggerty, but he would try.

"If you must arrest him before we find out who his handler is, please wait until after the handler is out of sight before you make the arrest," said the Prince. "That way, we can continue our surveillance of the handler without him knowing that he has been made."

John agreed and then quickly left so he could brief Dominic Santorelli and get the surveillance teams combined. He called Dominic and asked to meet him at the Ministry of Interior with his team. They were at the Ministry within half an hour. They met the Deputy Minister of Interior, General al-Rubayan, who had been brought up to speed by Prince Mohammed. The two teams began to coordinate so that they could communicate while in action. The Saudi side was able to bring many more resources into action because they had static surveillance at various points throughout the city as well as many more surveillants than the Americans did. Very shortly thereafter, the joint surveillance teams were on the streets and in position.

The American side decided that they did not want to delay the arrest of Haggerty. The decision was made that if there was a request from the Saudi side to delay, meaning they did not know the handler, the Bureau would wait until after the handler was out of sight before arresting Haggerty but they would wait no longer than that.

CHAPTER XXII

I t didn't take Tim long to signal his handler, a Pakistani accountant working for a Saudi construction company. Haggerty's signal indicated that he wanted a meeting at 9 PM that evening. It had been pre-planned that emergency meetings would take place near Tim's home, and in most cases, it would be a simple brush pass and not a verbal meeting. Haggerty rarely had sit-down meetings with his handler, preferring to prepare whatever intelligence he had in a written document. Tim wanted to spend as little time as possible with the handler and thus minimize the possibility of being compromised.

Tim lived in a nice villa within the DQ of Riyadh. The area he lived in was populated with mid-sized homes along well-maintained, brightly lit streets. There were small patches of lawns in front of each home, and the sidewalks in front of the homes made evening strolls a common practice. The Bureau placed teams of two or three men in ubiquitous white Toyota Land Cruisers parked strategically along this street, interspersed with the oc-casional Range Rover. The surveillants lay prone in the back of the vehicles where they had drilled out holes through which they could both watch and photograph. Each vehicle also had a Saudi team member. Each group of sur-veillants had secure radio contact with all other team members.

Just before 9 PM, Tim left his home via the front door and proceeded along the sidewalk. He had not walked for more than a block when a thin, dark-skinned man appeared to be walking toward him. At about the same time when the surveillance teams began to get reports of Haggerty leaving his home for a walk, another team reported that an individual who appeared to be a Pakistani was approaching Haggerty on foot. In very short order, the Saudis stated that the Pakistani was unknown to them. As the distance between Tim and the Pakistani narrowed, one of the Bureau teams reported that they had close visual and photographic coverage of both individuals. To the casual observer, it would appear that the two did not communicate at all as they passed each other. However, the team that had indicated they had coverage suddenly announced, "Exchange copied."

This meant that they had captured a brush pass from Haggerty to the Pakistani. The Pakistani continued to walk in the same direction, but after walking for a block, Haggerty turned around and began to walk back to his home. The two were now walking in the same direction, but they were about two blocks apart. Finally, the Pakistani turned right onto the next street where he had apparently parked his vehicle. Within a couple of minutes, the radio reported, "He's out of the area."

This was the signal for the Bureau to move in and arrest Tim. The back ends of Land Cruisers along the street began to open, and out came several men with very intent looks on their faces. Tim looked around and immediately sensed what was about to happen. He broke into a sprint to his house and got there before anyone was able to apprehend him. He locked the doors and retreated to his study. The Bureau quickly surrounded the home and tried to enter from the front door. It was locked. The team leader knocked loudly on the door and shouted, "Mr. Haggerty, this is the FBI. Open the door!" There was no response from inside, so the team leader called for a battering ram to break down the door. Before they could get the door opened, they all heard what appeared to be a firearm discharging. Quickly, they smashed the door from its hinges and entered the house. They raced into the study and found Haggerty slumped down in his chair with a 9 mm dangling from his hand. There was a small hole in the right side of Tim's head, but the left side was splattered all over the rear wall.

Meanwhile, the Saudi surveillance team continued to follow Reza Khan, the Pakistani who was Tim's handler. Khan possibly had some rudimentary training in surveillance detection, as he circled back several times to look for surveillance. But the Saudis had too many men on the street. Khan was an amateur and could not detect the many moves and switches the Saudi team made to remain undetected. Eventually, he led them to Abu Iyad's apartment. The surveillance team was under instructions to take no action other than to follow Khan.

While waiting for Khan outside Abu Iyad's building, the team leader reported back to General al-Rubayan at the Ministry of Interior. The General told the team to split in two: one to follow Khan and the other to keep Abu Iyad under surveillance. After a quick check, the Saudis discovered that they had a large dossier on Abu Iyad. They had suspected that he was an ISIS sympathizer, but they had no proof. The decision was made to arrest Khan once he was in his home, and they could then determine if he lived alone or with possible ISIS companions.

It turned out that Khan lived with two other individuals: one was another Pakistani, and the other was from Bangladesh. All three were taken into custody where the gloves came off. It didn't take long for all three to spill their guts. But they knew very little about ISIS' activities in Saudi Arabia. Apparently, they were not considered trustworthy and were only given very limited information by Abu Iyad. All three told the same story. They knew each other, Abu Iyad, and "another sadist just like him named Ali." The other Pakistani and Bangladeshi's only job was to rent safehouses for ISIS. Naturally, they provided complete details of the safehouses they had rented. One of these safehouses was where they normally met Abu Iyad. Khan was the only one of the three who had ever met Abu Iyad at his home.

Khan was grilled more than the other two because it was assumed that he knew the most. After all, he was Haggerty's handler. But their interrogation of Khan indicated that he had very limited knowledge of what ISIS was doing. Almost all his meetings with Haggerty were brush passes without any words spoken. On a couple of occasions when he did have verbal meetings with Haggerty, the latter simply used him to convey short cryptic messages to Abu Iyad.

So, the Saudis planned a major coordinated assault on all the ISIS locations they knew about. Abu Iyad's home and the safehouse where he met others were to receive the most attention.

No one knew that Abu Iyad had attended an ISIS meeting in Yemen the previous week. While there, he had learned that the security situation in and around Sana'a was very dangerous for ISIS members. At the high-level meeting Abu Iyad had attended, it had been decided that all future meetings would take place in Ta'iz. So, when he received Haggerty's report from Khan, he knew that something was wrong. He surreptitiously surveyed the street below for about 15 minutes before he was sure that he was being watched. He had made plans long ago for his family to be able to leave their apartment and retreat to another apartment within the same building. He decided that now was the time to implement that plan.

Abu Iyad's family quietly moved up one floor, leaving Abu Iyad alone in their apartment. Of course, the Saudis had placed a couple of men inside the building just in case there was an attempt to avoid detection. They watched the family creep up the stairs but took no action.

Hours later, after the interrogation of Khan and his two roommates, the Saudis decided to take down Abu Iyad. So, an action team joined the surveillance team outside Abu Iyad's apartment building. All this was noted by Abu Iyad from his apartment. He was not going to allow these Saudis to take him to their interrogation center. For as much as he loved to torture others, he had no stomach for enduring it himself. He decided to barricade himself in his apartment, and if they forcibly entered by knocking down the door, he would take out the first few.

Indeed, that is what he tried to do. The Saudis used a battering ram to knock down the door, but once the door was down, they did not charge in as Abu Iyad had anticipated. They threw a flash grenade into the room, which blinded Abu Iyad for about five seconds. The Saudi assault team rushed into the apartment a second after the flashbang did its job. Abu Iyad knew that they were coming, but he could not see them. So, he wildly discharged his 12-gauge shotgun, hoping to kill a few of the attackers and hoping they in turn that would kill him. But it did not work.

The Saudi team was disciplined enough to avoid the shotgun blasts and render Abu Iyad harmless in less than five seconds. They achieved their objective of taking him alive.

Abu Iyad trembled with fear, knowing that he was going to be subjected to severe torture. Once the interrogation began, he could not tell his captors fast enough all that he knew, and it was plenty. The information he provided allowed the Saudis to wrap up the entire ISIS organization in Saudi Arabia. They also obtained detailed information on ISIS individuals throughout the Middle East, which they shared with friendly intelligence services in the area as well as the CIA. Simply put, this was an intelligence coup that would cripple ISIS for years.

EPILOG

Denise Haggerty, who was upstairs in her bedroom when her husband shot himself, came racing down to the study and shrieked, "What's happened?" The agent nearest to her replied, "Your husband just saved the U.S. taxpayers a whole bunch of money and the U.S. Government a lot of grief and embarrassment." The lead agent quickly stepped in and said, "Please come with me, Mrs. Haggerty. You really don't want to see any more of this."

Taking her into the next room, he explained that they were there to arrest her husband for committing espionage on behalf of an enemy of the U.S. Denise did not appear at all surprised by his words. She told the agent that she did not know that Tim was doing something nefarious, but she said she was not surprised. In the past year, their relationship had soured, and the once patriotic Tim had begun to speak disparagingly about his country. Additionally, he hated the new COS. He had also become very secretive in the past year, spending hours locked up in his study. Denise said she had challenged him about his moods and activities, which typically resulted in a torrent of anger toward her. He had become very emotionally and verbally abusive, so much so that she had begun corresponding with a law firm about a divorce. The Bureau verified all that Denise had imparted to the agent. Subsequently, the investigation proved that she was telling the truth, and she was no longer under investigation. Since then, she has reverted to her maiden name and is living quietly somewhere in the Midwest.

Having wrapped up a large ISIS contingent in the area, the Saudi Security forces put Reza Khan and his roommates in a Saudi prison for an "indefinite" period of time. Abu Iyad was not so lucky. On a Friday after prayers about two months later, he met Mohammed al-Beshi in Deera Square, which was commonly known as "Chop Chop Square." Mohammed al-Beshi was the Saudi executioner who was quite adept at chopping off heads with one swing of the sword. Most often, the person to be executed was drugged so that he was spared the reality of what would happen to him. But once again, Abu Iyad was not so lucky. They neglected to provide him with a drug.

The investigation by the joint CIA/FBI task force led to the uncovering of an ISIS group in England that was very sophisticated. The group in England was extremely adept at hacking computers, and they had developed the scheme of manipulating online betting sites in such a way that the unsuspecting player was bound to lose. Once they got their claws into someone addicted to gambling, it was easy to control the individual. The task force was able to discover many others who had been targeted and exploited by this group, but Tim Haggerty was the only CIA employee who had been duped in this way. All of this information was turned over to Britain's internal security service, the MI-5, which eventually arrested the entire group.

A task force established by the CIA to investigate and act on the banking transactions reported by MONEY was able to deplete almost all the accounts that were supported by Prince Talal. Many charities in the world were pleased to receive large, anonymous donations. Friendly intelligence services arrested the fund's recipients and were able to disband their organization. Reports surfaced throughout the Middle East that Prince Talal had channeled funds to support sex slavery in Europe. These reports appeared to be very credible, so much so that Saudi authorities eventually arrested and convicted Prince Talal who was lucky to escape a meeting with Mohammed al-Beshi.

George Willis and Amal Ansari never returned to Riyadh. George divorced his wife Amy, and per their pre-nuptial agreement, relinquished any rights to hundreds of millions of dollars. George and Amal got married after George's divorce, and Amal assumed the name "Willis." Since George and Amal were active targets of ISIS or what was left of it, the Agency assigned

George to a Far East Station, and he will remain there for a cooling-off period of several years.

John Thorne contacted GREASE, the Saudi working in the Ministry of Petroleum, and told him that his friend George Willis was CIA and that George's contacts may have come to the attention of ISIS. Thus, there was the remote possibility of GREASE becoming a target of ISIS. It was felt that the Agency owed it to GREASE to warn him of this possibility. Furthermore, the Agency had solicited the agreement of a large U.S. Petroleum company to offer GREASE a very rewarding position in his field. GREASE readily accepted this offer and left Saudi Arabia with his wife and children.

Kim Malloy was offered a position in Europe as a case officer to work against the Iranian target. Utilizing his experience in Riyadh, he has recruited a significant number of Iranians. NE, his home division, is anxious to get him back after a suitable cooling-off period.

The CIA and Homeland Security identified the Lebanese member of ISIS who was casing targets in Atlanta. There were only three Lebanese Green Card holders who had traveled from Atlanta to Beirut in the time frame indicated by Ahmad Dijani. Two of them were over 70 years of age and only one was in his 30s – the latter was arrested and is currently awaiting trial in Atlanta.

Prince Mohammed bin Nawwaf was replaced as Crown Prince and Minister of Interior in June 2017. The King's son and the new Crown Prince had Prince Mohammed placed under house arrest, but no charges have been levied against him.

John and Alice Thorne remained in Riyadh for another two years. John was still debating whether to retire from the Agency, but if he did, he wanted to go out on a positive note. So, he completed his tour. During the remaining two years of his tour, the Riyadh station recruited a significantly large stable of assets, making it one of the most productive and meaningful stations. The image of the 13-year-old boy continued to be the last thing John visualized before sleeping every night.

NOTE FROM THE AUTHOR

The names of all the individuals in this book are completely fictional except for a couple of well-known Arab officials. As a senior CIA officer who specialized and served many years in the Middle East, I have attempted to recreate the atmosphere of a CIA station and the thought process of the COS. I realize that switching from original names to cryptonyms can be cumbersome and, perhaps, confusing for many readers, and I apologize for that. However, I did not wish to deviate from how conversations are conducted in a real Station. As an aide to the reader, I have provided here a list of characters in the book and another list of abbreviations, acronyms, and cryptonyms used. Additionally, footnotes have been inserted in the text for a more engaging reading experience. I hope you enjoyed reading this!

CHARACTERS

Abd-al-Aziz Numari: Saudi agent who penetrated AQAP

Abdullah al-Saud: Willis' developmental and an MFA official

Abu Ayub: Head of the station's local surveillance team

Ahmad al-Tuwayjari: AQAP leader from Yuwan

Ahmad Dijani: ISIS operative in Beirut

Ali: ISIS thug in Riyadh

Alice Thorne: John Thorne's wife

Amal Ansari: Palestinian developmental of Willis (28) – cryptonym **MONEY**

Amy Willis: George Willis' wife

Bill Lucas: Ex-JSOC trooper and recon specialist in Riyadh

Chloe Malloy: Kim Malloy's wife

Dan Clark: Chief of CIA's Counter-Terrorism Center (C/CT)

Denise Haggerty: Wife of Tim Haggerty

Dominic Santorelli: Lead FBI agent in Riyadh

Fred Wagner: U.S. Ambassador to Saudi Arabia

Faisal al-Awad AKA Abu Iyad: Head of ISIS in Saudi Arabia

Gabriella Saint-John: Disguise tech in Frankfurt

George Willis: Ops Officer in Riyadh

Ghaith: ISIS assassin in Riyadh

Gregory Whitehead: COS Geneva

Hasan al-Sudari: Saudi Captain

Hassan al-Asiri: AQAP bomb maker

Hisham an-Nassar: Malloy's developmental in Saudi Ministry of Energy – cryptonym **GREASE**

Hussein al-Biladi: Engineer working for Aramco – cryptonym **FLAG**

Jay McGovern: Head of CIA's elite entry team

JoAnn Sabinski: COS' secretary

John Thorne: COS Riyadh

Kim Malloy: Ops Officer

Lt. Col Brad Armstrong: JSOC team leader in Riyadh

Marcie Lucas: Bill Lucas' wife

Mick Dreggar: TECHNICAL SERVICE tech visiting Riyadh

Mike O'Leary: Polygraph operator out of Frankfurt

Mohammad al-Masri: Egyptian diplomat recruited by Willis – cryptonym **CHANCE**

Mohammed bin Nawwaf: Saudi Crown Prince and Minister of Interior

Norman Halderman: Riyadh station's military specialist

Paul Brant: Director of National Clandestine Service (D/NCS)

Prince Meshal al-Talal: Saudi Prince supporting radical movements

Reza Khan: Pakistani handler of Haggerty

Rifat al-Biladi: Cousin of Hussein and ISIS Jihadi – cryptonym **COUSIN**

Sam Butterfield: Ex-JSOC officer assigned to Riyadh and recon specialist

Stan Wolsky: Geneva station officer

Tim Haggerty: DCOS Riyadh

Jay McGovern: Head of the elite entry team

ABBREVIATONS AND ACRONYMS
USED IN THIS BOOK

AUB: American University of Beirut

AQAP: al-Qaida in the Arabian Peninsula

CHANCE: Egyptian Diplomat Mohammed al-Masri

C/CTC: Chief, Counter Intelligence Center in the CIA

CNE: Chief of Near East Division in the CIA

COS: Chief of Station

DCOS: Deputy Chief of Station

D/NCS: Director of the National Clandestine Service. Also known as the
DDO or Deputy Director of Operations.

DOD: Department of Defense

FSO: Foreign Service Officer

CAPTURE: Cryptonym for the operation in Yemen

JSOC: Joint Special Operations Command

POA: Provisional Operational Approval

RSO: Regional Security Officer

SDR: Surveillance Detection Route